T0125680

IN THE CARDS

By the Author

No Experience Required

In the Cards

Visit us at www.boldstrokesbooks.com

IN THE CARDS

by
Kimberly Cooper Griffin

2020

IN THE CARDS

ISBN 13: 978-1-63555-717-6

This Trade Paperback Original Is Published By
Bold Strokes Books, Inc.
P.O. Box 249
Valley Falls, NY 12185

First Edition: August 2020

Credits
Editor: Barbara Ann Wright
Production Design: Stacia Seaman
Cover Design by Tammy Seidick

Acknowledgments

Thank you, first and most importantly, to Radclyffe for inviting me to become a part of the Bold Strokes family.

I owe so much to Barbara Ann Wright, my editor. She makes my dull words shine and teaches me new things with each new book.

Thanks goes out to Tammy Seidick for creating the perfect cover.

So many thanks to my writer friends with whom I've had writing dates during the course of this book. I love to hear you typing away on our video calls, keeping me writing when distractions would have me stop. A little bit of your DNA lives in these pages. You know who you are—Beth, Renee, Millie, Nicole, Jaycie, and Ona.

Michelle Dunkley, my Michelle, my favorite beta reader, you are there for every book. I wait every time, holding my breath. Your feedback is a treasure.

Thank you to my readers. It's a tremendous gift that you read my humble words.

I dedicate this and everything to Summer

Chapter One

Daria

I slipped my sunglasses on when the bright mid-spring sun reflecting off the skyrise windows across the street nearly blinded me as I left work for the day. Hefting the strap of my computer bag to hang more securely from my shoulder, I merged into the stream of business people on the sidewalk who were making their daily escape from whatever white-collar hell they worked to pay the bills.

Or was it just me?

Judging from the snippets of conversations around me, I realized it was just me. I didn't even want to think about my dreary after work plans...if you could even call them plans. I rolled my eyes at the two twentysomethings walking in front of me as they squealed with excitement about the dance club they planned on hitting later. In the middle of the week. Where did they find the energy?

"The bar next to the dance floor is completely glass, with a frozen strip of metal running along the top to keep your drink cold." The woman on the right shook out her brown, flat-ironed hair and squeezed the other's arm as they walked.

"I wonder how many people get their tongues stuck to it," the other woman asked, running her fingers through her shiny blond hair.

The first stared open-mouthed at her friend. "What? Gross. People don't lick bar tops."

Did people really have these kinds of conversations without dying of boredom?

"It's a thing, you know. People putting their tongues on frozen metal and getting them stuck. My dad saw it in a movie, and he brings it up every time it snows." If I had to guess, I'd say the two were barely over legal drinking age. I listened to them move on to their outfits and makeup and rolled my eyes.

We stopped at the corner to wait for the light. I couldn't remember the last time I went dancing on a work night. Who got excited about the color of eyelash extensions? And did her lashes really have to match the sexy top she'd picked up at the mall on her lunch break? When one of them pulled said top from her bag to show the other as the light changed, I shouldered past without saying excuse me. They didn't care. Squealing about the shitty shirt, they didn't even notice. Typical.

I caught myself. I wasn't mad at them, even though they were shallow and vapid. Also, I didn't hate my job. In fact, I usually loved it. And I wasn't invisible. I had lots of friends and a nice place to call home, where my precious doggo, Rowdy, waited to cuddle with me. Plus, my sister, Marnie, lived with me, so I wasn't lonely. My life was good. I was just having a bad day.

I didn't know why I projected my foul mood onto innocent Denver office dwellers, and I didn't even have a good excuse for it. It wasn't like I'd had a bad day or anything. Nothing had gone wrong. In fact, the opposite happened. Things had gone according to plan, as they always did. Today was no different than the day before or the hundred days before. So what was the deal?

I knew part of the deal. Something was missing, and I didn't know what it was.

While walking the block toward the outdoor mall to catch the free bus to the train, I tried to change my attitude. My life was good. I had friends, family, a great job, and a nice apartment close to where I worked in Denver, the best city in the world. If something was missing, it couldn't be major. I was just being stupid, which was so boring. Just like the conversation I'd just listened to, minus the going out, drinking, and all the dancing.

That was it. I was bored. That was the deal. I was so damn bored. All these great things going on in my life, but still, I was bored.

At work, I had streamlined processes so effectively since I'd started working at McSweeney and Price six years ago that I could perform my accounting job in my sleep. Maybe I should have taken the promotion to director Taryn had offered. Higher positions meant more political jockeying, though, and I'd always been terrible at politics. I normally rocked at all the other things, the people management, the work flow optimization, the budget stuff. The truth was, I was ready to move up. Maybe I could be the one person who made it to middle management, who avoided all the political stuff, and who got to be left alone to focus on the actual work. I'd have to think about it some more. A little of my dark mood slipped away, but not all of it. The thing was, while I knew my job played a role in my boredom, it wasn't all of it. Part of me knew what the other stuff was, but it wasn't anything I could change, so I chose not to dwell on it.

I turned the corner onto the 16th Street Mall, and the sound of music distracted me from my thoughts. A violin played the melody of a classic rock song, and a small crowd had gathered around the woman performing it. I caught a few glimpses of her between shoulders in the crowd, and what I could see captivated me. She swayed to the music and was clad in a colorful bohemian skirt and tank top. Her dreadlocks swung down her back, held by a loose tie low on her neck. With her violin tucked under her defined chin, she sang into a mic she wore against her cheek. Better than the other musicians I was used to seeing busking on the mall. She compelled me to stop and watch.

At five foot five, I couldn't see much from behind the crowd, so I wove through, stopping next to a concrete planter several feet away. I set my computer bag down and sat to watch.

The performer ended the song and started another classic tune, taking me back to my childhood. I wished Marnie was there to listen, especially when the crowd sang along. She would have loved this. She and I shared an appreciation of music, although neither of us played an instrument. I'd always wished I'd taken one up, but sports took up most of my free time.

The funky mood I'd been trying to shake started to fade. The sunshine and impromptu performance gave me the exact balm I needed. When the song ended, the violinist spoke quietly to a bedraggled man sitting on a bench next to all of his worldly possessions. She smiled and gave him a fist bump before playing her next song.

"Take It Easy" never sounded so relevant. I sat, listening, watching downtown workers getting ready to go home for the day. A group of guys in business casual drinking beer at a bar on an outdoor patio sang along loudly. I enjoyed the idyllic scene: an early summer evening, music, and people having a good time. More of an observer than a participant, I decided to heed the message and take it easy, enjoy the moment.

The enthralling singer played with abandon, swaying and singing in a mesmerizing performance, and I watched her interact with the small audience while she played. People dropped money into her instrument case, and I wished I had a little cash to do the same. I never carried cash, especially on the 16th Street Mall. So many people asked for change, and I could never say no. I had awful instincts when it came to picking out the people who really needed it from the ones who commuted from their homes in Aurora and Highlands Ranch, making a living on the generosity of strangers. Who was I to judge, though? I forced myself to abandon that line of thought. My mood was finally brightening, and the plight of the homeless was too fraught a topic to consider while listening to a fantastic musician. I wanted to enjoy watching her.

So I watched, and something about her drew me in. I wanted to sit here all day. But I couldn't. I had to rush home to let Rowdy out and to fix dinner for Marnie and me.

More often than not these days, I found myself wishing I didn't have to go home. It wasn't a terrible burden, really. Marnie always helped, and she did the dishes afterward, so it wasn't as if I did it all by myself. But as I watched the people in the outdoor patios laughing and drinking, I couldn't help but think it would be nice to hang out with friends after work once in a while.

It wasn't like I was turning down lots of offers to go out for a beer. My friends had stopped asking me spur-of-the-moment a long time ago. They knew I needed to plan a few days in advance. Marnie was good at fending for herself if she knew in advance. It was more about having the choice to go out on a whim if I wanted to.

The last notes of Linda Ronstadt's "You're No Good" faded, and I tried not to think about feeling so tied down. Marnie needed things to be routine. And I liked helping her manage that. When our mom and dad moved to California to start Dad's sabbatical year doing research on immigration and the effect on migrant farm workers, I'd happily taken over Mom's role of taking care of Marnie, not that she needed a lot of taking care of. It was just better if things were well-planned and stayed on track. Otherwise, she could take care of herself, and she did, mostly relying on me to ground her when her stress got too high.

Then one year became three, and my mom and dad still hadn't figured out when they'd be back. After the first year, they'd extended Dad's sabbatical, which had turned into a leave of absence funded by grants, and they'd gone down to South America to a small town in Ecuador to be teachers and to perform research in the Amazon. I'd always been supportive of their work, but as ashamed as I was to admit it, I'd harbored a little resentment about being my sister's sole support system.

Marnie, my younger sister by three years, had always seemed older than me. She'd always been so serious, giving her an air of being more mature. When Marnie was born, my mom had focused most of her attention on her, trying to figure out what she needed. Nonverbal until she was six, Marnie had presented a sizable challenge. This had made me self-sufficient at an early age.

Marnie had eventually learned to take care of herself, for the most part. Still, it left me filling in the gaps without any indication it would be anything other than the two of us for a while. Like I said, I tried not to dwell on it. But there I was, dwelling on it while a beautiful woman played music for me on the mall. I sat up straighter and pushed all of those thoughts away to give the musician my full attention.

Too soon, she finished up with "Rocky Mountain High." As the final strains washed over me, I wished for more, but the woman with the beautiful dreads gathered the money from her case and packed up her violin. I watched with interest as she discreetly handed the money to the bedraggled man on the bench. His eyes gleamed with gratitude, and my eyes welled up as I pretended not to see the private moment. So many questions about the woman leapt to my mind as I watched her kiss her fingers, pick up her equipment, and wave good-bye to him. With a vibrant swirl of her multilayered skirt, she walked down the street. I wanted to follow, but I stayed put. She disappeared around the corner, and the bustling after-work crowds absorbed the dispersing audience.

The outdoor patios—crowded with young professionals holding wine, microbrews, and tumblers of whiskey and laughing overly jovial laughs and flaunting their camaraderie—continued to fill up as offices closed for the night. I could be one of them, laughing and drinking with coworkers.

But who would make dinner?

I sighed and got up, hefting the strap of my laptop bag onto my shoulder, and headed toward the train station, walking slowly, taking my time. About a block from the station, I noticed a storefront I'd never seen before. Or maybe I'd seen it but not really noticed it in my hurry to get home every night. The sign bearing a big hand caught my eye. *Madamee Eugenie—Tarot Cards, Palms Read*, the sign said in red neon. I'd walked this block countless times and had never noticed the small shop before. A tiny table draped with a black cloth sat next to the front door, and an old woman dressed in a long black dress and a red shawl sat at the table shuffling cards. Her eyes tracked me as I slowly passed. She didn't say anything. The little hairs rose on my neck. Not in a bad way. More like an *aware* way.

I checked the time on my phone. Already a half hour late, I backtracked to the little table, curious.

The old woman shuffled her cards and smiled. She spoke just as I began to ask her how it worked. "Don't worry. Mercury is in retrograde now. When the planets go direct, you will be content again."

The little hairs on the back of my neck stood again. How did she know?

She waved a hand above the deck of cards, her silver bracelets jangling like little windchimes. "The three cards I'm about to show you represent the past, present, and future."

I shifted from foot to foot, unprepared for a reading. She picked up the deck again, her gnarled fingers shifting deftly through the cards before she set the deck back on the little table. She flipped the top card, laying it on a black cloth with faint stars printed all over it.

She tapped the card with her yellowed nail. "This card is your past, the Page of Wands." Her raspy voice held the trace of an accent I couldn't place. "You have been content with your life, but it lacks direction. You've been at peace with most relationships, your work, your activities, but you have not held the reins. Your life has led you."

She flipped another card while I processed what she'd said, knowing she was right. Most things simply happened to me throughout my life. I'd never been hard to please. In fact, I'd always been kind of proud about how most of the major things in my life happened as if the universe provided what I needed when I needed it with very little drama. It happened in college, when a scout came to watch one of my soccer teammates and ended up offering me a partial scholarship to a local university—so I went. The same thing happened with my job. After I'd passed my CPA exam and attended a school job fair, a recruiter from a prestigious local firm pointed me in the direction of openings in their accounting department. I applied and got the job. Most of my relationships even started as friendships, with another player on my soccer team or someone from work. For some reason, people just sort of integrated into my life for whatever time the relationship lasted and then moved on. No real effort. No real drama when things fizzled. Except once. But it only took once.

The old woman's raspy voice interrupted my thoughts. "The Eight of Pentacles," she said as she turned the next card. Her twisted finger rested on its smooth surface. "This is your present." She paused. "Ah.

You fight inside. Your passion is rising against your lack of motivation and inspiration. You wonder how you will fix this." She stared at the card. "It's like you've been stuck on a railroad track."

My heartbeat quickened. Had she meant I was in danger, tied to the tracks? Could I escape?

The old woman's dark eyes found mine. Kindness shone from them. She almost appeared amused. "Not a real railroad track. A metaphorical railroad track, going in one direction, hard to leave without a lot of effort." She shrugged. "So you haven't. It's a smooth ride. Not the most interesting but not so bad, either. You're bored. Your eyes are opening. But you don't know what you see. This is going to cause a lot of questions and longing for change."

My mind raced as I tried to make sense of what she was telling me. I hadn't said a single word, but it seemed as if she knew me.

"Let's see what the future shows." She flipped another card, but when she placed it on the table, there were two cards. "This is interesting. The cards are telling us your future is not a single path." She shrugged again. "The truth is, our future is never a single path. But you have decisions. Decisions that can bring different outcomes. The Two of Pentacles and the Two of Cups." She tapped the pentacle card. "Change and balance, a time to manage your priorities. This can maintain calmness in your life. Or it can shake things up, leaving you feeling overwhelmed.

"The other card, the Two of Cups, speaks of connection and partnership, maybe romance, something lacking in your life, yes?"

I fought the urge to shake my head. Partnership, romance, neither had ever been important to me. Conversely, balancing the priorities in my life had always been a huge focus for me. I had other things in my life, more pressing things, things making it hard to pursue a relationship. Thus, all of the brief connections I'd made petered out. At the time, it made sense that the pentacle card should be the path meant for me.

But...

A shift in perception surprised me when I considered the two paths she suggested. A sense of something sliding to the side, revealing something I never wanted to analyze before that moment. It was true. I craved something more in my life, and I thought the "something more" could be the connection the old woman mentioned. I nodded.

"To ignore the connection can cause great tension, problems with communication, a sense of uncertainty and imbalance."

Her eyes darted across the cards as if she read a compelling story.

She looked up at me and smiled, transforming her face into something almost beautiful. The lines and wear on her face were the fine brush strokes of an artistic master. If her words hadn't been causing me to reevaluate the foundation of my life, I would have easily been lost in studying her. Thankfully, she spoke, breaking me from the spell.

"There is music and dancing. Color and laughter. Good things. Love." Her raspy voice drew out the last word, making it sound like something special, magical, necessary. I hadn't known I wanted it, but now I did, more than anything else. This was the thing causing my recent…I didn't know what to call it. Ennui? Yes, ennui sounded right. I'd been suffering from the gray dissatisfaction of ennui.

The woman took my hand, her grip light and her hand warm. She pressed the cards into mine. "You will choose the right path." Her smile and words calmed me.

"Thank you," I said, pulling my wallet from my bag.

"No charge. You'll come back for a full reading. Remember the music." She waved me off.

I turned, about to walk away when I realized I should at least give her a tip, but she'd vanished when I turned back.

I tucked the cards into the pocket of my jean jacket.

My phone vibrated again. I almost ignored the new text, but I sighed and pulled my cell out.

Where are you?

I peeked at the time: forty-five minutes past the time I usually arrived home. I thought about not replying. Home was less than fifteen minutes if I caught the next train.

Rowdy's hungry.

I'll be home soon. I sent the text before I changed it to something snarky. Marnie didn't deserve my frustration and probably wouldn't even pick up on my impatience anyway. She only wanted to know when I would be home. I should have sent her a text telling her I'd be late.

Okay, she responded.

I didn't expect her to ask what caused me to be late. I arrived at the train station as the train pulled in and boarded. I had my choice of seats, a benefit of catching the train later than usual.

My phone vibrated again.

Rowdy had an accident by the door.

Of course he did. I walked him in the mornings and after work. Marnie walked him at bedtime. She wouldn't have thought to take him out.

Is it bad?

Just pee. When do you think you'll be home?

I shut my eyes. I was an asshole. Poor Rowdy. *I'll be there in ten minutes. Can you take him out?*

I've already taken off my shoes.

I closed my eyes and pictured Marnie in our apartment. She always came home from work, leaned her computer bag against the table next to the front door, slipped off her shoes, put them on the tray next to the table, got herself a glass of water, went to her desk, slipped on her headset, and started an online game. Always that routine. Always in that order. There was never a deviation. I knew this because I was always home first, and I watched it every day. Because I hadn't been there, Rowdy, my good dog, had waited at the door before losing the battle with his bladder, after which, he'd curled up by her feet, ashamed of his accident. He loved her, but even with a full bladder, he wouldn't expect care from her right after work. That was my job. Of course he peed on the floor.

I got off at my stop and quickly walked the two blocks to our LoHi apartment, appreciating the freshly planted flowers in front of the buildings I passed. The sun sank low over the Rockies, and the blue sky hung overhead. A perfect mid-spring evening in Denver. I took the beauty of the evening in as I rushed home to Rowdy because I knew he hadn't let it all go. I swiped my card to enter the low-rise building and forwent the elevators, like usual, to take the stairs two at a time, stopping at the third floor. My watch vibrated, telling me I got all of my steps in.

The tarot card reading occupied my mind when I opened the front door. Rowdy sat a few feet away, unable to make eye contact. I stepped over the puddle and scratched his head. Poor guy. I grabbed some cleaner and paper towels from the kitchen and cleaned up the mess. Marnie's issues with germs meant she couldn't clean it up.

I regarded my little sister. She was sitting exactly where I'd pictured her: at her desk in front of two enormous monitors, a game playing on one side and green lines of code streaming down the other. I imagined her knit brows, eyes darting over the monitors, the tip of her tongue poking from the corner of her mouth. At the same height, with shaggy-cut brown hair and brown eyes people have always said she looks exactly like me, only more serious. Other than our appearance, we couldn't be more different.

The muscles in her shoulders moved as she manipulated a

controller with one hand and typed with the other. Every so often, she'd type something into her nearby laptop, open to a development window, probably giving her access to the back end of the game she played. The green lines of code looked like a bunch of unintelligible text to my uneducated eye. I found it amazing how many things she could do at once when she was in her zone, and games were definitely her zone, being both her job and her hobby.

I quickly finished the cleanup and threw the wet paper towels away before I washed my hands.

She didn't overtly acknowledge me, though she'd turned her head a little when I entered, indicating she knew I'd come home. A less intense part of the game must have come up because she moved one of the earphones from one ear. She still didn't turn around. "Hey, Dar."

Her hands moved rapidly across the keys of her laptop, performing her job. She tested video games for a living, and she played them after work for fun, alternating between using one of her various controllers or using her keyboard and gaming mouse. She needed the impressive setup to do her job and to play in her free time. She'd built her gaming PC all by herself.

I used to think she had one of the coolest jobs. But now, I basically hated it. Maybe "hate" was a strong word. Tired of it would be a better description. Gaming occupied Marnie's world and was basically all she did. She played games and talked about them all day at work and came home and either talked about them with her online friends or played them all evening. She usually didn't talk to me about them. I tried to be interested when she did, but not being a gamer made it difficult. Her focus made for an uninteresting existence for me sometimes, but I'd accepted it a long time ago. An image of train tracks flashed through my mind.

"Hey, Mar," I said, grabbing Rowdy's leash from the hook next to the door. Apparently, he'd gotten over his shame because he was now dancing at my feet. I'd be lucky to get him all the way out of the building before he peed again—or worse. I checked to ensure the dispenser attached to Rowdy's leash contained poop bags. I didn't have time to change from my work suit into jeans and a T-shirt.

"He's happy you're home." Marnie slipped her headphone back over her ear and concentrated on the game while I put on Rowdy's harness and leash. He continued to dance but didn't jump when I kneeled before him. He rested his head on my forearm as I attached the leash to the harness, giving me his version of a patient hug. I loved him so damn much. If not for Rowdy, I'd have been so lonely. I thought about the dancing and love the psychic talked about. Rowdy kind of fit the description if I thought about it. If so, as much as I loved my pup, I didn't imagine the ennui going away any time soon.

Marnie grunted. "Shooter on the left," she said to whoever she was playing with online.

I took Rowdy downstairs.

CHAPTER TWO

Phaedra

I set up my equipment on the 16th Street Mall a little early. I usually waited until later in the evening so I wasn't in the middle of the five o'clock rush. But it was a weird day—not bad but not good—and I craved a little music therapy.

"Can you play some Eagles, Phaedra?" Taco Bill asked, shrugging out of his backpack and putting it on the bench next to the garbage bag containing the rest of his possessions.

He looked good today, which lifted my spirits. The pneumonia he'd contracted over the winter had taken a big toll on him, and I'd been worried, but he'd finally kicked it and was gaining back a little of the weight he'd lost. I'd offered to let him stay at my place, but the old dude was stubborn and proud and maybe a little paranoid, so he'd refused. I tried to understand, but to me, life on the street was scary. To him, it was home.

"Sure, Bill," I said, returning the fist bump he offered before I rested my chin on the cradle of my violin. Goose bumps covered my skin when I pulled the bow across the strings. The music sounded ethereal on the mall. It echoed between the tall buildings on either side of the pedestrian path and vibrated down, wrapping around the people walking between them. It buzzed through me, giving me a natural high.

I'd been looking forward to counteracting the dullness of work all day. It always amazed me how playing a few songs on the mall helped with that. Work wasn't usually a drag, but with Mercury in retrograde, little challenges had tested my patience all day, and I needed a pick-me-up. I usually played on the mall Tuesday nights when weather permitted, as a way to kill time between work and the weekly judo class I'd started taking down at the Buddhist temple. Playing live had always been one of my favorite things, seeing the smiles, giving a break from the never-ending negativity of the recent news cycles.

I'd been playing live since I was a teenager, but playing on the mall started as a lark a couple of years ago. I had my violin and amp with me because Barb had asked me to play during an all-hands meeting. Barb Daniels, founder and CEO of Calamity Graphics, where I worked, liked to bring fun into the workplace, and part of it was showcasing the talents of the employees. I played at company meetings a lot, along with a handful of other employees who liked to rock out. Blending music with work helped keep the activity that paid the bills tolerable, so I could focus all my other time on making music, which I'd been doing since I was four years old.

On the mall, I mostly played cover songs. That particular audience enjoyed hearing music they found familiar, at least based on the engagement I usually got from people who stopped to listen. Even now, young men enjoying a few beers after work on one of the restaurant patios sang along after a few drinks. The Eagles were a favorite, right after John Denver. Go figure. John Denver continued to be a hit in Denver.

Every once in a while, someone who followed my band happened to catch me doing a mall show and would ask me to dance while I played. I didn't dance anymore, though, so I usually just smiled and played something fun to get their mind off my dancing. The requests stung, but I'd almost gotten used to it. Almost. Today, no one asked, and I was glad since I'd been in a bit of a funk earlier. Playing always helped pull me out of a bad mood.

As I sang, I watched a pretty woman sitting off to the side. It took her a couple songs, but she finally relaxed. I noticed her right off and was a bit bummed when it appeared she was going to walk by, but when she took a seat on the planter, a flutter went off in my stomach. She tapped her foot to the music, and I wanted to know more about her. Why was she so serious? Why did she hold herself away from the rest of the crowd?

I always did this. I'd always been an unashamed voyeur, a watcher of people, someone who tried to figure out what made them tick. People fascinated me. Not just the pretty women, either. Did the trio of guys at the patio bar work together? Did the kid with the skateboard have a home to go to? Was the woman talking on her phone fighting with her husband or yelling at a subordinate? But mostly, I couldn't help but rest my eyes on the pretty woman with the big brown eyes and fashionable, professional clothing. I sensed a lot bubbling under her put-together surface. In a previous time and place, I would have taken it upon myself to find out more. Not so much these days. Tonight, I played music.

I knew the songs by heart and barely had to concentrate to perform. This allowed me to watch the people and wonder if their interest in me matched my interest in them. Today, however, my eyes kept wandering to the business woman sitting on the planter.

CHAPTER THREE

Daria

I took a bite of my tuna sandwich and watched a kid on a skateboard in front of the coffee shop across the street jump the curb. A pair of mounted policemen stopped near him and told him to pick up his board or leave the mall. The kid kicked his skateboard up and tucked it under his arm as he moodily slumped around the corner. He'd be back as soon as the cops and their horses moved down the block. They performed this dance regularly, as he hung out on the mall almost every day. He seemed harmless enough, just a kid who wandered around downtown. I wondered where he went during the winter. I hated to think about the homeless in the cold, or any time, for that matter.

In an effort to think of other things, I thought about the woman I'd seen performing the night before, as I'd been doing obsessively in between musings over the impromptu card reading. Both events consumed me; the card reading for obvious reasons, and the woman because there was something about her that made my heart race. Her beauty? Her talent? Her kindness toward the homeless man? Probably all of it.

Taryn pulled out the chair next to me in front of the sandwich shop and sat, interrupting my thoughts. I knew what was coming.

"Why do they insist on putting tomatoes on my sandwich every time we come here? I clearly say no tomatoes, but still, they put them on." Her expression indicated her disgust as she held the offending garnish between finger and thumb.

"You asked for a number two. It's a bacon, lettuce, *tomato*, and avocado sandwich."

"But I specifically asked for no tomato."

"I don't think they register anything after the number you order. They're kids, probably working their first job. You need to ask for a build your own." I wanted to attribute this to the whole Mercury retrograde thing the tarot card reader brought up the night before. I'd never heard of it before, so I googled it, and supposedly, Mercury in retrograde affected communication and the ability to think clearly for some people. I wouldn't say I was one hundred percent convinced about the whole tarot card thing, let alone that the position of Mercury could cause people grief, but when I read up on it, it appeared lots of people did. Either way, it seemed like it was right on the nose for me. I thought about running it by Taryn, but not right then. I'd wait for a time when she wasn't all fired up about her sandwich order.

"It's not rocket science, Dar. And build-your-owns are a dollar more." Taryn picked up the bread, examining inside the sandwich. She dropped the bread and sighed dramatically. "Mayo on one side of the bread but not the other. I specifically said mayo on both slices. I hate this place."

"Yet we always come here. At your suggestion."

Taryn dropped her head back, pouting. "They make a delicious BLAT. When they make it right, which is maybe one out of five times."

I took a bite of my delicious sandwich. "I wouldn't know."

"Right. You don't eat animals. And apparently, you're saving yourself some stress."

"I don't eat animals who have the capacity to love," I corrected. "I eat meat."

She gestured toward my sandwich. She didn't need to ask what it was. I always ordered the same thing. "What about the dolphins caught in the tuna nets?"

"I only eat hand-caught tuna." I held up my hand. "But let's stop here. I can't think about the origins of my food while I am eating it."

"Oh yeah. Right." She dropped a tomato slice into the bag her sandwich came in, muttering her displeasure. "Tomatoes are disgusting. They taint everything they touch."

I barely heard her as I stared at my sandwich. Fish had died for this lunch. "Shit."

She rolled her eyes before she took a bite. "Why aren't you a vegetarian?"

"I've tried. My body craves animal protein. A psychological thing clicks on and grosses me out when I think about the actual animal I'm eating. I want to let them live their lives. But my body says, 'Daria, feed me meat.'"

She chewed and swallowed. "It's a disorder."

I picked up my bag of chips. "I am totally aware of that."

"I still love you." She rubbed my arm.

"For which I am grateful." I ate a chip. I could always count on potatoes.

I had to get my mind off the fish thing before I barfed up the three bites I'd taken. The woman who played the violin yesterday commandeered my mind. For the first time, I wondered if anything the psychic had said pertained to her. "Have you ever noticed the little tarot card shop down at the end of the mall?"

"Which end?"

"The west end. Down by the train station."

"Oh, you mean Madamee Eugenie's, the little one with the neon signs? It's been there forever."

"Have you ever gone?"

"Once, a couple years ago. A few of us were coming back from a Rockies game and thought it would be cool to check it out. You and I should go sometime. They take walk-ins."

"Do you believe in that stuff?"

She squinted, looking at the sky. "I don't know. I did a palm reading. It was more on target than not, I guess."

"Was it the old lady doing the palm reading? What did she say?"

I wanted to talk about my reading, but it weirded me out, and I needed to process it some more. I thought about the cards. I'd tucked them into my jacket pocket, and even though it was hanging in my closet at home, I imagined them emitting a mysterious energy with some sort of pull over me. I'd be the first to admit I'd seen too many horror movies.

"I can't remember exactly. She mostly talked about general things, I think. But she told me I'd get a promotion at work, and a couple weeks later, they gave me the director position. Remember?"

"Yeah. She predicted it? Or did she say something more ambiguous like, something good will happen at work, and you just connected it to her prediction?"

"I remember her exact words. You will get an unexpected promotion. She also said I would break up with Scott."

"But you didn't."

"Yes, I did. Remember when he flirted with the girl at Rock

Bottom right in front of me, and we had a huge blow up? I kicked him to the curb that night."

"Oh yeah. It lasted all of a week before you let him come back."

"But she got it right. We broke up. She couldn't have seen it coming. *I* didn't even see it coming. When she told me, I was, like, no way. I was gaga over him."

"You still are."

Taryn flashed a big cheesy grin, and I wished I'd ever felt half as much for anyone as what shone in her eyes for Scott. "True. But the point is, she sees things no one can see or guess. It's been on my mind ever since, and I've wanted to go back for another reading."

"Sounds kind of scary. What if she sees something you don't want to know?" I'd said it without really thinking, but I realized finding out something terrifying was my main concern. What things did she see but didn't tell? And would I want to know?

"I know, right? It's the primary reason I haven't gone back."

She ate her sandwich, and I nibbled on my chips. I couldn't stop thinking about it. When I'd gotten back from walking Rowdy the night before and had started dinner, Marnie had come to help. Normally, I tried to get her to talk about her day since she rarely offered work stuff on her own. But last night, we'd worked on making dinner and had eaten without exchanging more than a dozen words while I wondered about the meaning of everything the old woman had said. The main thing on my mind was the whole train track thing. My eyes had been opened, and now I couldn't close them. I was stuck neck-deep in a rut—or on a train track I couldn't get off of—and I didn't even know if I wanted off it, let alone what I would do if I did.

"Earth to Daria. Come in, Daria." Taryn's voice interrupted my thoughts.

I looked up, confused.

"Jeez, girl. You were circling Neptune there for a minute. What are you thinking about?"

"I'm thinking I might go visit the tarot shop." Maybe a full reading would give me some clarity.

Her eyes widened. "Really? I never thought *you'd* be into it."

Even my friends thought I was boring. "Why wouldn't I be?"

She looked me up and down. "No offense, but you're pretty straitlaced."

I hated to admit it, but my first thought was, I was turning into Marnie. I used to be fun. I used to be spontaneous. I used to do unexpected things like checking out mysterious shops. What had happened to me? Indignation and guilt wove together to create a dark cloud in my mind. "No offense, huh?"

"You know what I mean. I just never thought you'd be interested in something like tarot cards."

"Me neither." Her words spurred me on even more. "But let's do it. You said they allow walk-ins? Or do we need to make an appointment?"

She finished her sandwich and cleaned up her mess. "We walked in when I went before, but I'm sure we can make an appointment."

"Let's go on Friday. We'll walk in. If it works out, it's a sign. Besides, it will make it harder for them to do any internet searches on us before we go." There was no way the old woman had dug up any info on me before last night, but I couldn't shake my skepticism.

She smiled. "You're getting all mystical on me, girl. I never suspected this side of you."

I lifted an eyebrow. "There's a lot you don't know about me, Taryn. I'm a mysterious conundrum."

She eyed me with an unconvinced squint. "Yeah, right. Conundrums don't have a meal plan mapped out for every day of the week."

I frowned. I didn't want to be predictable and boring. How did that happen to me? It just convinced me I needed to make a change. How long did Mercury retrogrades last, anyway?

CHAPTER FOUR

Phaedra

I dropped the sandwich wrapper into the bag beside me on the bench and stood to brush the crumbs from my blouse and lap. I rarely left the office for lunch, but Barb said we couldn't deny the beauty of the day, so she'd dragged me out to a cute little sandwich shop on the mall. Our bench wasn't far from where I'd played the night before, and I thought about the pretty woman I'd seen. I wondered what building she worked in and how close she might be right now.

I stretched, and the new muscles I'd discovered in judo class last night made themselves known. I rubbed my thighs, and a piece of shredded lettuce stuck to my hand. I could be such a slob. Apparently, an out of shape slob, too. I groaned. "I swear, I end up wearing half my food. Do I have any mustard or mayo on me? I'm too sore to fix it." I pulled the bottom of my shirt down to check out the situation.

Barb flicked another piece of lettuce off my skirt. "You are free of stains, Phaedra. But the pattern on your skirt would hide it if you weren't. You'll get used to the exertion soon, by the way."

She would know. She was the one who'd turned me on to the classes at the Buddhist temple. She'd achieved her second-degree black belt before having to give it up due to a torn rotator cuff she refused to get surgery on.

"Dang, I hope so." I straightened my arm, pulled it across my chest, and held it closer with the other arm. Ow. Ow. Ow. "Why do you think I lean toward multicolored clothing? I've been a slob since I was a kid. If I were a man, I'd be the guy who always has hot sauce on his tie."

Barb waved her hand dismissively. "You are definitely not a slob. I work with you, remember? Your desk is immaculate."

My mother's voice rang through my head. "I can't take you anywhere. You end up wearing more of your food than you eat." I shook my head. Mom was long gone, but her voice was always in my head. Even her memory was a nag, but there was a certain comfort in it. I missed her, even the naggy part.

"I make up for my bad luck with food and clothing by being a neat freak elsewhere." I tossed our lunch sacks in a nearby recycling bin and left the unopened pack of chips on the bench. Hopefully, one of the homeless kids would find it.

Barb checked her watch. "We still have thirty minutes. Are you up for a loop up and down the mall?"

It wasn't like her not to want to get right back to work, so I knew she wanted to talk. "Sure, my boss is out of the office, so I can slack off." I laughed at my own joke. Barb was far from a taskmaster.

"I won't tell if you don't." She winked.

The busy lunch hour on the mall provided a myriad of interesting things to look at, and it didn't look like we were the only ones who'd escaped from the office to soak up a little fresh air and brilliant sunshine. We strolled along the sidewalk, gazing into shop windows, watching people. The muscles in my bad leg screamed at me. My lower-leg prosthetic was usually extremely comfortable, but all the recent work in the dojo had made muscles I hadn't used in years scream at me. The walk was helping, though, loosening it up. Judo was harder than I'd thought, but I needed my strength back. Seven years of no real exercise would require a lot of make-up workouts, but it was time to make some changes.

Barb looped her arm in mine. "How are you doing, love? Is everything going okay in Phaedra's world?"

Had she picked up on my recent sense of disquiet? I thought I'd kept it reined in. "I'm fine. Why do you ask?"

"You're preoccupied all the time, and your energy is a little dialed back. I'm used to you going a million miles an hour, especially in early summer when you start planning all your camping and music festival trips."

"I'm not into it this year, I guess." I stopped to admire an acoustic guitar in a music shop window. I had two at home, but it didn't keep me from wanting more.

"What's keeping you from being into it?" she asked.

I usually didn't like to talk about my problems, except with my best friend Leigh. But Barb had a way of getting me to open up, at least about most things. "All of my friends are paired up this year. I'm the only one without a partner to do things with."

She lifted an eyebrow. "Well, your singledom *is* self-preserved. Do they really require a plus-one to hang out with you?"

I laughed. "Not at all. But they all have someone, and I'm the lone wolf. I don't like it when I'm the one sitting by the campfire after everyone else has retired to their tents for sexy time."

"This is interesting coming from you. You've never been the type to need a girlfriend. Besides, I've heard musicians rarely have trouble getting chicks. You could have a new one every night if you wanted."

She was funny, perking up, talking about "chicks," and basically advocating for my promiscuity. I didn't talk about my love life very often, mostly because it was nonexistent, so this had to be exciting for her.

I stopped before one of the touristy shops, where a cute knit cap on sale caught my eye. The big stylized C from the state flag sort of ruined it for me, but I liked everything else about it. We started walking again. "I don't want a string of strangers in my bed. Besides, you know I don't trust women to be honest with me."

She only knew part of where my distrust came from. "Loredona really did a number on you, didn't she?"

I nodded. "I wasn't even in love with her, but I was having a good time. I sometimes thought we'd end up together."

"Except she's straight."

I pretended to glare. "Thanks for reminding me."

She laughed. "I wish you told me you were seeing my assistant on the sly. I could have told you she was married and saved you the heartache."

My face grew warm thinking about all the sneaking around Loredona and I had done, in and away from the office. Being eight months removed from it, I could admit the sneaking contributed to most of the excitement. I never would have imagined being one of those people who conduct illicit romances in the office, especially with a married woman. "The thing about secret office romances is they're secret. Either way, I think I'm completely shut down and have been since she went back to her husband in November."

Barb made a huffing sound. "I'm glad she quit. It saved me the trouble of firing her."

"As much as I love your loyalty, she didn't do anything to warrant losing her job. We don't have a fraternization policy."

She raised a brow. "Aside from having intercourse on the premises, you mean?"

The heat of my blush could have ignited anything flammable within a ten-foot radius. "Okay, you have a point. But I was just as complicit."

"It's a good thing I'm the CEO, then." I loved her wicked humor, even at my expense.

I still felt bad about keeping my fling with Loredona a secret from her. But Loredona had begged me not to say anything. She'd claimed fear of losing her job, but now I knew the real reason. Barb had only found out because I asked her why Loredona wasn't at work following the whole embarrassing mess at my loft, except I didn't tell her what had happened. When Barb told me she'd quit, I broke down into a blubbering mess. I'd never told Barb the details. She'd thought Loredona had simply gone back to her husband. Only Leigh knew the real truth.

"I honestly can't imagine wanting to even try to date again," I said. "Women suck."

She glanced at me. "Present company excluded, right?"

"Always. You know I get first dibs on you if Bharat ever decides to turn you in for a newer model."

"Ouch."

"You know I love you."

She rolled her eyes. "As a wise old grandma, I know."

"As a hot and luscious woman." I could say things like that to her without her getting all weirded out. She might have been several years older than me, but she was far from the grandma type. I'd never tell her about the crush I'd always had on her. She was married, so nothing would ever come of it, but even if she grew a fondness for the fairer sex, I liked being sweet on her from a distance. Why did I torture myself with straight women, anyway?

She smiled. "Nice backpedal."

We arrived at the end of the mall where 16th Street allowed cars, and we turned to walk up the other side. On the cross street at Wynkoop, a block up from Union Station, the slight smell of incense tickled my nose. A small table with a black cloth draped over it sat before one of the little shops. An old woman with long white hair, dressed in all black, sat in the single chair, staring at me. As we passed, I sensed her tracking me. I looked over my shoulder to see her still watching. It should have been creepy, but other than feeling a little on display, I didn't sense any

・34 ・   KIMBERLY COOPER GRIFFIN

malice. The psychic's store made me think of my mother, who'd been from Haiti. She'd handed down some of her fear and awe of magic and witchcraft to me, things intrinsically woven into the tapestry of her life. Although I'd grown up in Colorado and I didn't share the depth of her superstition, I didn't mess around with powers I didn't understand.

A shiver passed through me. "Have you ever noticed the psychic place?"

Barb turned, as did I. The old woman must have gone inside. "Madamee Eugenie's. The shop is a Denver treasure."

"How have I never noticed it? Did they just add the neon signs?" A red light in the outline of a hand over the words "Palms Read" glowed in the window.

Barb shook her head. "Nope. It's been the same for decades."

"Have you ever gone?" The thought of her, with her pearls and perfectly coiffed hair, consulting a psychic almost made me laugh.

"A few times, actually."

I almost tripped. My mom would have crossed herself just for thinking about going. "Seriously? Is the place legit?"

"I think so. I went the first time right before I started Calamity."

"Did the reading help?"

She nodded. "I wanted to do a check-in to see if I could make the company work. Madamee Eugenie took one look at the cards and told me I had to go through with it to feed my soul. I didn't even know my soul needed to be fed, but it did. It was the first business I started on my own."

I squeezed her elbow. "You were never on your own."

She shoulder bumped me. "You're right. You've always been there for me to lean on."

I spun in a circle, my skirt flaring around me. "All twenty-two years of knowledge and wisdom I was back then." I laughed.

"You've been my sounding board since the beginning, and I appreciate you more than you will ever know." Tears glistened in her eyes. I was probably the only person, aside from her husband, who knew what a real softie she was.

I looped my arm around hers. "Let's go get our palms or cards read sometime." I couldn't believe the words came out of my mouth. My mother would have had a heart attack.

CHAPTER FIVE

Daria

Walking the mall in the afternoon always felt a little weird, but it felt especially weird today since Taryn and I skipped out of work early to visit Madamee Eugenie. The outdoor mall wasn't as busy as I was used to without the high energy hustle and bustle of the lunch hour crowd or the business folks going to and from work. Without the crowds, I noticed colorful murals and planters with new flowers, making it appear both familiar and new at the same time. This quieter mall seemed like a place I'd like to hang out and explore. I needed to get out of the office more often.

Taryn and I walked casually, enjoying the afternoon, and I caught myself thinking about the street performer I'd watched earlier in the week. I'd have gladly postponed the card reading I'd promised Taryn to watch her sing again. Maybe I had nerves about the reading, but I knew it had more to do with the crush I had on a woman I'd never even met. Either way, I barely recognized myself with all this pining over a stranger and going to psychics. I kind of liked stepping outside of my comfort zone and the sense of anticipation it gave me.

We'd made it almost to the shop when a young man sped past on a skateboard, close enough for us to feel the breeze in his wake. It was startling, but not unexpected with all the foot traffic. I recognized him since he was on the mall all the time.

"Hooligan!" Taryn walked backward, shouting and shaking her fist, but she was laughing. We'd never been in danger. She was just being funny.

The kid had the grace to appear apologetic and slowed down. "Sorry, ladies," he said, glancing back and pinching the rim of his flat-billed trucker's cap featuring the Avalanche hockey team logo. He flashed a captivating smile before he kicked off again.

"You know," I said to Taryn, "I can envision that kid five years from now, sitting in an interview for a new movie based on yet another comic book hero, explaining how he was discovered while loitering in Denver's 16th Street Mall. It'll be a great story. His fans will eat it up."

Taryn nodded. "He's a good-looking kid. I see him out here all the time."

"Have you seen the singer who plays the violin?" I tried to say it like I hadn't been thinking about her off and on since I first saw her.

"The one in the bohemian skirts? Totally. She's amazing. I think she plays in a local band, too." Her expression grew thoughtful. "It must be nice to pursue your passion. I'm too addicted to money and nice things to do something like that."

"What are you talking about? Your passion is bossing people around. You live your passion daily."

She looked at me sideways. "I'm offended. You know what my real passion is."

"I beg your forgiveness. But I believe you'd get arrested for quitting your day job to have carnal knowledge of your boyfriend in public on the mall."

"You're awful. I meant wine, and you know it. It would be great to just chuck it all and buy a vineyard or a wine bar. What would you do if you could quit your job and follow your dreams?"

"What's your guess?"

Taryn furrowed her brow and studied me. "I honestly don't know. You like to read, but I wouldn't call it a passion. Netflix? You tell me."

Now *I* was offended. How freaking sad it was that my best friend couldn't name my passion. She'd known me for almost ten years, and she couldn't name a hobby I liked? I opened my mouth to give her shit but realized I couldn't tell her what I'd do given the chance to pursue my passion. My life was boring. I worked, and I took care of my sister.

"Just for that, I'm going to keep you guessing," I said, hoping my voice didn't betray the sadness I felt at realizing I couldn't name a single hobby or pastime I was passionate about.

Taryn chuckled knowingly and didn't act as if she sensed my inner turmoil. "Oh, honey. I can have loads of fun with guesses. You'll wish your passion could live up to my imagination."

Just in time to change the subject, I spotted the neon hand glowing against the black backdrop. I wondered how I'd never noticed it before the other evening. I'd walked right by it almost every day for six years. I stopped a few doors down. Something tumbled in my stomach. "There it is."

Taryn backtracked to me. "Having second thoughts?"

"No. Not at all," I lied. I didn't know what it was. The impromptu reading had been interesting—a little nerve-racking in its accuracy—but not scary. I wanted to hear more insights from Madamee Eugenie.

"Are you afraid the psychic lady will read your inner thoughts?"

I laughed hollowly. "I don't have any inner thoughts. Nothing I'm afraid of anyway." I chewed the corner of my thumbnail, a habit I thought I'd kicked years ago. Maybe she'd tell me I was destined for the very life I was leading, which filled me with disappointment. I wanted off the train tracks. Pretty sure it was the primary cause of my ennui, I needed help to figure out some changes. But how could I when I was responsible for more than just me?

"Let's do this thing," I said, walking toward the store even though I wanted to run away. Taryn fell in beside me, making me grateful I wasn't doing this on my own.

A crystal ball sat in the center of the unattended table outside. Taryn opened the glass door with black cloth draped over the back. The tinkling of bells sounded from a chain hanging inside. A thick aroma of perfumed incense enveloped us as we stepped in, and the door swung shut behind us. My eyes struggled to adjust to the dimness after the bright sunshine of late afternoon. As things came into focus, I noticed more black cloth on the other windows, and all the walls and ceiling were painted black. A large round table ringed with high-backed chairs took up half of the narrow room. Maybe for seances? I estimated that the room could accommodate several people at a time, but for now, it held only the two of us.

"Have a seat." A voice came from behind a dark piece of fabric hanging in a doorway. Faint symbols in silver sparkled like the tablecloth outside.

I glanced at Taryn. We both shrugged and sat on the red velvet couch near the door.

A haphazard pile of eight-by-ten laminated cards lay on a low coffee table before the couch. I picked one up. The front featured a menu of services such as palm and tarot readings, runes, and aura readings along with a variety of prices. The back listed other services like past-life readings and exorcisms. The type of services that kind of scared me, making me worried that dark spirits might be involved. No prices were listed for these services. In large bold letters on the bottom, someone had made sure to note, "No Voodoo!" I let out a relieved snort before I could help myself. It helped my nerves knowing that even psychics had boundaries.

I checked out the tarot listings, which described several options. Above the section, a description interested me. "Unlock your inner wisdom. Use your own intuition, access your subconscious to understand yourself. Apply what you discover to guide yourself on your personal journey." I liked the idea of being part of the discussion, and it didn't sound like it would be someone telling me things I already knew. The prices were reasonable.

"What brings you to Madamee Eugenie?"

I jumped and dropped the card. A young woman with long dark hair and a flowing black dress stood before us. Ropes of silver chains festooned with different pendants hung around her neck and down her front. Like Madamee Eugenie, she adorned her wrists with a multitude of silver bracelets.

I exchanged glances with Taryn, who looked as startled as I felt. I cleared my throat. "We were hoping to get a reading."

"You came to the right place." She gave us a warm smile. My edginess faded a little. "Do you have an idea of what you'd like? We offer quite a few."

"I'm new at this. Maybe a tarot reading?" I said.

"I came here once a few months ago," Taryn said. "I had a palm reading. I think I'll try tarot this time."

"Will this be together or separate?"

Taryn and I passed glances. I wanted her to take the lead since she'd been here before, but she just shrugged.

Well, I didn't want to be alone. "Separate. But can she be in the same room?"

Taryn nodded. "Me, too." She looked relieved.

"Certainly. Come with me." She turned and moved to the cloth-draped door. She appeared to glide, adding to the mystical vibe I'd picked up throughout the shop. She held the cloth back, indicating we should enter. A string of twinkle lights lit a hallway leading to three different doors.

She led us into the only open one. I admired the intricate weaving of her dress and head covering, and I wondered what the other rooms contained. A purple light barely illuminated the small room that someone had painted black. A small, cloth-covered table sat in the center, with three chairs around it, one facing the other two. Another chair sat in the back corner. The woman rounded the table and sat on the opposite side. Made of dark, heavy wood and upholstered with worn red velvet, it seemed more like a throne. The other chairs were shorter, with wooden arms and worn velvet seats. She gestured for us to sit, and Taryn and I obliged.

"What's your name?" I asked.

She smiled. "All of the women in my family are named Eugenie."

I wondered if the old woman was her mother or grandmother, but something kept me from asking.

This Madamee Eugenie placed her hands on the table with a deck of cards. I hadn't seen them earlier, and she hadn't stopped to pick them up. The door to the room clicked shut behind us. The sound was startling in the otherwise quiet room, and I checked behind me. There was no one there.

"You seek answers." Her eyes were large, the whites stark against the nearly black irises.

No shit, Sherlock. Apparently, nerves caused me to lapse into juvenile sarcasm even in the privacy of my own brain. I hoped she didn't read minds.

"Bring your questions to the front of your mind, and the cards will provide insight."

I was glad she didn't ask me to say them out loud. Somehow, giving voice to them would be disloyal to Marnie. Nothing in this world would cause me to hurt her. Nothing.

Madamee Eugenie split the deck. "You don't need to tell me. The cards will tell us."

I exchanged more glances with Taryn as Madame Eugenie shuffled the cards, and I noticed her long nails were painted a dark color I couldn't discern in the dim light. She fanned out the deck on the table and asked me to select a card. I pointed at one somewhere in the middle of the deck.

Her face remained impassive as she split the deck at the place I'd pointed to and set it back on the table. I admired her slender fingers adorned with rings as they slid the top card from the deck, turning it over. An unexpected image of Madamee Eugenie using her beautiful fingers in intimate ways invaded my thoughts. Ashamed for letting my thoughts go to forbidden places, I closed my eyes and shook my head. Until that moment, my thoughts had been as far from erotic as they could be. Now I couldn't stop thinking about her doing delicious things to me, to herself, to others. *Stop this.* My mind went blank. When I opened my eyes again, Madame Eugenie raised one corner of her mouth. *Could* she read my thoughts? Heat rose up my neck, and I forced myself to think about other things, though the passion in me persisted. I squeezed my legs together, and a pulse spread from my center, making my fingers—and other places—tingle.

I forced myself to think about my life and the role Marnie played in it. The inappropriate images stopped. Thank God.

Madame Eugenie placed the card on the table, facedown. "The reading I'm about to give you is from the ten-card Celtic Cross spread. This configuration provides a view of the bigger picture by observing how the cards interact. Do you have any questions before we start?" I'd been watching her hands, and when I lifted my eyes, hers bored deeply into me. Or was my imagination running amok in this mystical setting? A tingle, barely under my skin, started at the crown of my head and spread in a wave down my body. I couldn't stop the shiver it caused, so I shook my head in an attempt to mask the response I was having.

She nodded with a knowing smile and focused on the deck, turning over the first card. She arched an eyebrow and my heart started to race. "This card represents the present. It may provide insight into your perception of the situation on your mind. The Tower. A major arcana card that speaks of sudden change, perhaps an awakening. This portends big revelations, maybe chaos?" She looked at me, maybe to read my reaction. I tried to keep my face still, but my mind was racing. Big revelations? Were my feelings of discombobulation merely the beginning of something else? Madameе Eugenie dropped her gaze to the deck, and I took a deep breath. "Let's find out what the next card brings. The remaining cards will help bring context to the situation."

She selected another card from the top of the deck.

I couldn't tell what she thought about the reading so far, other than what she'd said the cards meant. "Another major arcana. The Lovers. This card represents the challenge you seek to find answers to. The meaning can be literal, about love and relationships. Or it can be figurative, about physical or emotional well-being, harmony, choices." She squinted. "You, though, you're healthy. I think you are seeking insight about your heart." She laid the card atop the first one, crossing them. "Either way, the Lovers can signify a crossroads. With the Tower, it appears you may have a choice to make."

I didn't want to lead her down a specific path by giving affirmation to her guesses, so I sat there, hoping my expression remained as impassive as hers. A matter of the heart in regard to me seemed far-fetched, especially as I wasn't in the market for romance. My life didn't have room for it, even if I wanted it, which I didn't.

"We'll understand more as the cards are laid." Madame Eugenie selected another card. She rested her hand over it before turning it over, watching me intently. "This third card is your past. Knowing how your challenge came to be can provide direction on how to solve it."

I already knew how my challenges came to be. I had responsibilities. They'd increased big time when my parents had moved to California. That was when my choices had been drastically limited, through my own decisions. At the time, and even now, well beyond the one year I'd agreed to, I'd taken the responsibility willingly. I loved Marnie, my sister and, in a way, my child, too. I couldn't imagine life without her. But the decision had meant big changes for me.

I had responsibilities.

Madamee Eugenie's long fingers flipped the card and placed it to the left of the other two. "The Magician," she said.

I almost snorted. *This is where she goes wrong.* Magic had nothing to do with how I'd arrived in this situation.

"In most cases, this card indicates you deliberately made your way into the situation you seek information about. You tapped your power and took strong action."

Well, I'd been wrong before.

"However, this card is upside down, and your path is likely uninspired, your talents not fully realized. You landed where you fell."

How did she know? How did she develop this laser precision in describing my life? I tried not to let the surprise show as she picked up another card. I stared at the three on the table. Everything she'd said made sense now, except the heart stuff.

"The fourth card is your future. This card, like all the rest, does not necessarily predict the final outcome but simply provides insight about the next step in your journey. This will manifest itself in the next few weeks or month." She flipped the card and moved it to the right of the others. Her beautiful finger tapped the face. My stomach clenched. A person hanging by their feet from a tree. "The Hanging Man," she went on. "This card is often mistaken as a negative signal."

Do you think? I almost croaked out. It sure looked negative to me.

"But it's the opposite. It's the card of letting go and finding new perspectives. The Hanging Man encourages us to pause and take stock. It is probably why you're here today, trying to divine your future.

Hanging upside down by one foot, searching for a different way to see things. But look." She rested her finger on the card. "The face is calm. The man doesn't mind being there. He's there by his own choice. This is the card of ultimate surrender. It appears your future may depend on you releasing something. A person? A feeling? A way of seeing things? Perhaps all three and maybe more."

I nodded before I could stop myself. There was no use in trying to keep my expression noncommittal when she already knew my inner struggles. She wasn't a danger to me, but did I need to fear the information she knew?

She drew another card, laying it on the table. I remained silent. She focused on the cards, her eyes flicking between the four she'd placed in a vertical line, her lips moving slightly. As if she'd become aware of my study, she raised her eyes, and they flashed across my face, perhaps gleaning something from the directness of my gaze. Tempted to look away, I didn't. I met her scrutiny, her eyes shining with intention, alive with the workings of her mind and whatever gave her the vision she used to read the cards. She wasn't smiling, but her stare held no challenge.

She rested her hand atop mine. The erotic sensations I'd fought against earlier rushed through me again, but they weren't centered on her. Someone else, someone familiar, but I couldn't tell who. Her eyes switched to an inward gaze, and she closed them. I didn't fight the feelings. Amid the desire, a vast peace fell over me. I took a deep breath, released my shoulders, and closed my eyes. My awareness of the room, of Madamee Eugenie and Taryn, remained, but I also sensed the mall outside the shop, the city around it, the world surrounding us, and the endless space beyond. In a strange and electric moment, I clung to the connection of everything around me. I was expanding, floating, conscious of everything and anything. Sublime calm filled me.

Whispered words brought me back to the moment, and I opened my eyes. Madamee Eugenie removed her hand. Her eyes were half-closed while she uttered words in a beautiful language I didn't understand.

Taryn cleared her throat. Madamee Eugenie opened her eyes and stared at the card beneath her fingers, sliding it into position above the first two cards she'd read. She began to speak as if the moments of expanded consciousness never happened, except the peace persisted.

"Ah, the Sun. In the fifth position, the card represents what is above the surface and active in your mind. It reflects the goal you seek for the situation on your mind. Whether or not you are aware, this is what you are consciously working toward to resolve the issue. The Sun is a symbol of positivity, fun, warmth, and success." She caressed the card. "The female figure in this card is naked, on a white horse. The essence of purity and innocence. She has nothing to hide. Success is at her fingertips, and life is a gift." Her eyes flicked across the cards. "In concert with the preceding cards, it is apparent you know what the happy path is for you, but something you hold on to keeps you from realizing it."

She spoke the truth, and I sensed her disappointment. I came here for insight when I knew I'd never act on it. Pursuing happiness didn't release me from my responsibility. I wanted to cry.

I pointed to the deck. Madamee Eugenie flipped the top card over.

"That which completes the cross, the sixth card, Justice, representing the subconscious realm. It explores much further, examining the core of the situation. What is driving you? It could bring unexpected results if insight is not developed. This card, when upright, speaks of the law, of fairness and truth, cause and effect. But it is upside down, thus, all is reversed. Unfairness, lack of accountability, lies. Maybe you, maybe not. Maybe someone close to you. Either way, it is not intentional, coming from the domain of the subconscious. The double-edged blade signifies what you think it does. Actions always carry consequences. But her eyes are wide open. She sees all. The pillars behind her represent the duality of the situation, right versus wrong, good versus bad." She studied the cards. "Balance can be achieved. But will it? I think yes, but you must make what is below, above. Insight is required. In parallel with the card representing your future, this tells you to let go. Let go of that which is above but also that which is below."

What did she mean? Unfairness? Lies? I considered myself an open book, what you saw was what you got…mostly, anyway.

Madamee Eugenie rested her hand on the deck. How many cards would we use? We'd only done a few, but the amount of information overwhelmed me. I'd already forgotten much of the first few she'd read.

"I know it's a lot to take in. Remember, the detail isn't important. The general impression you receive from the reading will guide you."

"Thank you." My throat felt raw. Probably from all the words I held back swirling in my head. I didn't know why I held back. Was I afraid she'd use my words as a tool to dupe or con me? I didn't think so.

"We've completed the cross, and now we reveal the staff. As you will see, the Celtic Cross formation takes us through all the aspects of the situation. The cross explores the details close to you. The staff, made up of the last four cards, divines the details beyond you."

She kept answering questions without me asking. It freaked me out. She drew four more cards and arranged them in a vertical line to the right of the others. She flipped all four over and scanned them along with the ones we'd already discussed. One perfectly shaped eyebrow rose, and she looked up. "I've never seen this before. All ten cards drawn are major arcana."

"What does it mean?"

"The cards are made up of major arcana and minor arcana. The minor arcana consists of the four suits: wands, cups, swords, and pentacles. The major arcana tells the story of the journey of the Fool, who represents us all. The major arcana can be considered the big things in the journey of life, and the minor arcana are the day-to-day things, which is a good way to view them. The major arcana represents important choices. These choices affect the rest of your life, or at least, guide your path in a certain direction."

"I guess it means my question's a pretty big one, then?"

Madamee Eugenie tilted her head. "You can say the rest of your life depends on it."

Pressure filled my head as if the atmosphere in the room became enormously denser.

"Remember, what you seek may simply be the top layer of a deeper, more fundamental question." She tapped the sixth card. "When you explore what lies below, the question may metamorphize into something else."

What the hell did she mean? I wanted to call her out for leaving herself an out, but my mind teemed with everything she'd said so far. I tilted my chin at the cards. "What do the rest say?"

Madame Eugenie raised her perfectly sculpted eyebrow again. That was when I saw it. Death. The next card on the table actually said Death. What the fuck?

"The base of the staff, or the seventh card, is the root of what you came here for. Advice. It provides the guidance regarding the approach you might take to address the issue you seek answers to."

Dread filled my belly. Death as the outcome could not be good. Was I fated to be unhappy? Or did she mean it literally? Did it mean I'd die if I didn't address the issue? I could feel the train barreling down on me while I was still on the tracks.

Madamee Eugenie's hand fell over mine again, and the peace

from before fell upon me. A smile shone in her eyes. All the stress evaporated.

"This particular card is not what it appears to be. It's important, have no doubt, but it's not sinister. It's good, at least when it is not reversed. And it is not reversed for you. This card speaks of the end. Which can mean many things. It could be change or transformation. There are endings, and there are new beginnings. It talks about letting go of the past and coming out of unknown darkness. This is a good card for you. If your question is about sadness, this will lead to happiness. If you seek answers for a broken heart, it will mend it."

My skepticism became a faint memory. "What advice do you give?"

Madamee Eugenie scanned the cards. Her hands hovered over them, and her beautiful fingers…why couldn't I stop obsessing over her fingers? Finally, she spoke.

"Do what you already know is needed. Seek beyond what is before you and learn more, trust your instincts. If you follow your heart, you will never go wrong."

Hadn't I been following my heart, which held love for my sister, already? Wasn't it my heart that had landed me in this chair hoping for advice in the first place? Of course, I hadn't really expected a fortune-teller roadmap to be given to me, but some of what she'd told me had been directly on point. At times, it seemed like she'd plucked knowledge straight from my mind. I had to admit, I was disappointed with the almost trite, follow your heart, message.

"She'll take it differently than you expect, and after some confusion and a big misunderstanding, you will find happiness again. The music will guide you."

What? Wait. Happiness? Music? I must have missed something. She who?

Madamee Eugenie's finger rested on the next card. "This card tells us of external influences, highlighting the energies or events affecting the outcome of your question beyond your control. Reversed, the High Priestess indicates there are secrets. The position and reversal both indicate the disconnect from intuition, where insight is blind, signaling withdrawal and silence. Hidden influences are at play." Her finger swept across the pendant holding the Priestess's robe closed. "Normally, the cross she wears, with arms spread wide, represents balance, but upside down, it means the opposite. Be careful. The upside-down High Priestess can destroy you if you aren't careful." Chills ran down my arms. Madame Eugenie's fingers drifted across the card. "The black and white colors of the card symbolize duality and knowledge, and truth will only be revealed when the seeker is ready to see beyond the material realm."

"Am I the seeker?"

Madamee Eugenie's eyes, unfocused and turned inward as she spoke, regained their focus. "You are *a* seeker."

I wasn't sure what she meant. I guessed I had to figure out what seeing beyond the material realm meant.

"The next to last card, the Star, represents your hopes and fears." Madame Eugenie tapped it. "This position is complex to read. It depends on the context gleaned from all the other cards. Moreover, hopes and fears are opposite sides of the same coin. Often, what we hope for may also be what we fear. If fear is stronger, it can push away true hope."

She'd been so confident with the other cards, but something told me she might not be sure about this card. I wondered what she saw but didn't say.

"What does it mean?"

She pursed her lips. "It's hard to tell. Your question, I think, merely touches the surface of what you truly desire." She pointed to the Justice card. "Until you know your true desire, there's no telling what hopes or fears may arise. Or maybe you already think you know, and there will be a struggle. It's not clear how it will resolve itself, but one thing is clear. You will choose the path you walk. It is your choice and your choice alone."

What she said sounded as if I would have some sort of control over things, which gave me relief. To a certain extent, despite her suggestion that my question might not be the real question I wanted to ask, I knew what I wanted to know, and as she went on, it became clearer to me. I wanted to know if I could extend my life beyond the focused boundaries of my sister's comfort. Did I have to work so hard—and limit my life in the process—to maintain the structured routine we'd established to keep her from becoming overstimulated?

Marnie couldn't "fix" her autism. It was as much a part of her as her arms and legs. What choice did I have? And honestly, did I even want to change her if I could? No. I loved her for all the facets of what made her who she was. There was no better feeling in the world than being the center of her attention or knowing I had the unique ability to ground her in an instant when she needed it. And it went both ways. Sure, she couldn't read me the way other people could read me; she couldn't tell the difference between excitement or anger most of the time. She took things absolutely literally. But her logic often guided me to the core of whatever issue we had. If I told her I needed her help, she dropped everything, even her games. I loved our connection. That was why I made a promise to my mom and dad to watch out for her. I could never ask her to help me with this particular thing because in doing so, she'd discover my favorite thing in the world—being her rock—was also one of the causes of my discontent. I felt selfish even thinking about it. Why did I even come here, getting glimpses of a future I could never have without causing her distress?

I cleared my throat to release the tightness gathered there.

Madamee Eugenie faced me with compassion, as if she knew my thoughts, and I wondered how long I'd been lost in them.

"The Star is a card of contrasts and universal effect. It represents everything at once. When upright, as it is here, it speaks to hope, renewal, and inspiration. It also speaks to faith and spirituality, but not necessarily in a religious way. If you pay attention to the silence when the mind is at peace, the truth will be revealed."

She waited as if she expected me to say something. I didn't, so she continued. "She is pouring two containers of water. The jar in her left hand represents the subconscious. The jar in her right, the conscious. With her right hand, she pours the water into the lush greenery around her, nourishing the Earth, always aware of what she is doing. The other hand, representing her subconscious and out of sight, pours the water onto the arid land, where it divides, making five streams often interpreted as the five senses. Even her feet represent the duality of reality: one foot on the ground, displaying her practicality and common sense. Her other foot is in the water, where intuition and inward vision create an inner voice to guide her. Unclothed and vulnerable, she depicts trust under the enormous night sky."

Madamee Eugenie fell silent, staring at the cards as if trying to figure out what the Star really meant relative to its position among the other cards. I sure as hell had no idea what all of it meant even after her description. And again with the conscious and subconscious thing. My hopes and fears were in a tug of war with one another. But weren't everybody's?

She waved her hand at the last card. "The outcome. If you did nothing differently from what you've been doing, this card tells you where the situation is headed and how the issue will be resolved, if it gets resolved at all. This doesn't mean you are locked into what we talk about here today. You have free agency. You can change your path and change the outcome."

"So basically, none of this is set in stone?" I asked.

She pressed her hands together and rested her chin on the tips of her fingers. "Nothing is set in stone except the past."

"What's the point of reading the cards, then?" But I knew the answer. Insight. She'd used the word several times. I'd hated philosophy in college, but here I was, staring directly at the age-old philosophical question of existential truth. Fate versus free agency. Destiny versus charting my own path.

Instant headache.

I sighed. "Forget I asked. I get it."

She smiled. "This last card, the Wheel of Fortune, is one of my favorites. It represents good luck, karma, life cycles, destiny, a turning point." Wait. Destiny? Hadn't she already said I had the power to change the outcome if I wanted? "You'll notice the symbols for certain elements; mercury, sulfur, water, and salt. These are the foundations of life. Then there is the Sphinx, who is knowledge and strength, the gate-keeper. Other aspects noted in this card are stability amidst change, wisdom…all good and positive things. While it's possible to change your path, it occurs to me, you may not want to. We go back to the first cards making up the cross in our spread." She gestured toward the first few cards. "You already know what you need to do. Listen to the silence to understand more. You know what is needed. If you continue on your current path, the outcome will be positive."

"Thank you," I said. My head was spinning, and I knew I wouldn't remember a fraction of what she'd said.

"Do you have any questions?" Madamee Eugenie leaned forward, taking both of my hands. Her eyes were magnetic. I couldn't look away. The faint sensation of the earlier desire swirled within me, but it was background to the other thoughts taking over my mind. None of them questions but none of them answers, either.

"I can't think of anything."

She held my hands for a moment more before she turned to Taryn to read her cards. I mulled over what I could remember. Two things stood out. The first, that I should continue on my current path. What did she mean? Maybe she meant for me to turn inward and listen to the silence for answers. My mind was anything but silent. The second, that the outcome would be positive. What did she consider positive?

By the time my thoughts settled down, Taryn's session was over, and Madamee Eugenie was seeing us out. When I stood, I noticed the old woman from my last reading sitting in the chair in the corner. She smiled and nodded, and I returned the gestures. So strange. I hadn't noticed her, and I thought I would have noticed the door opening when she came in. She remained seated as we exited.

"I recorded your session with my phone," Taryn whispered as we passed through the veil into the front room, and I fished cash from my wallet, still wondering about the old woman. "I remembered how few details I could remember after my first session. I'll run it through a transcription app and give you the recording as well as a printout."

I wondered if I'd have the guts to listen to the session again.

CHAPTER SIX

Phaedra

I weaved through the crowd milling around the long bar, careful not to step on toes. "I'll have the Vanilla Nitro," I mouthed to Buck the bartender.

Happy Hondo's was lively and packed. Most of the crew from Calamity took off early today and was here celebrating a big new customer. I was in charge of making sure everyone got something to drink and a little food in their bellies so the alcohol didn't go straight to their heads. But if it did, I would also call a ride for anyone who ended up being overserved. We used to keep beer, wine, and liquor in the office for occasions like this, but as the company got larger, Barb put the kibosh on it. I wholeheartedly agreed with this decision. It was always so embarrassing when the newbies tried their first taste of beer at their desks and took it too far. About three of five would make fools of themselves at least once before learning to dial it back. When Hondo's opened downstairs, it was a great way to transition that kind of fun out of the office, and Hondo's was a natural choice as the adopted company bar. They enjoyed the business, and the team enjoyed being taken care of as loyal regulars.

Buck slid the beer to me and winked. "On the house, m'lady."

"You know free drinks won't get you anywhere with her," Ralphie, one of our new guys, said in a loud voice, the swagger of someone being in the know. "She dates women."

Buck gave him an exaggerated look of surprise. I held back a snicker. "It's a way to say thanks to her for not being competition for the men *I* want to date." Buck winked at Ralphie, who had the decency to blush.

"Was he flirting with me?" Ralphie asked when Buck turned his attention to another customer.

I did snicker this time. "Would it bother you if he did?" I wondered if we'd made a mistake hiring Ralphie. He'd come with plenty of experience, and everything pointed to him being a good fit in the interviews, but if he was going to be a bigot, I wasn't down with it.

"Not at all." His eyes were glued to the back pockets of Buck's assets. "He's kinda cute. I just pegged him the wrong way."

It appeared I'd pegged Ralphie wrong, too. "He's single and ready to mingle," I whispered in his ear as I walked out to the patio.

When I made it to the section of tables the team had taken over, Barb was standing on the sidewalk, talking over the metal railing to a couple of folks from IT.

"I thought I kicked you out of here half an hour ago," I said to her.

"I forgot to give you this." She waved a credit card and handed it over as the folks from IT wandered away.

"Ah. You didn't need to come back down here. I was going to expense it. I know you and Bharat have tickets to *Wicked*."

"It's no trouble. It's on the way." She leaned close. "Plus, I wanted to give you a heads-up about the new woman in marketing."

I tried to think of who she meant. A cute but very young face came to mind. "Josie?"

She nodded. "The very same. She's interested."

"Interested? You mean in me?" I scoffed. "I seriously doubt it."

She swatted me with her wallet. "Don't act like you aren't the hottest piece at Calamity. I heard her asking Ralphie about you today. She wanted to know about fraternization policies."

No way. I laughed to hide my discomfort about having a woman ten years younger than me asking about me. "Did you call me a piece?"

"Don't change the subject. The girl is into you."

I glanced around the bar, searching for Josie. She was next to Ralphie, but she caught me glancing her way. She waved and smiled. It had been so long, my gaydar must have broken. I would have bet my bonus on her being straight. Embarrassed and totally not interested, I waved back. I hoped I wasn't sending the wrong signals. I turned back to Barb, who was smirking.

"She's a kid."

She gave me the side-eye. "She's old enough."

"We do have a fraternization policy. I wrote it when Calamity was just the two of us."

"Then you'll remember it only applies if you're in the same department. You're under sales. She's in marketing."

I waved her off. "No thanks."

She sighed. She did that a lot. Not about my work. I kicked ass there. Only when we talked about my nonexistent love life. "Don't say I didn't try. I hate thinking of you not enjoying your camping and music getaways."

I cupped her chin. "While I truly appreciate your deep desire to improve my vacation time, I don't need you to pimp for me. What's the saying? You shouldn't poop where you sleep? I think I'll stay away from an office romance."

She took my hand from her chin and pretended to bite it. "I think the expression is 'you shouldn't shit where you eat.'"

"Even better. And apt. I'm going to take your advice. Enjoy your show." I crossed my arms. "I'll be here babysitting the crew, working hard. Don't you worry about me. Yep..."

"I am immune to your guilt trips."

I laughed and flapped my hands toward the performing arts complex only a few blocks away. "Seriously, go have fun. Give Bharat a hug for me. Where is he?"

"I'm meeting him there. What plans do you have after this?" she asked over her shoulder.

I leaned against the patio railing. "I don't know. I might go to the psychic shop."

She turned, walking backward a few steps. "You should do it. Maybe she'll point you in the direction of Ms. Right."

I surveyed the area to see if anyone else heard her. Everyone appeared preoccupied. I shooed her away and snorted. "Go find your hubby."

She rolled her eyes. "This conversation isn't over."

She left, and I turned toward the bar. Great. Josie walked toward me with a glass of wine and a pint of stout.

She offered me the stout. "Buck said you like this."

Somehow, I'd already finished my beer. I didn't want another, but I didn't want to appear rude, so I took it. Young and beautiful, Josie put off a totally hip energy. I'd appreciated her intelligence and confidence in the interviews. She had star employee written all over her, I already knew it. I hoped Barb had it wrong. "Thanks."

"Cheers." She held up her glass. I tapped the pint to it, and we took a drink. "How's the right-hand woman to Barb Daniels?" I swallowed and tipped my head. "I can barely keep up with her." She nodded. "I joined Calamity just to work for her, you know. She spoke at a women's leadership seminar in January about how important it is for women to give a hand up to other women in business. 'Her Hand in Mine' was the name of the session. I was in the front row. She's an inspiration. My boyfriend leaves the room when I talk about her now." Her eyes sparkled with admiration, peering down the sidewalk in the direction Barb went.

I couldn't wait to tell Barb how mistaken she was.

Buck handed me the check, and I was working out the tip. Almost everyone else had left the bar—some had gone home, others had headed over to the pool hall down the street—and it was only me, Josie, and Ralphie left. Ralphie was busy chatting Buck up, and from all appearances, Buck was enjoying it. If he and Ralphie hit it off, they would be an interesting pair. Someone came up beside me. I knew it was Josie before I saw her. She'd been my shadow all night. It hadn't been unpleasant, and after I'd found out that her interest in me was purely for professional growth, I'd relaxed a little. I appreciated a woman who was open about what she wanted. She was also interesting and easy to talk to, but it was the end of a long week, and I was ready to head out.

"Hey. My boyfriend went out with his friends, and I was gonna grab something to eat. Do you want to go with?"

It was sweet of her to ask, and I might have said yes if I hadn't already made the decision to go visit the tarot card reader. It was a solitary kind of experience, especially with the questions I had. "Normally, I'd say yes, but I have a thing to do tonight. Raincheck?"

Disappointment crossed her face, but she recovered quickly. "Sure. Definitely another night." We walked out together. "Have a good weekend." She headed one way, and I headed the other.

The mall was busy, as it usually was on a Friday night. A sense of apprehension crept into me as I neared the psychic's shop. I attributed it to the ingrained distrust of fortune tellers I'd picked up from my mom. I paused by the handle of the glass door before I pulled it open. Regardless of my mom's advice to stay away from psychics, I always trusted my gut over everything else, and my gut said I really needed something to lift me from the funk I'd been in since my accident. I took a deep breath and pulled the door open. The heel of my shoe caught on the threshold as I stepped into the shop, but I was able to maintain my balance without much of a wobble. All those years of dance and the new foray into judo were my saving grace. Interesting, though. It had been on my good foot.

Just as I'd imagined, inside the shop proved to be dark and mysterious. The tinkle of bells, the scent of incense, and the vibrant splash of red velvet added to the ambiance. I picked up the faint smell of perfume mingling with the incense, a unique fragrance I'd smelled before but couldn't place. Something about it reminded me of music.

Not seeing anyone in the front room, I took a seat on the couch and picked up a laminated page from the low table and scanned the list of psychic services Madamee Eugenie offered. I'd come in thinking about a palm reading, but the tarot cards sounded interesting.

"Thank you for visiting Madamee Eugenie's."

The gentle voice startled me, as I hadn't heard anyone enter. I stood to meet a young woman dressed in black. I'd expected an older person like the woman I'd seen when Barb and I passed the shop earlier in the week.

"Hi," I said. "Do you have time for a tarot card reading?"

She smiled and dipped her head. "We do. Follow me."

She pulled back the fabric on the rear wall, revealing a dim passageway, and I followed her into the back of the shop to one of three rooms. The old woman I'd seen out front sat in the shadows in the corner. She smiled and nodded. I smiled back and sat in one of the two chairs situated on one side of the table, while the young psychic took her seat across from me. I wondered if the younger woman apprenticed with the old woman. Was either of them Madamee Eugenie?

She shuffled the cards as she watched me. The expression on her face was interesting, as if she knew all about me, which shouldn't have been weird, considering her line of work, but it was a little disconcerting.

"I think I met someone important to you today," she said, placing the deck before me. "Please rearrange the cards as you like."

Huh? Important to me? I cut the cards and restacked them. "What do you mean?"

"It's just a feeling I have. It could be nothing. It could be everything." She pulled the deck closer and flipped the first card onto the table.

CHAPTER SEVEN

Daria

My apartment door appeared before me, and I had only the foggiest recollection of how I'd gotten there. Preoccupied didn't come close to describing me. About to press the code to open the door, I found myself wanting to turn around and go somewhere else. Where? I didn't know. Maybe I could sit at the bar at one of the gazillion trendy restaurants populating this part of town, have some tapas, get a drink, and ponder the reading. I'd asked Taryn if she wanted to go to a coffee shop to talk, but she had to get home. I definitely needed more time to really understand how to deal with my path forward.

Marnie knew about my plans to be home late. She'd had a few days to get used to it, and we'd written a list. Although wicked smart, Marnie needed lists when her routine was broken. Without one, she had a tendency to get focused on something to the exclusion of everything else. Lists kept her on track, especially if time played a part. Without specific times annotated, she'd eventually get the list completed, but it could take much longer than expected.

She had a short list tonight, consisting of taking care of Rowdy, making dinner, and doing the dishes. With taking care of Rowdy on the top of the list, I knew he was fine. The other stuff didn't matter as much, since Marnie would eat when she got hungry, even if she forgot about it. All of this meant that I didn't need to be home yet. The possibility of taking some real time to myself loomed before me, and a twist of excitement flared within me.

I stood before the door, debating whether to go back out. Finally, I had the chance to be spontaneous, and I had no idea what to do. How'd I become such a stick in the mud? Okay, I knew how. But seriously,

I didn't want to squander the chance. Being tired and contemplative didn't help.

But I could do anything I wanted.

Rowdy's whine from the other side of the door became the decision maker. He'd smelled me. I couldn't just leave him. I dropped my head and took a deep breath before I let myself inside. So much for my big chance to take time to myself.

Rowdy danced on the entryway carpet, part excited that I was home, part trying not to pee. I knew the dance by heart. Poor guy. I grabbed his leash and gave him some love as I affixed it to his harness.

Marnie sat on the couch with her gaming headphones on, laptop before her, mumbling into the mic on her cheek. In a rare moment of acknowledgment, she told the other players to hold on and paused her game. Although she played all day, every day, she joined a group of friends every Friday to play *WoW*. Often, it went late into the night. So she'd been playing for a few hours already. A couple of beer bottles sat next to her on the end table. I didn't want to overthink it, but the little detail made me happy. Marnie very rarely did anything outside of her routine without prompting. Maybe one of her online friends suggested it.

"Hey, Dar."

"Hey," I said, giving Rowdy one more tussle before standing. I shrugged my bag off and leaned it against the table next to the door.

"I wasn't expecting you until later. Did you and Taryn have fun?"

She never asked me about my day.

I hadn't told her about seeing a psychic, simply that Taryn and I had plans, and I'd probably be late. By late, I'd meant somewhere around nine o'clock, which for most people wasn't late at all. Since it was only eight, it proved I was a total loser.

"Yeah. It was interesting." I grabbed the doorknob but turned before I took Rowdy outside. I thought about telling her about the visit to Madamee Eugenie's. Much of what the psychic had said coursed through my head, but I didn't feel like talking about it right now. "Did you have dinner?"

She drummed her fingers along the top of her laptop. "I forgot. I know it's on the list, but SamBot420 talked me into one more fight and, well…" She shrugged. It was an expression she'd made since she was a little girl, and it still made me smile.

"I didn't have dinner, either. I'll make us some veggie burgers when I get back."

Rowdy didn't take long, maybe fifteen minutes. Time enough for him to pee, investigate each corner of the off-leash dog park near our building, and say hello to the other dogs and their owners. There weren't many people there. It *was* Friday night, after all, but the few who were out, I liked, and we chatted for a few minutes. At least I wasn't the only one home on a Friday night.

Rowdy and I tromped up the stairs, and when I opened the door, the aroma of cooking delighted my senses. We always had veggie burgers on Friday night if we didn't go out, which didn't happen often since Marnie didn't like crowds. Plus, it would impact *WoW* night.

Marnie stood in front of the stove with a spatula in one hand and her cell phone in the other. "Hey, Mom, Daria just came back in with Rowdy...Oh, okay. I'll tell her...I love you, too."

I hadn't talked to our mother in a couple months, so I met Marnie in the kitchen, excited to talk to her. I held out my hand for the phone, but Marnie set it on the counter instead.

Disappointment wisped through me. "Were you talking to Mom and Dad?"

"Only Mom. Dad was..." She looked up and to the right in a classic expression she used when trying to access a memory word for word, an amazing talent. "'Wrestling with the goddamn bags, trying to get them out from under a goliath mess in the back of a pickup truck piled at least as high as three fucking times its own height, even though they told the porter they would be getting off at the first stop and have a very important boat to catch.'" She sounded exactly like Mom.

My spirits sank. "Great. Now it'll be another two months before I talk to them."

Marnie flipped the burgers three times each. "Probably not. They'll be home before then."

What? "Really? Where are they now?"

She was staring intently at the burgers. "I don't know. She wasn't sure. All she said was they're still in the Amazon and doing well."

"When are they scheduled to be back?" Excitement made me bounce up and down.

"The first part of September. Dad already has his classes assigned."

"What else did she say?" I wished I'd talked to her. I would have asked all the important questions. I checked my phone, and sure enough, I had a missed call from her. I should have taken it with me to the dog park.

"Not much. She only had a couple minutes on a borrowed satellite phone. But they're on their way out of the jungle, and she'll call with more info when they get to civilization." She pressed down on the burger. "Perfect," she mumbled. "Oh, and she loves you."

I leaned on the kitchen island and realized I still had Rowdy's leash. I bent to unharness him. He gave me kisses and went over to flop in his bed. I barely noticed. Mom and Dad were coming home. I almost didn't know what to do with the information. I missed them so much and couldn't wait to see them. After three years, it didn't seem real.

A small clatter of plates roused me from my thoughts. "Thanks for starting dinner." I hadn't had to ask, and this was different.

"It's on the list, and SamBot420 said we could take a break from playing."

She'd mentioned Sambot420 once already tonight, and the gamer handle had come up a couple times before. She never mentioned players outside of play, so I pondered the significance. I didn't know how I felt about it. Protective played a part. Curious did, too.

"You've been mentioning SamBot420 frequently lately. Is this a new player?"

"Pretty new to the game. But Sam is from work."

From work, huh? "Do I know Sam?"

Marnie blushed and flipped the burgers three times each. I didn't push. She'd tell me if she wanted but wouldn't if I made a big deal about it. I suspected SamBot420 might be more than a fellow gamer. If my guess was right, this would be a pretty interesting turn for Marnie, who had never shown interest in anyone romantically before.

"You haven't met Sam, but…"

I waited, watching her flip the burgers three more times.

"I think I want you to."

"I enjoy meeting your friends."

The burger flipping became constant, so I lightly stroked the back of her short hair. The flipping stopped, and her shoulders dropped into a more relaxed position.

"I'll ask him to come over for dinner. Thursdays are the best, followed by Wednesday. Fridays are the worst because we have *WoW*. I'll send you an email with details about him, so you'll know what to talk to him about."

I wanted to tell her she didn't need to send me an email but refrained from it, more for her comfort than mine. But as soon as I thought about it, I realized the information might be useful. This was new territory for us. Her email description would probably be insightful about her feelings for him as much as it would tell me about him.

"Sounds great." As much as I wanted to ask more, I could tell I was on shifting sand, and she would shut down about the subject if I pressed at all. I'd have to wait for the email.

The timer on the oven went off, and Marnie silenced it before opening it to reveal sweet potato fries lined evenly on the baking sheet in three rows, alternating longest to shortest. Most people—like me—would have dumped them on the pan. But Marnie took the time to put them into orderly columns. Something about the way she went about the organization made them crisp up perfectly. I'd tried to do it her way, but my fries never turned out as perfectly baked. A big part of it was that Marnie would not leave the kitchen with the stove or oven on. It was one of her ways of overfocusing. I never had to worry about her burning the house down.

"Thanks for making dinner."

"My pleasure," she said with a smile.

When we sat down to eat, Rowdy roused himself and inhaled the kibble and canned dog food mix Marnie had put down for him in, like, two gulps. I gave him another half cup of kibble in the hope that he would take more time with it and not sit by my chair and beg. He wasn't allowed most kinds of people food because it caused him gastrointestinal distress.

Marnie tucked into her food and finished before I was halfway through my burger. I wanted to talk about Mom and Dad coming home or about this SamBot person, but she didn't like to talk while she ate. She'd read that lack of focus and taking too large bites and swallowing without chewing enough times contributed to choking. She always chewed her food thirty-two times before swallowing. Despite the number of chews for each mouthful, her concentration caused her to eat quickly. As a result, she almost always finished before me.

While she put her dishes in the dishwasher, I pondered Mom, Dad, and SamBot. A neat cook, she'd cleaned the mess as she went, so she had the kitchen back in order and had taken her place back on the couch to play her game before I finished. I heard her speak to SamBot, but her expression didn't belie the possible crush she might have.

After dinner, I sat at the table, thinking about the tarot reading. Not that I'd stopped thinking about it since I'd left the shop. It had been processing even through the call from Mom and the revelation about

SamBot. Especially the part regarding the train tracks and how it all affected Marnie. It occurred to me that Mom and Dad coming home made things a little easier.

Immediately, guilt consumed me. What kind of person did it make me if I considered handing off Marnie as a burden and not a person with feelings? I reminded myself that thinking it didn't mean I loved her any less. It didn't. Not even a little.

I got up and tossed a bag of popcorn into the microwave. While it popped, I had an epiphany. If Marnie had a "special" friend, maybe I'd have more room for spontaneity. I snorted about the irony of planned spontaneity. No matter what, I needed to get off the tracks, and I needed to do it gently for Marnie's sake. Hopefully, I wasn't getting ahead of myself. Who knew what SamBot420's intentions were? Was he even ready to date a person as complex as Marnie?

I poured the popcorn into two bowls and tossed a few fluffy kernels into the air for Rowdy, and he followed me in hope of more. I knew better than giving him more than two or three. Otherwise, there'd be extra trips outside in our future. I left a bowl next to Marnie on my way to my bedroom.

"Hey, thanks for the popcorn, Dar," Marnie said before saying something to someone online.

I went into my room and picked up my laptop, thinking I'd do a little work I hadn't gotten to since I'd left early. But before the login screen had a chance to fully resolve, I shut down the computer and tossed it onto the bed. Crunching numbers and fine-tuning reports, while intriguing most other times, didn't sound appealing tonight.

I turned on the television and wandered through the overwhelming menu options, stopping when I found *Sleepless in Seattle*. Romantic comedies didn't usually do it for me, but I could relate to characters feeling pulled between their responsibilities and their dreams. Plus, Meg Ryan was a hottie, so there was that.

CHAPTER EIGHT

Phaedra

The keys jangled loudly when I tossed them on the kitchen counter, and I dropped my bag on the couch on my way to bed in the partitioned area of my open loft. It was dark outside, but the ambient light of the city filtered in through the multipaned floor-to-ceiling windows taking up one entire wall. My apartment was one of the only units in the converted textile building that hadn't been remodeled into smaller spaces, and I had the entire tenth floor to myself. I'd bought it for cheap when the old brick buildings near Blake Street had become dilapidated and barely habitable, with dreams of one day turning part of it into a recording studio for my band, Washtub Whiskey. Fifteen years of gentrification and a few iterations of the band later, I still hadn't built the studio.

My living space took only one corner of the large space. Most of it was open with instruments and sound equipment arranged in another corner. Aside from having the occasional practice when Calamity was still in start-up mode and before the other floors were converted into more conventional apartment spaces, we'd had a few of our holiday parties here. It had been a while, though. The company was too big to fit in my apartment these days, and the band usually practiced in a warehouse off Walnut where Leigh, my best friend and our drummer, had her software development company. Also, since they'd broken the floors into separate units, I didn't know all the tenants anymore, and it was hard to get everyone on board with how loud a band could get. We mainly played bluegrass with a heavy dose of rock, so it wasn't too noisy, but the box drum could be pretty loud even without the pick-up on it. I missed the old days, when I only had to knock on a couple doors, one above and one below, and tell them we'd be practicing and they could come have a beer and hang out if they wanted to. These days, if the weather was good, we dragged our stuff to the rooftop common space if we wanted to jam at my place. It was still fun but not nearly as spontaneous. I couldn't afford this loft if I wanted to buy it today. Not even close. I made pretty good money at Calamity, but the real estate market was out of control in Denver.

I usually loved having room to chill, but tonight, all the open space just made me lonely.

I kicked off my shoes, hopped over to my bed, and dropped onto it, kneading below my knee where the prosthetic had been. Trance, in his mysterious, catlike way, appeared from one of his hiding spaces and jumped up beside me, rubbing his head across my arm. I scratched the short black hair behind his ears. Loud purring rumbled from his little body as he licked my arm and tried to extract all the love he could. Even though I'd come home at lunch, it was evident that I'd spent too much time away from home. His insistent rubbing was a sign that I had neglected him terribly.

"I'll bet you're hungry." At the sound of the magic word, he turned into a darting shadow, leaping across the room toward his dish. "I see how it is, you greedy bastard. You don't love me. You love your food."

I sighed dramatically, but he had me trained well. I grabbed the crutch I used at home when I wasn't wearing my prosthetic, went into the kitchen, and opened a can of his favorite food. He attacked his bowl like he hadn't eaten in a week.

I leaned against the counter in the kitchen and watched. It was only 9:45 p.m., and I was tired. When had I become an old lady?

I'd left a few of the windows open when I'd gone to work, and music poured in from the rooftop bar across the street. I went over and peered down. They'd opened the outdoor bar when the weather turned nice, and the rooftop was bustling with twentysomethings blowing off all the stress from the week. There was a time when I'd have been one of them, doing shots of Patrón and laughing with my friends. Leigh dragged me out to the bars once in a while, but I didn't party like I used to, like it was my second job. These days, I preferred to go somewhere fun but quiet to hang out with my friends. They'd mellowed, too. Well, everyone but Heloise, our steel guitarist. She was probably at one of the bars down there, raising hell. She didn't drink, not after the rest of us threatened to kick her out unless she got some help. She'd surprised us all and kicked it cold turkey, but she still loved to dance. Not many years ago, I'd be putting together an outfit and getting ready to hit the dance clubs, too. These days, when the band didn't have a gig, I was usually in bed by nine.

Thinking about dancing reminded me of the card reading. Madamee Eugenie's statement that I'd find love when I let the music move me again struck me as poignant because of the reference to the one thing I was most passionate about in life. Plus, it was poetic and beautiful, if not ambiguous. The thing was, I played music all the time, and the act moved me every time. Did she mean love of the music? Or something else? There was no way she meant romantic love because I was definitely not looking for that.

My stomach rumbled, pulling me from my reverie. I realized I'd made sure everyone at Hondo's put a little something in their stomach, but I hadn't. Not since lunch. My stomach growled again. I didn't bother to search the behemoth Sub-Zero Leigh had talked me into getting. For what? Sure, it was the perfect accoutrement to my open concept kitchen, but the only things in it were condiments, a couple beers, and a container of parmesan cheese. I picked up my phone and ordered my regular from Diner to Door food delivery. Tomato basil soup and an apple walnut spring salad with chicken was perfect for when I was hungry but uninterested in what I ate, like tonight.

After I placed my order, I opened a beer and sat at the kitchen island, scrolling through the newsfeed on my phone. Scenes from the work gathering floated through my mind. It'd been fun. I'd gotten to know some of the newer folks a little better, which I enjoyed. I'd always gone out of my way to make sure I got to know all the new hires, but it was getting difficult as the company grew. I replayed the last few minutes with Josie in front of Hondo's and laughed with embarrassment at my idiocy. To be fair, Barb had set the tone with the "she's into you" remark. But I'd been unfair to judge Josie without getting to know her first. Not that it made a difference. Barb had read the situation wrong in her eagerness to pair me up with someone when she knew I didn't want to date.

Trance jumped on the counter and set to grooming himself right in front of me. On the phone in my hands, to be exact. I squinted at him. "I'm not using my phone or anything." That didn't stop him, but he did open his eyes and watch me as he licked his butt.

I knew the expression. It said, "Nothing is as important as what I'm doing right now. I'm taking care of me. You should do the same thing." He was right. I hated it when he was right.

The buzzer sounded on the key pad next to the front door. I extradited my hands and phone from under my cat and pushed away from the counter, buzzing the delivery woman up and shrugging into a hoodie. The chilly late-June night air coming in the open windows made the tank top I'd worn to work less than effective at keeping me warm, but I wasn't going to close the windows. I lived downtown so I could be a part of the greater human organism. I loved sitting in my own space, listening to life below. Besides, I loved wearing hoodies. They were the epitome of comfort, and I had to be comfortable when I wrote music, which was what I was planning on doing as soon as I finished my dinner.

Writing on Friday nights was my thing. I looked forward to it all week. I sometimes got a little writing in during the week or over the weekend, but Friday was my dedicated night if we weren't playing somewhere.

A knock at the front door told me the delivery woman had made it up the elevator, and I slid the metal door open.

"You were quick," I said with a smile. I'd never seen her before.

"I guess it doesn't take long to make a salad and pour soup," she said while I tried to juggle my phone and my crutch and take the plastic bags from her. "Do you want me to bring it in?"

"That would be great," I said, grateful for the help. "If you could drop them on the counter, I'd be grateful."

"This is a great place," she said, coming in and glancing around. She was cute. Super cute. "I've delivered to other apartments in the building, and most of the floors are split into smaller units."

I leaned on my crutch. "I was one of the first owners."

She placed the bag on the counter and backed toward the door. "Well, I hope your leg heals soon. I'll bet it's a bitch trying to get around in all this space on a crutch."

"Thanks," I said, letting her out and closing the door behind her.

Since I was still wearing my long skirt, there was nothing for her to see and I didn't feel like explaining. Not that she'd ask. People usually just stared when they noticed my missing leg. I thought I'd be used to it by now, but I wasn't. Especially when beautiful women were involved.

Battling the return of the funk that had been hanging around me lately, I ate most of the soup and salad, then settled at my keyboard, which was set up before the large front windows that overlooked Blake Street, and while the game had let out about half an hour ago, the lights from Coors Field were still on. I set the instrument to organ and played

"Take Me Out to the Ball Game" as I watched people wandering the street below. Many of them were heading to or from Union Station or the bars along the nearby streets. I loved living downtown. I couldn't imagine living anywhere else, except for maybe a cabin in the mountains. I'd get restless pretty quickly being all by myself and away from people, but the idea of being surrounded by pine forest, taking long hikes during the day, and writing music at night seemed like the perfect existence some days.

"You'll find love when you let the music move you again. Follow your heart." The phrase kept running through my mind. But I wasn't searching for love.

I watched the people below as I let my fingers wander across the keyboard. Although I didn't have the volume up too loud, it drowned out the music from the rooftop bar. The lights, the breeze, the smell of restaurants cooking food below, it all created the perfect ambiance for good song writing.

"Alexa." I waited for the light on the AI device to signal it heard me. "Play my indie-pop music station, please."

"Playing the enduring love music station," Alexa replied.

The crisp, sweet sound of Alison Krauss's soprano filled my loft.

"Alexa, stop," I said, though she was playing one of my favorite songs. I definitely was not in the mood for love songs. The music stopped. "Alexa. Please play my indie-pop music station." I made sure to clearly enunciate.

"Playing your endless love music station," Alexa said.

Two chords of a Lionel Richie song sounded before I shut her down again. "Alexa, play my hipster-cocktail party radio station."

Finally, the upbeat tempo of Magic Giant filled my loft.

"Alexa, thank you."

"It is my pleasure to give you what you ask for."

I used my right hand to pick out the melody but turned toward the cylinder of technology sitting on my coffee table. What the hell?

Whatever. I kept playing. The song tested my ear and got my blood pumping. The melody was fast but easy. My left hand picked out the chords without much effort, and soon I was playing along, adding some layering of my own.

As I played, my mind wandered back to when I'd first arrived at Madamee Eugenie's earlier in the evening. My thoughts coalesced, in particular, on the old woman who'd been at the table in front of the shop when I'd arrived. Minutes later, inexplicably, I had seen her again when the card reader ushered me into the back room. At the time, feeling a bit overwhelmed just being in the presence of a psychic, I'd figured she'd slipped in through a side door. But now that I thought about it, a woman as old as she was probably couldn't move that quickly. Of course, I had no idea how old she was. She could have been in her late seventies or one hundred and ten. She was a mystery to me. Her very fortuneteller-y demeanor gave me no doubt about her authenticity, though. No doubt at all.

I ran my fingers across my keyboard, and goose bumps ran across my body at the memory of the old woman. I heard my mother's voice reciting the rosary, warding off evil. It had taken everything in me not to turn and leave with the old woman sitting behind me and the young psychic sitting in front, getting ready to tell my fortune. The weird sensation of desire that had come over me had been surprising, but that had been mostly overshadowed by the sense of dread. I remember wondering, what if she told me something I didn't want to hear? What if she told me *exactly* what I wanted to hear? I'd seen enough movies to know that even good news derived from magical places came with a price.

Even now, playing my keyboard in my home, the visceral memory gave me shivers.

The vulnerability of my deepest thoughts being seen in detail had been, and still was, disconcerting, but I'd gone there to have my fortune told. I'd sought guidance, knowing I couldn't continue down the solitary path I'd been restricting myself to. And she'd given it to me.

Now I picked out the melody of a smarmy pop love song where the singer got the girl for a happily ever after. Maybe Madamee Eugenie had been talking about love songs when she told me I'd find love. But real love didn't happen in my life. Not anymore. Unless I wanted to believe her when she'd said I'd already found the love I was looking for.

"Follow your heart," she'd said.

Yeah, right.

First of all, I hadn't been aware I was actually searching. Yes, I'd done a lot of thinking about not wanting to be alone, but it wasn't the same as actively seeking someone to be with *right now*. I didn't want to risk rejection again. Plus, women kind of sucked.

God. That sounded harsh.

Bitter and thirty-six. I was too young to be bitter.

I sighed. I couldn't wrap my mind around the music. Tonight, it just reminded me of everything I'd lost.

I turned off the keyboard and moved to the couch, turning on the television, flipping through the channels until I landed on *Sleepless in Seattle*. I loved Meg Ryan. The main characters weren't perfect, either, which was a little more realistic for me.

CHAPTER NINE

Daria

Marnie and I stood on the curb, waiting for a break in the farmer's market traffic so we could jaywalk to the restaurant co-op across the street. We'd spent a couple hours at the market, dropped Rowdy and the vegetables off at the apartment, and headed out for lunch. The city skyline painted a geometric view down the hill from where we were standing, and the sun shone brilliantly in a sky so blue it appeared painted. I fucking loved these kinds of days, and I loved spending them with Marnie. Still, an unnamed sense of expectation fluttered in my gut, not uncomfortable but not pleasant either. It felt as if I was waiting for something to happen, but I didn't know what to expect.

A motorized scooter jetted past us on the sidewalk, and I jumped. Jesus. They were everywhere these days, and they didn't pay attention to pedestrians. Marnie turned when we got to the other side of the street, and the brilliance of her smile sent happiness through me. I didn't get to see that smile often, her being such a serious person, but the beauty of the morning seemed to have infected her, too.

"We should try those one day. They look fun," she said.

It was completely unexpected coming from her, but I had to agree.

I loved our Saturday mornings together. It was our thing. We ran errands, and then we usually went somewhere for lunch. I could live without the part afterward, when we went home and cleaned the apartment, and after which she gamed for a few hours before dinner. That was when I felt most lonely. But after dinner, we usually watched a movie, which I enjoyed. I wouldn't call it a bad routine, it was just…a routine, and in some ways, I was tiring of the repetition. My good mood blunted somewhat at the thought, and I tried to think about something else. Marnie didn't appear to notice the slight turn my mood had taken.

Sometimes, her inability to read emotions frustrated me, but right now, I was glad she didn't pick up on mine. I needed some time to unwind this new perspective on my life.

I hadn't slept much the night before, thinking about the tarot reading, which had underscored the ennui consuming me. As soon as the reading had supported my plight, several other things started to fall into place. I wasn't the kind of person who made spur-of-the-moment changes in her life. I was a thinker, a plotter. I weighed the pros and cons of everything. But for some reason, I now longed for the freedom to make a choice without turning it over a million times. I wanted to say yes to fun and excitement. And it didn't mean I hated my life. I simply wanted *more*. And that knowledge made me want to fix it *now*. But how did I do it without throwing Marnie's life into chaos? She needed me to protect the structured way she'd designed her life.

I remembered when Marnie started sixth grade. The school district had decided to rearrange the classes in our neighborhood due to an increase in the number of students. Sixth grade had been moved to the middle school where I'd been going to open up extra classrooms at the elementary school. Although Marnie had been mainstreamed into the general classes, she'd had the same team of support staff working with her since day one. The school, knowing her situation, made every effort to notify our family well in advance to ensure Marnie had time to get used to the idea and for us to start establishing new routines to make the transition easier.

Despite the care taken to prepare her, it hadn't gone well.

It started with the first day when we'd walked *past* the gate to her elementary school on our way to our middle school half a block up the street. She'd stopped dead in her tracks and had refused to walk past the gate. Nothing we'd tried worked. She wouldn't move. I'd stood humiliated while all my middle school friends streamed past us. When my mom, who had the patience of a saint, took her hand and tried to guide her, Marnie had tossed her head from side to side and had let out a keening sound. The sound had made the hair stand up on the back of my neck. And it had gotten worse from there. She wouldn't allow us to take her home or move forward. Finally, the only thing we could do was let her go into her old school and sit at the desk she'd used in fifth grade. Thankfully, the teachers had understood. It had taken two full months to get her established in a new routine at the middle school. A similar situation had occurred when she started high school, but by then, we knew we needed to start the new routine in the middle of summer. That was also when we'd started to write detailed checklists to help her through major alterations to her schedule.

Since then, she'd gotten a lot better at change. She still didn't like it, but she hadn't made a scene in a very long time. I wasn't sure how much was related to her growing out of it or all the work we did to prevent unexpected adjustments to her routine. Whatever it was, it was working, and I was thankful.

We went inside the restaurant. Containers was a large space. Very modern. Very spartan. With two stories around the perimeter and the middle area open to the ceiling, with large windows spilling sunlight throughout the space. Around the perimeter sat rows of steel train cars, complete with wheels. Each hosted a different little food truck with micro-menus. The concept was brilliant, giving diners a casual place to eat and many dishes to choose from. This kind of place would normally cause Marnie to shrink, but we'd been going here for a couple of years, so she was used to it. The co-op gave me a variety of food to choose from, so I didn't go batty with having a single menu, which was what happened before Containers opened, and the only restaurant Marnie would eat at had been a pizza place a block south. I still couldn't eat pizza very often. We went to our usual table and claimed our seats.

I studied the menus listed in the book at our table as Marnie pointed toward the stairs leading to her favorite pizza place on the second floor, saying what she always did, "Right on. I'm getting pizza."

If it was her choice, we'd have pizza every night.

I settled on a Mediterranean menu. "Falafel and hummus sound good."

"Okay, meet you back at the table." She took the stairs up to the second level.

I sighed. She was being the same person she'd always been, but for some reason, her very expected choice of pizza irritated me. It wasn't her fault, and I tried not to let the irritation mount, but it was proving hard. She'd made coffee and left coffee grounds and drops on the counter without cleaning them up, like usual. She'd left her pajamas on the floor in the bathroom after her shower instead of putting them in the laundry basket, like usual. She'd slurped her coffee noisily as she read the news on her laptop, like usual.

What the fuck was wrong with me?

One minute, I was seeing my sister as the awesome woman she

was, and the next, I was ready to explode. I was being a jerk, but I couldn't stop it. At least I hadn't taken it out on her yet. It was just a matter of time, though. I had to fix this before I ended up tearing her head off about something innocent like existing.

I ordered falafel and hummus along with chicken shawarma and went back to our usual table. Marnie joined me a few minutes later, her plate heaped with several slices of pizza.

"Got enough to eat there, Marn?" I asked, my mood swinging back to being happy with life. She could eat twelve whole pizzas if she wanted to and not gain an ounce. Her metabolism was incredible.

She chuckled and picked up the top slice. "They had so many kinds, I couldn't choose. I'll take whatever I can't eat back home for a snack later." She bit into her first slice, and her eyes rolled back. "This is so good."

I loved how much she enjoyed her food.

She nodded at my plate. "How's yours?"

It was unusual for her to ask about what I was eating, and for some reason, it touched me. I mean, tears sprang to my eyes. Jesus. I was swinging all over the place with my moods. Maybe I was about to start my period or something.

"It's okay. It's good, actually." I pushed my plate away and took a long drink of water. "I guess I'm not hungry right now."

She waved her hand. "We can save it for later. I'll get boxes. There's no way I can eat all of this pizza. We can do leftover night tonight."

I nodded and stared out the window. People were out, walking dogs, jogging, biking. I wished I was out there with them rather than sitting here.

Marnie wiped her mouth on a napkin. "I'd like to go by Best Buy to grab a new controller after we're done grocery shopping. It's right there in the same parking lot. We can run in and grab it. Should only take a minute. I researched it already and know exactly which one I want."

My thoughts did another swing. *You'll go in and spend half an hour browsing while I stand there, bored out of my head, and the groceries go bad in the car.* I was such a bitch. I cleared my throat and raised my arms to stretch, buying time before I responded. *Do not take your bad mood out on her.*

"Okay. But why don't we go there first, so we don't have to worry about the groceries getting too warm?"

I hoped I said it without letting my attitude out of the bag. Not that she'd notice. But I would. I didn't want to be a shitty person. She bobbed her head and took another bite. "Okay," she said around the food. I hated when she talked with her mouth full. I wanted to do a table flip right then and there. Really! What the hell was wrong with me? I wanted to get up and leave. Nonissues were getting to me. I hated it, but I couldn't control it. Marnie didn't deserve my anger. She hadn't changed. I had.

I had to tell her what was going on with me even though I didn't know what was causing it or what I needed to do to make it go away. I wondered if she'd understand. But maybe if I told her, it would take the power away from it. Even if she didn't understand. I needed to be careful, though. Being different didn't register with her, which was a cool aspect of her form of autism, so I wasn't worried about her internalizing any of my issues. My main worry was with me and the possibility that whatever I was going through would make me less connected to her. She'd register that, I was sure. Her capacity to love was probably bigger than most people's. She just showed it differently, mostly by trusting someone she loved, allowing them to touch her, and by doing small things for them. When Marnie broke her routine and did something out of her norm for me, my heart always exploded. I'd protect our connection with my life.

We sat without talking for a few minutes while she ate, and I tried to find the words to tell her what was going on with me.

"Hey, so, I…I have something to talk about," I said. I still didn't know how to say it, but something had to give. The sooner, the better.

"Are you going to tell me why you've been so mad at me?" she said, an uncharacteristically clued-in moment for her. I was used to her being blithely unaware. Still, she stared at her food as she ate, as if it was more important than the conversation. Guilt billowed through me. She'd known something was going on, and she'd never let on. It was so like her. Most people would have tried to talk about it. She internalized things, carrying on like nothing ever happened, and you didn't know when, or if, it would bubble up later. I should have said something earlier.

Despite saying she couldn't eat all the pizza, she was almost done with the last slice.

I cleared my throat. "I'm not mad at you, Marn. Not at all."

"Good." She met my eyes, which was a good sign.

"I didn't know how to bring it up. But since we're talking about it..." I swallowed hard. "I think I need to branch out a little."

She wadded her napkin and took a drink of water. She didn't seem agitated. Another good sign. "Branch out like what?"

My heart beat so hard I could hear it in my head. "I need to find something just for me, I guess." I laced my fingers and squeezed my hands between my knees. The food I hadn't been able to eat looked super unappetizing, and I pushed the plate farther away. "I think I might want to date."

I watched her expression, afraid of what I might see. She'd stopped chewing while she listened, and then she resumed and finally swallowed. She gazed out the window, and I watched her eyes track people. Maybe she counted them. Or maybe she sorted them into groups: people in shorts and people in pants. Or perhaps she picked out the people with shirts with an E in the logo. Her ability to capture detail amazed me. She was the one who should have become a CPA. She'd helped me countless times to make sense of a spreadsheet that didn't add up.

Her lack of response enervated me. "Say something," I said.

She pushed her empty plate away and stood. "Hmm...um. Well. I have to go to the bathroom. Be right back." No response to my statement. No indication of what might be going through her mind or how she felt. I watched as she walked toward the bathrooms. Nothing in her movements gave anything away.

I wanted to leave, but I stayed. I had to make sure she was okay.

When she came back, she'd brought a to-go box and started scraping my uneaten food into it. There was no indication I had suggested a major change to our routine, and I didn't tell her I wasn't going to eat the food. She stacked our dishes and leaned back in her seat, rubbing her stomach. "I'm stuffed. I think the last piece was a little too much." She picked up her phone. "You ready to hit Best Buy and the grocery store?"

I couldn't tell if she'd accepted what I'd said or ignored it, and I didn't know how to check in to figure it out.

She got up. "You ready?"

"Did...did you hear what I said?"

She finally made eye contact. "I did. I'm processing. You ready to go?"

"Okay." I stood. "Let's go." Her response felt a bit anticlimactic, but I'd said what I needed to, opening up the conversation. Bringing it up released a little of the pressure, and I didn't feel like exploding anymore.

We retrieved my car from the apartment parking garage and drove to Best Buy, where, as predicted, Marnie took forty-five minutes browsing before she picked out her new controller. After that, we went to the grocery store.

Marnie acted like she always did, making stupid jokes, talking about our purchases, basically acting as if I hadn't told her I wanted to shake up our routine. Part of me wanted to let it be, but the chance remained that she'd have a reaction later. So I wanted *some* sort of response, just so we could talk about it. I wanted her to be her usual logical self so we could walk through how it might work. But she gave me nothing. Regardless, I didn't want to push her into a conversation she didn't want to have.

By the time we got home, I'd settled down a little, but the lack of discussion fueled a sense of anticipation that felt a lot like anxiety.

"I'll take Rowdy for a walk if you put away the groceries," I said, grabbing Rowdy's leash.

Marnie put spaghetti noodles in the cupboard. "Sure," she said without turning my way, which didn't mean much because eye contact wasn't her thing. Of course, I read into every little thing, and I couldn't dismiss it so easily.

I took Rowdy to the little park at the end of the street so he could run around. He danced around me when I took his leash off until he spotted his beagle pal, George, and dashed off. Normally, I'd have gone to chat with George's dad while the dogs played. But I stuck to the edge of the park and thought about how to access what Marnie felt about our conversation.

When I got back to the apartment, she was already playing a game with her new controller. It looked almost exactly as some of her other controllers. She had quite a collection since she used them for work. But apparently, this one did something different. She didn't acknowledge me when I entered and took Rowdy's leash off, but she did pet him when he galloped through the living room and stopped at her feet. Afterward, she went right back to her game without a word. It was normal behavior, but I couldn't help but worry about her wrestling with thoughts I didn't know about. I was totally projecting, and I knew it.

I stood. "Do you have anything on your mind? About before? If you want to talk, I'm all ears."

Her brow furrowed as she rapidly clicked her controller. "About what?"

Maybe she didn't consider it a big deal, and I should have been relieved, but I couldn't let it go. "You know. How I might want to start branching out, like dating and going out with friends more often. That kind of thing."

She rolled her shoulders but continued to play her game. "I think you should do it. I always wondered why you didn't. I thought maybe you were ace or something. I can support that." Her eyes stayed on the game, but she sort of turned her head toward me, which indicated her engagement in our conversation.

I raised my hands and let them flop back to my sides. I didn't know if I should be amused, confused, or another emotion. What did she know of ace, or any orientation for that matter? She'd never shown interest in anyone before, and we'd never discussed it. Maybe I'd been remiss about certain conversations as her big sister. More than that, though, she sounded so…worldly. I hadn't expected it.

"I'm not ace, but I'm glad you'd support it if I were. I just… well…" How was I supposed to tell her I hadn't dated because I thought it would be too disruptive for her?

"Look." She took her headphones off and dropped the controller onto the cushion beside her when she finally made eye contact. "I think you should date. Love is awesome. You of all people deserve to have love in your life."

I barked out a hollow laugh at the last thing I'd ever expected her to say. I didn't know how she knew anything about dating except what she'd seen on television or in the movies. "Really?"

She raised her shoulders. "Yeah. You're awesome. Anyone would be lucky to have you in their life. I know I am."

I shook my head. Not how I expected this to go at all. I needed some time to think. "So…um…are you cool if I go out for a while?"

She shrugged. "Sure." She put her headphones back on and picked the controller up.

I put Rowdy's leash back on and went outside. It was still a beautiful day, but I didn't notice. I couldn't believe Marnie's reaction. I hadn't known how it was going to go down, but I totally didn't expect her to be supportive. It was messing with my sense of reality.

I walked a few blocks and came to a street temporarily blocked from traffic. Vendor tents lined the sides, and the delicious scent of different foods permeated the air. Music rose from somewhere farther down the street. Rowdy and I made our way toward the sound and found a small stage taking up space at the end of the block. Chairs and picnic tables sat in front of the stage where people danced to a cool type of zydeco/bluegrass/pop kind of music I'd never heard before. Bobbing my head, I sat at a picnic table close to the beer truck in the shade. The signs near the stage said the band was Washtub Whiskey. Rowdy planted himself next to a dog dish filled with water.

To my delight, the lead singer happened to be the woman from the mall. As beautiful as I remembered, she had on a tank top, and another long, flowing skirt of bright colors swirled around her ankles. She swayed to the music and interacted with the band, exuding a free-spirited energy. She had a powerful presence, like a magnet, and I couldn't take my eyes off her. God, her smile. It transformed her beautiful face with a radiance that nearly knocked me over. I leaned against the table and enjoyed the show.

The music sounded different from the songs she'd played on the mall, which had mostly consisted of covers. With a band behind her, her energy expanded, infecting everyone around the stage, bringing them to their feet to dance. Everything about her spoke of soft sensuality, drawing me in. A little overwhelmed by the power of the attraction, I pried my eyes from the gorgeous lead singer for a minute and checked out the other four members of the band, all women. Each had several instruments set up around them, and they played well together. I imagined they'd been together for a long time by the subtle body language with which they communicated. Attractive in an androgynous way, one played a box drum near the edge of the stage, performing directly to a little fan club of women clustered at the front of the stage. As hot as she was, I found the lead singer more to my liking.

The dance space grew crowded, and the applause was thunderous after each song. My mood lightened quite a bit as I watched them perform. The singer's voice was a smooth alto with an effortless ability to rise into soprano. I liked her style, too. Her thick dreadlocks, which fell almost to her hips, were pulled back by a colorful headband, leaving a couple smaller ones to hang free about her face. While she stood in one place, her upper body moved lithely to the music while she sang and played her violin. All the fabric and long hair made her movements flowy and graceful. And that smile. I couldn't get over her smile. She was so beautiful, so much livelier than her performance on the mall.

I couldn't stop watching her. It had been a very long time since I'd enjoyed myself like this.

An older man dancing nearby offered his hand, and I took it. I didn't know why. I'd normally be too self-conscious to dance with a stranger, but the music had me in its grip, and I went with it. Rowdy's leash was wound around the leg of the picnic table, so I didn't worry about him wandering off as I followed the old man into the crowd. For someone who was probably in his late seventies, he could really dance. He swung me and spun me, and somehow, I was able to keep up. I couldn't remember the last time I'd had such fun dancing. I noticed the lead singer watching, and I hoped we looked as good as I imagined, but it almost didn't matter. This kind of fun made everything else fade away…almost. My awareness of the lead singer stayed strong.

We danced through three songs before I begged off. He'd tired me out. I collapsed onto the bench, leaning against the table behind me and catching my breath. The band continued to play, which gave me the opportunity to watch the lead singer again. While I seriously considered getting a beer, I didn't want to miss a single minute of her performance. With so many things about her to like—her beauty, her talent, her style—a certain energy she put off enthralled me. I'd never been captivated like this, yet I'd never even spoken to her.

Finally, she announced a break, and the crowd broke up to get beer, food, or wander through the rest of the fair. I watched the other band members jump off the front edge of the stage to mingle with the crowd, but the lead singer walked to the side and took the steps. While her style was quite bohemian, she maintained an intriguing graceful elegance. My obsessive attention on her bordered on ridiculous, but no one knew, and nothing would come of it, so I didn't care.

Getting ready to leave, I bent down to rub Rowdy's head and untie his leash. His wagging tail and puppy smile told me he was having a great time, too. Part of me didn't want to go home. I was considering whether I should get up to buy a beer when someone sat on the bench next to me. My breath nearly left me when I sat up and saw the beautiful singer.

She pulled her dreads back and tied them in a knot behind her head while fanning the back of her neck with her hand. A light scent of essential oils wafted toward me.

She smiled, and my heart sped up. "I know you. You stopped to watch me play on the mall the other day."

I was surprised. Surprised she'd approached me but more surprised she remembered me from all the other people in the crowd. "Do you remember everyone who comes to see you perform?"

Holy hell, her smile. Up close, her teeth were even and white, and her lips were full and... I cleared my throat. I'd only recently decided to *maybe* start dating, and here I was, drooling over the first woman who spoke to me. Super cool.

"Not everyone. But I have a pretty good memory for faces. I'm Phaedra." She held out her hand, seemingly unaware that I was silently scolding myself about my attraction.

I shook her hand. "Daria."

"I loved watching you dance, Daria. You and your boyfriend sure know how to boogie."

Boogie? What an interesting word. Using the word "boyfriend" in relation to me was even weirder. "I don't know him. He just asked me to dance."

Phaedra laughed, the sound so melodious, I could listen to it all day. She watched me out of the corner of her eye while she pushed her stray dreads into her headband in a gesture that showed how at ease with herself she was. She probably didn't even know how sensual she looked. "Redd's one of our equipment managers. He says he likes to pick the prettiest woman in the audience and get her to boogie with him. His words, not mine." She glanced at me and then looked away. "Although the description definitely fits."

I was fairly sure she'd just called me pretty. I didn't know what to say. Thankfully, she changed the subject before I could scramble for a response.

"And who's this handsome boy?" She reached to scratch Rowdy's head. He leaned into her touch, soaking up the attention.

"This is Rowdy." I scratched near his tail. He was in hog heaven with all the petting while I reveled in her calling me pretty.

"Rowdy wasn't with you when I first saw you." She stopped petting him, and he sat up, resting his head on her knee, begging for more attention.

I pushed my hair behind my ear. "I was leaving work, and he was at home."

"He's a love." She stood, and I expected her to leave, but to my astonishment, she put her hand on my shoulder, sending a buzz through my entire body. "I need a beer. Can I get you one?"

"Um." It had been a while since someone offered to buy me a beer. But here a beautiful woman said she wanted to buy me a drink, and I was suddenly tongue-tied. A beer sounded great in the midafternoon heat, and I was parched from dancing. "Um, sure. I mean, no. I should buy the beer to say thank you for playing such awesome music."

She seemed pleased with the compliment, and I about patted myself on the back with my smoothness. She shook her head and leaned so close, her warm breath tickled my ear as she whispered, "I drink for free, so let me get it." When she pulled away, my ear tingled, and I enjoyed the essential oils scent again. I also noticed the dimple in her left cheek. Oh goodness, she was something else.

It only took a minute, and Phaedra came back with a couple plastic cups filled with amber liquid. I was slightly disappointed when the woman who played the box drum followed with a beer. Were they together?

Dressed casually in faded jeans with holes in the knees and a simple black tank top, the drummer was more fashionable than most people, probably without even trying. She smiled at me as they drew closer. I could understand why the women gathered around her. Several watched her without trying to hide it. She acted like she didn't notice, but she had to see it. I wondered if it made her uncomfortable because she didn't show it. I was two years shy of turning thirty, and here I was, feeling all special hanging out with the cool kids. I was so uncool.

"I got you a Blue Moon," Phaedra said. "It was a toss-up between it and Coors. With all the great microbrews in Denver, they always seem to have the mass market stuff at these things. But I can't complain if it's free." She placed a plastic cup full of frothy liquid before me and sat beside me. She rubbed her lower leg as if it was bothering her, and she nodded toward the drummer, who took a seat at the table, putting her cowboy-boot-clad feet on the bench of the table next to us. "Daria, this is Leigh. She's our drummer."

I said hi, and Leigh took a sip of her beer and flashed a sexy smile. "Hey, Daria."

I couldn't see her eyes through her mirrored sunglasses, but I was sure they'd be sexy, too. Why was I all of a sudden noticing the sexiness of women? This needed to stop. But I didn't do anything to stop it. I was enjoying Phaedra's company. "Thanks for the beer." I grimaced behind the cup. Was that all I had? I was such a dork.

Phaedra smiled. "My pleasure."

"Do you play at a lot of these kinds of things?" I asked. Another brilliant conversational piece.

Phaedra tilted her head and glanced at Leigh as if for confirmation. "Two or three a week during the summer. It's picked up a lot lately. The weather is nicer, and I think we're getting a little more notice these days."

Leigh snorted. "I would have given my left nut to play this festival last year."

Phaedra laughed. "Don't you mean ovary?"

"Same diff." Leigh tossed her shaggy hair back.

Phaedra playfully slapped Leigh's thigh. Again, I wondered if they were lovers. "Yeah. Last year we had to hustle to pick up gigs. But this year is a little different. We've declined some work because we can't do it all."

I sipped my beer. "Well, you're good. This was different than what you played on the mall."

"Yeah. Our original stuff doesn't resonate with the mall crowd so much. They like stuff they're familiar with, stuff they can sing along to."

"You write your own music?"

Phaedra nodded. "We do."

Leigh leaned over and winked. "Don't let her modesty fool you. There is no 'we' except for performing it. She writes it all. We just play it."

Phaedra punched her lightly on the shoulder. "You guys tweak it to fit during rehearsals."

"Whatever." Leigh drank and scanned the crowd.

As we chatted, a few people came by the table and asked Phaedra and Leigh to autograph CDs. "That never gets old," Phaedra said as the last one left.

I expected someone who exuded such confidence on the stage to be bored with the attention of fans. Her modesty came off as endearing.

She laid her hand on my shoulder. "Will you and Rowdy be here for a while?"

I hadn't told Marnie how long I'd be gone. I checked my phone, which had no messages, so I assumed she was fine. "Rowdy said he wanted to stay near the beer truck and check out the lady dogs for a while, so I guess we'll be hanging out here."

She winked. "The beer truck is a great place to meet beautiful women." She grabbed Leigh's hand and pulled her toward the stage. "You ready to hit the stage again, hot stuff?"

I watched them get ready for their next set and wondered what she meant by the wink and comment before calling Leigh hot stuff. Maybe she thought *I* wanted to cruise women near the beer truck. I'd meant it to be funny. It took me a few minutes to remember she had met *me* at the beer truck. Maybe that was what she'd meant. Either way, I was overthinking things and getting way ahead of myself. I still had my own situation to figure out before I could start worrying about beautiful musicians and what might be on their mind.

Rowdy and I enjoyed the second set, and I loved that I could openly watch Phaedra do her lead singer thing without having to pretend I wasn't staring. When their set ended and they broke down their equipment to make room for the next act, Phaedra and Leigh came back over, and we had another beer. It had been so long since I'd made a friend outside of work. Not having expectations or professionalism guide the interaction was kind of freeing. And Phaedra and Leigh were so chill, they made it easy to be myself.

We ordered another round—three drinks were more than I'd drank in the past month—and strolled around the vendor tents. Phaedra found a long skirt, and Leigh found a leather bracelet. I didn't think I could pull any of it off, so I just browsed.

Finally, at around ten, the street fair started to wind down, and I had a small panic attack when I realized how late it had gotten, but with no messages from Marnie, in a rare instance of me not falling into an anxiety spiral, I chose to assume she was fine. I'd had so much fun with Leigh and Phaedra, I didn't want it to end, but Rowdy could barely stand, and I didn't want to appear too clingy to my new friends. And even though I tried to not worry about Marnie being home alone all afternoon, I was still worried.

Rowdy was fast asleep at my feet. "I guess I should get this boy home."

Phaedra reached down to pet him. "He looks like I feel."

Leigh stood and stretched in the casual way that cool, lanky people who are also infinitely confident stretched. "I was thinking about going down to George's." She turned to me. "They allow dogs on the patio if you want to come."

I was flattered…no…I was *tickled* that she asked me.

Phaedra laughed. "Why am I not surprised about you going to George's? Wait. Is the cute bartender working tonight?" She pointed as if she was on to her. "She's the reason, isn't she?"

Leigh hung her head in a shy gesture I would never have thought she'd use. "I hope so."

I finally had an answer about if they were dating. I felt more relief than I had a right to.

Phaedra rubbed her knee. "I need to get home and off my feet. I've had a long day. I'm so glad Kyle and Redd took the equipment to the warehouse."

"How about you, Daria?" Leigh raised her eyebrows. Did she really want to continue hanging out? I was doubly tickled that she'd want me to go even if Phaedra didn't. I almost went simply because I was so flattered, but I had to get home to check on Marnie.

I sighed. "Maybe a raincheck? I need to head home, too."

"Sure. Either of you want a lift?" Leigh asked.

"Sure." Phaedra stood and pulled her bag onto her shoulder. She wobbled a bit, and Leigh took her elbow. It couldn't have been the beer. We'd finished the last one an hour ago.

"I live a couple blocks in the opposite direction, but thanks," I said. We'd spent hours together, but part of me still didn't want it to end.

"I parked on the other end. I'll bring my car around," Leigh said, and she loped away, leaving me alone with Phaedra.

"I had a good time hanging out with you," she said and gave me a hug. The scent of essential oils surrounded me, and her body heat made me aware of every point of contact. When she stepped back, I fought an urge to pull her back. "I guess I'll see you around?"

Wishful thinking had me imagining her reluctance to leave, too. "Yeah. I'll try to come watch you play again." I wanted to play it cool, but I had every intention of going home and checking out their website to find out when the next show would be. Or maybe the one after that. I didn't want to appear *too* fangirly.

Her eyes lit up. "We're playing at the Royal Standish on Wednesday if you want to come."

I wanted to go, but, like I said, I didn't want to come off as too eager. Also, I wasn't sure what the home situation would be like on Wednesday. "Can I get back to you? I have to check my calendar." I would make it work.

She tilted her head in a cute way I'd already started to think of as her thinking posture. She was trying to figure me out. I liked the way she saw me, as if she really cared.

"Sure. I'll put your name on the list. All you have to do is tell the doorman you're on it, and they'll let you in for free."

"Thanks. I've never been on a list before." Our eye contact was continuous and intense, almost physical.

She winked. "I can hook you up with free beer, too." Her comment was light, but our attention on each other was anything but. Somehow, we'd drifted closer, and she held my hands. I hadn't even noticed it happen.

"How can I say no?" I stared at her mouth, perfectly shaped, naturally dark, and curved up at the corners. I drew my teeth across my bottom lip, wondering what it would be like to kiss her.

"I'm hoping you can't."

I drew my gaze back to her eyes and saw her staring at my mouth. She lifted her eyes to meet mine, and I knew we were thinking the same thing. "Um…" My turn to respond, but I'd lost track of the conversation, focused on bridging the few inches separating us. Our bodies seemed to be doing it on their own as they leaned ever so slowly toward each other.

"I should have taken the longer route."

Leigh's voice broke me from the intensity of the moment, and I watched Phaedra snap out of whatever hypnotic pull she'd been experiencing, too. We stepped away from one another and dropped hands.

Leigh stood beside Phaedra, looking amused. She bent down to pet Rowdy, who I'd almost forgotten about.

"Sorry to interrupt, but I told Morgan I'd be there by now."

"Oh, right." Phaedra ran her hand down my arm and backed up another step. She seemed as reluctant to leave as me. "I hope you come Wednesday."

I watched them drive away, and Rowdy and I walked the couple blocks back to the apartment while I thought about the last several hours, especially the last several minutes when the world had completely dropped away, leaving just me and Phaedra. As with a dream, I recalled the weird, almost hypnotic sensation of falling into her eyes, about to kiss her, but then my toe caught something, and I almost fell. Somehow, I'd crossed a street without realizing it and stumbled over the curb.

Already in front of my building, I had no memory of getting there. It was a wonder Rowdy and I hadn't been hit by a car.

I took the stairs up in a wonderful mood. I hadn't had an afternoon like that in, well, ever. I'd forgotten the heady feeling of hanging out with new friends, one of whom my attraction for grew stronger with every passing minute, without worrying how Marnie was getting along. Well, not worrying as much as I thought I would. I wanted to do it again. Wednesday might be too soon, even though I wanted to see her again. It depended on how the week played out.

Unsurprisingly, I returned to find Marnie playing a game. She and I usually watched a movie on Saturday nights, but if she had her way, she'd game all day, every day. Rowdy ran to her, and she scratched his head before he went straight to his bed, walked around in four circles and plopped down, wiped out. He normally made ten.

"Hey," I said to Marnie as I hung up the leash and left my shoes at the door.

"Hey, yourself," she said, clicking away with her controller. She turned her head a bit without taking her eyes off the screen.

"Sorry I'm late. I went to the street fair over on North Pecos and lost track of time."

"No worries. Did you have fun?"

"I did. I made a couple of new friends and checked out some music."

"Sounds like fun. Rowdy's exhausted."

"He is." I made it to the doorway of my bedroom and turned to say good night when she glanced at me.

"There's a grilled cheese sandwich on the counter if you're hungry. You can heat it up in the pan I left on the stove if you want."

She'd made me a sandwich? I'd expected her to have eaten snacks or a bowl of cereal. I didn't think she'd ever cooked something without being asked to. I went into the kitchen, and sure enough, she'd made me a grilled cheese. It transported me back to when we were kids. My mom had made the best grilled cheese in the world, and she'd make them for us on cold winter days or when we were home sick from school. I wasn't sure Marnie and I had ever made them at home. I wondered what had inspired her to do it today.

I turned on the burner to reheat it and transferred the sandwich into the pan. It was cooked a perfectly toasty brown. "This looks delicious. What made you make them?"

"Mom and Dad coming home." Her fingers continued to manipulate her controller, and her eyes flew all over the screen.

"Did Mom teach you how to do it? This looks just like hers."

"SamBot420 walked me through it. It's pretty easy."

"SamBot, huh?" Had she talked to SamBot about missing our parents? That surprised me.

"Yeah. He said it's his specialty and told me his secret process. I can't tell anyone, otherwise he'll have to kill me."

What? Had he threatened my sister? I flipped the sandwich and walked into the living room. "SamBot actually said he'd kill you?"

"It's a joke, Dar." She didn't even pause her game, and I'd never heard her scoff before.

I returned to the sandwich and finished heating it, wondering once again who this SamBot was and what he meant to Marnie.

CHAPTER TEN

Phaedra

I should have been exhausted. We'd played two sets at the street fair, and then Leigh and I had stayed until ten to hang out with Daria.

Daria.

Wow.

Something had happened between us, something super intense and powerful. Leigh tried to get me to talk as she drove me home, but I still felt the spark, so I didn't want to talk and ruin the feeling. But by the time I got home and had some distance from it, I felt just the opposite. I liked the feeling, but I didn't want to like it, and when I got upstairs, I took out my violin and danced, trying to forget.

God, I'd missed this kind of immersive playing, where the music played me as much as I played it. I missed it so much sometimes, my chest hurt. Not now, though. I'd become a whirling dervish in the open space, with my arms and legs keeping time, my heart free, my body infused with the magic of the music, and I let it flow through me.

It felt like torture, sometimes, standing onstage in front of everyone, playing my violin without letting my body move the way it wanted. It'd been a while since I'd let the music dance me away, and right now, I relished the uninhibited movement while the bow did its own dance across the strings of my violin. I had energy coursing through me, and the music kept it flowing. My fingers were getting sore, and sweat dripped down the sides of my face. A couple of my dreads had come free of my hair band, yet I continued to play and dance, feeling too good to stop.

I dragged the bow across the G string, and the flat note stopped me mid-spin. I played the note again, and the same flat sound issued into the room. I plucked the string and tightened the tuning peg. I plucked again, adjusted a tiny bit more, and tested the string again, drawing my bow to release the perfect note. I positioned my bow to begin a new song, but the sound of clapping stopped me in my tracks. The hair on the back of my neck stood up, and I held my bow in front of me like a sword as I scanned the loft. The only light came from the streetlights and electronic signs on the buildings across the way. Shadows fell across the open space. The silhouette of someone leaning against the arm of my couch spooked me at first. But I'd recognize that lanky frame anywhere. Leigh had keys to my place.

"Now, that's the Phaedra I remember. Damn, girl! I miss your dancing." She got up and approached me.

I took a deep breath and lowered my violin and bow. I ignored her comment. "Why aren't you down at George's, chatting up your cute bartender girlfriend?"

"I stayed until closing and walked her home. When I passed your building, I heard the music. I'd know your playing anywhere."

"And you ditched her to come up?"

"I took her home first."

I arched my brow and laughed. "And she didn't invite you in? That's gotta be a first. Have you lost your touch?"

Leigh tossed her shaggy hair back. "She asked, but I told her I had to get up early."

"You don't get up early. Besides, it's never stopped you before."

Leigh shook her head and studied the ceiling. "I know. I want to take it slow with this one. She's different, Phay."

I could barely make out her face in the dim light, but I didn't need to see her expression to hear the yearning in her voice. The tilt of her head told me she thought this girl was special.

I gently tapped the bow against my leg. The rhythmic near-metallic sound filled the quiet space. "What's her name?"

"Morgan."

"Well, I'll play something nice at your wedding."

Leigh laughed and threw up her hands. "Don't jinx it, lady!"

"Why are you here?"

"I told you. I heard you playing."

It hit me then. The quiet. So sedate for a downtown Saturday night. The music had stopped blaring from the rooftop bar, as had the ambient sound of crowds walking the streets, and even the constant rush of traffic was quiet. I moved to the window and peered down. A few people wandered the sidewalk, and a single car sat at the light at the intersection.

"What time is it?"

"Almost three a.m."

Shit. I was going to hear from my neighbors. I didn't have the electric pickup on my violin, but it was loud enough when I played. I wondered why I hadn't gotten a call or a knock on the door yet. I saw some major cookie baking and deliveries in my near future.

"How'd it get so late?"

"You were lost in the music."

"I guess so." I tapped the bow against my leg again. I enjoyed the vibration up through my thigh.

She grinned. "You were dancing."

"I was."

"It's been a long time."

I knew there were a bunch of questions underneath the comment, but I shrugged, hoping she would let it drop, knowing she wouldn't.

"This can't be the first time you've danced in seven years. Is it?"

I tapped the bow against my leg again.

"How is your leg? I noticed you favoring it a little today."

The cool breeze from the open windows chilled the sweat drying on my face. One of my smaller dreads fell forward. I shook it back. I backed up and fell onto the couch and lifted my skirt, pulling my right leg up and dropping it on the coffee table. It landed with a bang, a little more dramatic than I'd intended. "The other one gets a little heavy when I walk a lot. I got fitted with this new one a few months ago so I can do judo."

Leigh switched on the lamp next to the couch.

"Why am I just now seeing it?" She studied my new leg, and I hated how the scrutiny made me feel, even from her. Seven years, and I still couldn't stand it when anyone looked at my leg, even doctors. She ran her finger along the edge of the curved flat spring. "It's all space-age and shit. You weren't wearing this earlier."

"No. I'm still getting used to it. It wears completely different, and my muscles are adjusting."

I tilted the prosthesis left and right to let her take in the carbon fiber spring and socket attached to my leg below my knee…where my leg ended. It was completely different than my usual prosthesis, which was comprised of an aluminum rod with a foot attached so I could wear shoes. The realistic ones with a molded calf didn't appeal to me. Wearing one of those would feel like I was trying to be the old me, the whole me, which would be a lie. I still wore the old one most of the time so I could wear high boots and people couldn't tell I was sporting a fake leg under my skirt.

The new carbon fiber spring felt amazing. Made for athletes, it was lighter and gave me a lot more movability, with a sprinter sole on the end for traction. The blade wasn't made to wear with a shoe, and the sparse hardware was way more noticeable under my skirt when I moved. But I could pivot on it with so much more grace than the clunkier rod and shoe. The thing was, I didn't want people to see my challenge and feel pity for me. So I only wore it around my loft. At least for now.

Leigh examined the blade. "It seems lighter and springy, giving you some bounce." I could tell she wanted to study it more closely but wouldn't dare. She knew how I felt. "I'll bet you could run like the wind with this."

"I've never tried."

"You were dancing like a wild woman on it. I didn't even notice it in the dark. Have you been practicing?"

I tossed the skirt back over my leg and shook my head. "I've only walked around the loft and worn it for judo. It's so much lighter and infinitely more graceful. Tonight was the first time I've danced."

"You reminded me of your old self."

Her comment took my breath away. I'd felt like my old self. The one who used to dance all over the stage while I played, the one who used to take running leaps into the crowd without missing a note. But those days were gone. I couldn't stand to be known as the peg-legged violinist or whatever the city beat mags would call me if they saw my prosthesis. It was okay for them to wax poetic about my earlier performance days, and I didn't even mind when they wrote about the accident, explaining my more sedate performance style. I'd more than made up for the transformation by becoming a better musician. Before, I'd coasted on my so-so talent by making up for any weaknesses with dancing. But when I'd been on my ass, recovering from surgery and learning how to walk again, I'd numbed myself with incessant practicing. It had made me a far better musician, and I enjoyed the reviews. I didn't need the dancing, or so I thought. Not to please the audience, anyway.

But when I saw Daria dancing with Redd earlier today...My God, she was beautiful. The familiar tug of the music had pulled at me. I'd wanted to be the one dancing with her. My heart sped up at the memory. She'd caught my eye, and I'd recognized her from the mall. It'd been so long since I'd been attracted to someone this strongly. At first, I thought it was just pleasure at watching her dance with Redd. They'd danced well, but then again, Redd made anyone look good. Daria had some moves, too. But the euphoric expression on her face was what really got me, reminding me of how I felt when I used to dance onstage. It had taken everything in me to stay in one place and play while I'd watched them. So when I got home, I'd danced. And it was the best I'd felt in years.

"So…what did I interrupt between you and Daria earlier?"

A shiver spread through me, transporting me back to the last few minutes Daria and I had spent together. My first response—after the shiver—was to deny there was anything happening. I didn't want whatever was happening to be anything. But it was. And I hadn't figured out what to do about it.

I pulled my hands down my face. "I'm not sure."

"It looked intense."

I squeezed my eyes shut against the memory. When I opened them, Leigh was watching me.

"You're not ready to talk about it."

She knew me so well. "Is that okay?"

"Yeah. It's cool. I get it. But for the record, I'm not sure you want to let that thing happening between you just float away."

We chatted about other things for a while, and Leigh drifted off to sleep, fully dressed, arms crossed, and feet kicked up on my coffee table. I envied her ability to sleep wherever, whenever. I turned off the light and draped a blanket over her. She didn't even move. As tired as I was from the long day, I wasn't sure I would sleep at all.

CHAPTER ELEVEN

Daria

"What did you two get up to yesterday, Marnie?"

Harper, the captain of our soccer team, trapped the soccer ball and kicked it back to Marnie, who was helping her warm down after our game. I was on the bleachers, changing out of my cleats into sports slide-ins. I loaded our equipment bag slowly, curious to hear Marnie's answer. Harper was her only other confidant. Would she talk about us? Or about me leaving for the afternoon and most of the evening? Did she even care?

Marnie toe-popped the ball, bounced it off her knee, and head-bumped it back to Harper. Her natural athleticism, intensity, and focus gave her an edge. Soccer was a good sport for her because of the lack of contact, and we'd been playing on the same league for so long, most of the players knew to give her space. "You know. The usual. We ran some errands, had lunch at the pizza place across the street, and went to Best Buy to pick up a new controller so I can play the new first-person shooter my company wants me to test drive. Then I played games the rest of the day."

I don't know what I expected. I guess I was relieved she didn't mention me going out. It meant that she wasn't upset about it, right? She still hadn't gotten worked up about me wanting to date again, either. I thought of Phaedra, and a tingle ran through my body. But I'd just met her, and even though we'd shared a moment the evening before, it didn't mean anything would actually happen.

What had I been thinking about again? Oh, yeah.

I worried about Marnie getting anxious about my desire to start dating, but I hadn't expected it to not faze her at all. Was she actually processing it, like she said she'd do? She might be ignoring it, as she did sometimes when something was too big for her to deal with. It made me wonder if we were in for a bigger blowup at a later time.

I zipped up our bag as players from the next game started to congregate on the field. The next set of games started soon after ours ended, so we said hi to the players we knew and cleared the aluminum bleachers.

Harper walked backward the last few feet to her truck. "Meet you at Grub Street for lunch?" she asked everyone on the team within earshot.

"Sure," Marnie answered before I had a chance to beg off. I really didn't feel like going, but hanging out with the team after games was the only social thing Marnie really did.

Harper juggled the soccer ball with her knees next to her truck. "Good. First round is on me. You guys ran your asses off today. With us playing one player down and them with four subs, we still kicked their asses. We were on fire!"

A cacophony of woots and hell-yeahs filled the parking lot as everyone got into their cars.

The ride to the sports bar was short and quiet as I tried to figure out how to bring up what I'd started to talk about yesterday. More needed to be said because I had all this responsibility and guilt moldering in me. I needed Marnie to tell me if it was okay with her or if she had problems with it. Both answers had consequences, but at least I would know where Marnie stood. I wondered if I should talk to Taryn first.

With all of this churning in my head, I pulled into the parking lot of the restaurant and parked my Subaru Outback. Marnie went to open the door, and I almost grabbed her arm before I checked myself. She couldn't stand to be grabbed. Touching her had to be extremely casual, like in passing, or telegraphed in advance and moved in on slowly.

I drummed my fingers on the steering wheel. "Wait. I want to check in with you about the talk we had yesterday."

She smiled and opened the door. "We're cool. Like I said, I think it would be good for you to start dating." She smiled at me like she meant it. "They're waiting for us, Dar."

I watched her shut the door and cross in front of the car on her way into the restaurant. Was I making a big deal out of nothing? And was that disappointment or fear I felt?

I sighed and followed her.

❖

Marnie sat between Harper and Courtney during lunch, listening to them talk about the game and adding short observations. I chatted with some of the others, but I was trying to subtly watch her. It was a normal after-game lunch, and she seemed as if she was in a good mood. We were both quiet on the way home. Quieter than usual, I should say, since Marnie wasn't a big talker. I was probably being overly sensitive, but I sensed a disconnect between us. Conversations were generally on her terms, so I usually waited for her to be in a receptive mood. There was a possibility that she'd said all she wanted to say on the topic of me dating, but I needed to be sure. I figured she'd bring it up when she felt ready or when I caught her in the right mood.

As soon as we parked in the underground lot, she checked her watch, mumbled something about being late to join a game, and bolted. I knew it didn't have anything to do with our talk since she'd done the same thing the last couple of weekends. She'd always been into online gaming, but lately, she'd been a bit obsessive, even for her. But who knew? Maybe she'd been reacting to the energy she said she'd been getting from me. I hoped not.

Or maybe it had something to do with SamBot420. I still didn't know how I felt about that whole thing. As much as I wanted to change up our life, I wasn't sure how to handle the uncharted territory of a burgeoning romance. Maybe that had something to do with how blasé she was being about me starting to date again.

I got out of the car and took the stairs even though my legs were still spaghetti from the game. Marnie had already taken one of the elevators. I stopped on the landing below our floor and gazed out over the city, not because of my tired legs but because of the view. Our building sat on a small hill on the west side of town, and the higher elevation gave us fantastic views of the city, especially at night when all the lights from the skyscrapers, stadiums, and Elitch's amusement park lit up the horizon.

Sometimes, I'd stare at the view and think about all the people living their fascinating lives, doing amazing things, and I'd get the feeling that there had to be more to life than what I had, and I had that feeling bad right now. The tarot reading came to mind for the hundredth time since Friday, and I wondered if Madamee Eugenie's words were actually making my weird mood worse.

I called Taryn. I needed someone to talk to, and she usually gave good advice.

"Hey, sexy," she said. She flirted with me incessantly. People at work didn't get to see this side of her. It wasn't that she was stuffy at work, but she sure didn't go around calling other people sexy. I felt special for being one of the few who were allowed to glimpse this side of her. The funny thing is, *I* was the stuffy one at work. I would have liked to blame it on being an accountant, but so was Taryn, so that theory didn't hold up.

"Whatcha doing?" I asked.

"Laundry, toilets…you know, the normal glamorous stuff I get up to on Sundays."

"Sounds riveting." I leaned against the low wall of the landing.

"You have no idea."

"I don't know about you, but I can't stop thinking about the tarot reader the other night."

"Me, neither. She was right on the money, right? Scary accurate. I want to go back, but I don't want to, either. You know what I mean?"

I bit my thumbnail. "Do you think it's real, though?"

She paused. I imagined her pursing her lips and tapping her chin, her thinking pose. "Well, it mostly makes you think about what's going on in your life and helps you make logical connections. So, yeah, I think it's as real as you let it be."

"But she said other things, too. You know? Like about me having already met my future love. How could she know?"

"It got you thinking, right? Like maybe you're more interested in dating than you let on? Please make it true."

"Those were her words, not mine." I didn't want Taryn running away with this whole dating thing. She'd have me auditioning for the lesbian version of *The Bachelorette* before I knew what happened.

"By the way, I still need to send you the recording. Hold on." A fair amount of rustling occurred on her end, and I imagined her pressing buttons, trying to find the audio file. "Shit."

It didn't sound good. "What?"

"The file is too large. I can't send it to you. I have to upload it somewhere."

"You can put it on your cloud and give me access."

"Who has a cloud thing just hanging around?"

I laughed. Taryn's wizardry with Excel spreadsheets didn't extend to most other technology. I'd actually been surprised when she'd thought to record the session in the first place. "Oh, only about half the world, my simple luddite friend. Why don't I come over and listen to it?" My eyes drifted toward the next floor, where Marnie had most definitely logged on to her game already. I couldn't bear the thought of stressing about her stress any more for the time being. "Maybe I could come now."

"Yeah, sure." She said it as if she was reconsidering her current outfit.

"Don't change your clothes on my account. I'm still in my soccer gear, and I'm riding my bike over. We can be grubby together. I'll be there in, like, fifteen minutes."

I shot off a text to Marnie telling her about going to Taryn's and asked her to take Rowdy out to pee. Why not? I'd gone out yesterday, and she hadn't complained or appeared upset. She had her online games, anyway. If this was how branching out happened, maybe I didn't have anything to worry about.

I went back down to the parking garage and unlocked my bike.

❖

"I've always known exactly how to communicate with Marnie, so it's weird being at a loss with this." I swept a hand toward Taryn, gesturing at her outfit. "By the way, how can you appear so put together cleaning your toilets? It's really unfair, you know." She'd answered the door with a toilet brush in hand but still looked gorgeous. It wasn't like those old black and white TV shows where the mom did chores in a dress and high heels, but it was close enough. I'd have been dressed in a stained T-shirt and cutoffs. Obviously, she didn't splash bleach all over the place like I tended to do.

Now Taryn and I were sitting on her couch, sipping lemonade. We hadn't gotten around to listening to the recording because I had other things on my mind, but I'd already told her about the conversation with Marnie about me dating. I didn't say anything about meeting Phaedra because I wanted to keep it to myself until I knew if it would go anywhere. Plus, Taryn had a way of blowing things out of proportion, and I wasn't ready to deal with it.

"What do you mean? These are my cleaning clothes." She waved her hands impatiently. "And don't change the subject. You have to let me catch up, girl. I'm still trying to get over the whole thing where you're unhappy with your life but never said anything to me. Are we friends or not?"

Looked like the introspection would start sooner rather than later.

"Of course we're friends." I stroked her arm. "It happened so gradually." I shook my head in frustration. "I don't know. I need… more. I can't blame Marnie for this. It's all me. She's the same as ever, with the exception of spending more time gaming these days. She talks to her gamer friends more than she talks to me." I was jealous about the last part and felt guilty for being grumpy about it. Plus, there was the possibility she was crushing on one of her game buddies/coworkers who I didn't know. There were all kinds of horror stories about people taking advantage of someone they met online on gaming sites…or worse.

Taryn rolled her eyes. "How can she game more?"

"Believe me, she is. Anyway, there's got to be more to life than work and hanging out with my sister." A paralyzing wave of guilt crashed over me. "Not that Marnie isn't awesome. She is. I love hanging out with her. Besides, my parents are going to be home soon."

Taryn leaned forward. "Why didn't you lead with the thing about your parents? Great news. When?"

"Not sure yet. My mom only had a minute to talk, and Marnie talked to her. She didn't think to get details."

"Well, having them home will help. Besides, even if they weren't coming home soon, you don't need to justify your feelings. I've been telling you to get out of your rut for years. Now you can."

"There's a disconnect in me, though. And it's definitely me." I gritted my teeth. I had to say it as much as I hated myself for thinking it. "I've started getting resentful of my situation, and I'm ashamed to say, some of the resentment is focused on Marnie." I hung my head.

"Why are you ashamed? If you can't resent your siblings once in a while, you aren't doing it right."

I stared. I was being completely disloyal by talking about Marnie like this.

She laughed. "What? You mean because she's autistic you're not allowed to have normal feelings?"

"Taryn—"

"Seriously, Dar. It would be weird if you never experienced a bit of resentment for the role you find yourself in." She shook her head with a smile when I shot her a look. "I know you love her. I know she's pretty much self-sufficient. I know you volunteered to care for her when your folks moved to California. But they extended a year-long trip to three years, and until recently, there's been no end in sight. It's always there for you. It's a responsibility, and good for you for taking it seriously. All siblings should possess that kind of loyalty. But you're human, Dar. It's natural for you to want a little more than what you've limited yourself to for the last few years."

My hackles rose. She was right, but we were talking about Marnie. And even if she was right, I didn't have to like it. "I haven't limited myself. It's just the way it is."

Taryn gave me a look. "You know what I mean."

"I don't, though." I did. I didn't know why I chose to be difficult.

She sighed. I could tell she had more to say, but she was trying to figure out a way to redirect the conversation. "Let me guess. You started feeling like this about two years ago?"

I squinted at her. "You're trying to link this to Lisa, aren't you?"

"I suspect it may have been a trigger of sorts, yes."

Lisa Taylor. I'd really liked her. Maybe more than liked her.

We'd met at an accounting conference a little over two years ago and had hit it off immediately. But for some reason, Marnie had a hard time with the whole thing. I'd never found out why.

Marnie had seemed all right when I introduced them. In fact, I'd thought she even had a little crush on Lisa at first. But it didn't take long before she'd started displaying signs of major anxiety when Lisa came around, and the anxiety spiked when I would leave to go be somewhere else with Lisa. If I tried to talk to Marnie about it, she would get upset, clam up, wave her hands, or walk out of the room. Eventually, Lisa got sick of how much maneuvering I had to go through just to be with her without sending Marnie into a bad place, and she'd broken up with me. It had devastated me. I'd liked her a lot, to the point where I even saw myself settling down with her. Over time, I'd realized it was for the best. Marnie was part of my life, and she wasn't going anywhere.

I settled back into the couch and pouted. "Hey, I know you minored in psychology in college, but you don't get to psychoanalyze me, lady."

"This doesn't take a therapy degree to figure out. You want to date. You want to meet someone. You're twenty-eight. It's normal."

Memories of the night before with Phaedra flooded my mind, and a little flutter filled my stomach. I had no idea if anything would happen between us, but the possibility was exciting. Despite my earlier thoughts about not telling Taryn about it, I wanted to share how excited

I was. I'd probably regret it later. "I actually might have met someone. It's early, but I kind of like her."

Taryn's eyebrows went up, and she leaned forward. "Tell me now. Who is she? Do I know her? Where did you meet her? I need all the details."

I got excited. I needed someone to talk to. I told her about Phaedra, and as I did, I started to feel stupid about it, like maybe I was reading too much into it. "I have no idea if she's even interested. I think she is, but who knows? And I keep thinking about whether Marnie will be on board with it because if she isn't…well, what's the use?" I sighed. "Listen to me, putting the cart before the horse. I shouldn't be worried about Marnie yet. I don't even know if Phaedra is into me. I've only seen her the two times, and the first time, we didn't even talk. But I'm worried. I have to be."

Taryn crossed her legs, shaking the top foot. "Phaedra, huh? I know this isn't about you and me, but it's weird how you haven't brought her up before now. You first saw her last week?"

I waved my hand to dismiss it. "We didn't even talk the first time, and we actually only officially met yesterday. There was nothing to tell. No big deal." Except it *was* a big deal because I thought I really could like her.

The shaking of her foot stopped. "No big deal? You haven't spent time with a new woman in a long time." She pointed at me. "I'll give you a pass on not leading with this."

I dropped my head back on the couch and groaned. "I think, more than anything, I have all this guilt about being a bad sister." I rolled my head back and forth. "I guess I want to be a good sister and have a life of my own, too."

Taryn smiled. "Perfect. You summed it up nicely. And I'll tell you, what you want is nothing to feel guilty about. You simply need to find a balance."

"But what if it means disrupting Marnie's balance in the process? I don't see how it wouldn't. She's used to having me to herself."

"You have to deal with it when it happens."

"I'm not sure I can do it." I squeezed my eyes shut, and a red landscape and blue skies flashed before my eyes. My heart started beating hard within my chest. "I've been down this road before."

"You've been doing a great job of it for three years on your own."

I couldn't tell her why it scared me. The memory from more than ten years ago filled my head. I'd just turned seventeen, and we'd gone to Utah on a family trip to check out some of the national parks. My parents had stopped in Capital Reef, and we were standing on a huge rock formation at a roadside viewing point down in the valley. The entire landscape looked Martian red and rugged from ancient waters now long gone. Marnie and I had gone exploring, and no one had been particularly worried about navigating the difficult terrain. At fourteen, Marnie understood heights and was sure on her feet. Besides, our parents were there and responsible for her, not me.

We were doing our own things, and I was trying to take a selfie to send to a girl I was crushing on hard from school, but Marnie kept trying to get in the picture. I only wanted me, so I asked her to move out of the photo. She wouldn't and leaned in even closer. If I moved away, she moved with me. I got frustrated, and since I was a teenager, I overreacted.

I pushed her. I shouldn't have. Pushing or pulling were sure ways to set her off, and I knew it. I simply didn't care. She stomped her foot and moved closer again to get in the picture. I should have just taken the stupid thing. But I stepped away again and gave her the stiff arm, holding her back. That was when she'd lost it. Full blown. Stomping feet. Yelling. Waving her arms. I gave a half-assed attempt to settle her down, but my frustration resulted in impatient gestures, which only made it worse. When she got near the edge, I panicked. I legitimately tried to calm her down. I asked her to move away, and then I begged, but she wouldn't listen. I was terrified, pleading, trying to soothe her, but nothing worked. Then, as if in slow motion, I stepped closer, ready to pull her away, but she stepped back again, and I watched her disappear over the edge. My stomach dropped with her, and I froze. My mom and dad came running. They'd heard her yelling and had seen everything but had been too far away to prevent the fall.

It had happened so quickly. Fear had paralyzed me, but my father ran to the edge and searched for a way down. I finally shook the paralysis and peered over the edge. It wasn't as bad as it could have been, and instead of falling all the way down the fifty-foot drop, she'd landed on a ledge about twenty feet down. I saw her there, motionless and so small, in her jean shorts, T-shirt, and white tennis shoes, and somehow, while my dad was still trying to find a way down, I scaled the smooth rock to get to her first.

When I'd kneeled by her motionless body, fully expecting her to be dead, the rise of her chest sent a wave of hope crashing over me, and

I'd screamed at her to open her eyes. Against all odds, she'd complied. By then, my dad had made it to the ledge. I lost it. I didn't remember many details except she'd acted like nothing had happened, and I'd sobbed when I'd found out she was okay aside from a few bruises and scrapes.

It had been the most terrifying thing I'd ever experienced. I'd been sure I'd killed her.

I'd cried uncontrollably while the sister who couldn't tell if I was annoyed or happy with her most of the time—and really didn't care—patted my back, stroked my hair, and murmured soothing words. She'd sounded just like my mom.

It had been a key turning point in our relationship.

I didn't want to release the memory from my private files, let alone put the whole ordeal on the table and analyze it with anyone, even Taryn, who would understand. No one needed to tell me how it had formed my future relationship with my sister. All I knew was I never wanted to risk another scenario like that again. I never wanted to be the cause, and I wouldn't let it happen on my watch.

So, yeah. I understood why protecting Marnie was my first priority and why it was extremely important to me. I just didn't feel like diving into the psychology behind it.

"Have you been arguing or something?"

Taryn's voice broke through the haze of memory. "Huh?"

"I'm trying to figure out why you're suddenly feeling at loose ends."

"Loose ends is a good way to describe it." Having words for it made it more...manageable.

"Glad I could help." She smiled and took a sip of lemonade.

"Actually, Marnie refuses to fight. She won't even debate. She's the master of ignoring. Kind of like she's doing now. And it drives me crazy." And a pang of guilt shot through me. "I'm being an asshole. I know."

Taryn shrugged. "You feel what you feel. Feelings don't make you an asshole. Actions do. And, you my dear, have never done an asshole thing in regard to your sister."

"You didn't know me as a kid. I was a self-absorbed piece of work."

"You know what I mean. You're a wonderful sister."

I sighed. "It's like being mad at her for having brown eyes."

Taryn laughed. "Not really."

"It is," I insisted. "She can't help how she is. I don't have the right to criticize it."

"There's a difference. Brown eyes don't trigger reactions. Actions, or lack thereof, *do* trigger legitimate reactions. You are having a reaction. You have needs and emotions, and her actions, whether they are intended to cause a specific reaction or not, will have consequences."

"I get it, but—"

"No buts, lady. You do a heroic job of managing your reactions. Give yourself a break and stop giving yourself guilt trips."

"Yeah." Easier said than done.

"I know what you're doing."

"What?"

"You're agreeing with me to shut me up, but you don't mean it."

"True. But—"

"No buts—"

"*However*, I have to be aware of her inability to deal with some things, and it's my responsibility to react accordingly. I don't have a choice."

"You always have a choice. And you're right. You do have a responsibility. But—"

"You said there were no buts."

She rolled her eyes. "*Nonetheless*, I don't think you give *her* enough credit."

My hackles rose. "What do you mean?"

"Down, girl! Do you remember the Halloween party last year when Scott was a dick, and I had to drag him from there before the Amazon on your soccer team squashed him?"

"Yeah."

"Before that mountain of a woman got involved, Scott was talking with Marnie about one of the online games she'd worked on. He got all worked up about how her company mediated the chat boards, calling guys out on their objectification and toxic masculinity."

I didn't remember this. "She can't talk about stuff like that. Politics and human rights, it overwhelms her. She usually blanks out. She stops responding, and her eyes go glossy."

"Yep. Well, this time, Mount Saint Woman—"

"Courtney."

"Huh?"

"The woman's name is Courtney, not Mount Saint Woman." I

wanted to tell her Courtney was sweet and quiet, as well as extremely sensitive about her six foot, five-inch height. But Taryn was trying to tell me a story, and she wouldn't hear anything else. Taryn had to figure out things on her own. The cool thing was, she always did.

"Whatever. The woman is an Amazon. Anyway, she stepped in to defend Marnie, but Marnie patted her arm and then patted Scott's arm, smiled, and said, 'Hey, it's okay if you don't understand. I don't understand a lot of things, either, but we can be nice to one another.' He was being a total asshole." Taryn shook her head as she did most times when talking about Scott. "But she totally took care of it."

"Seriously? *She* defused it?"

"Yeah. I reamed Scott a new one the next day. But the thing is, she took care of it herself. Maybe she's a little more self-reliant than we give her credit for."

I'd never seen Marnie handle anything like that. I usually handled those things for her. Well, people usually didn't act like douchebags. Most people quit when she didn't engage. Taryn's story had given me a new perspective.

"This lemonade isn't doing it for me," I said. "What do you say we go get a drink somewhere?"

Surprise flew across Taryn's face. I never suggested fun things. "You don't need to ask me twice. We'll talk about the readings while we're out."

I wasn't sure I had it in me to talk about the readings after the quasi-therapy session we'd just had.

CHAPTER TWELVE

Phaedra

Bikes and runners crowded the Cherry Creek bike path. It made sense. Who wanted to be indoors on such a beautiful day? The sun felt nice on the exposed skin of my arms and legs. Dressed in bike shorts for the first time since before my accident, I wasn't obsessing about people staring at my leg for once. Showing the new prosthetic to Leigh and seeing her response had given me confidence. In fact, I hadn't noticed anyone staring or anything. All the recent coverage of the Paralympics seemed to have normalized sports prosthetics. For the first time in forever, I felt outdoorsy, even a little athletic.

At first, using the spring to pedal the bike felt a little weird. I normally used the clunkier prosthetic. The new one slipped off the pedal a few times, but it didn't take long to figure out how to keep the pressure applied in a way to keep the rubber sole from sliding off. I wondered if I could get a better clip to ride farther and faster.

Leigh applied her brakes to fall in beside me. "Can we stop at REI to get coffee?"

She was a trouper. She normally didn't like physical activity outside of the bedroom, but she'd agreed to ride with me anyway. She'd crashed on my couch last night after our talk, and we'd had a late breakfast. More coffee sounded good, and I had my eye on a set of headbands I'd seen there. I already had about a dozen or so of them, but I needed them to keep my dreads back, and the sporty ones were vibrant and fun. Also, I could talk to the folks in the bike department about a clip for my pedal.

"Sure. I could go for some more coffee."

Leigh gave me one of the sexy half-smiles that made her irresistible to women. She knew it, too, although I don't think she did it on purpose. She just exuded a natural appealing charm. Even I wasn't completely immune, but we'd been best friends for so long, it would be weird for us to be anything else.

Daria was a different story. Her kind of sexy came out in a completely different way, and I'd enjoyed hanging out with her yesterday. I couldn't wait to see her again, hopefully at the show on Wednesday. Otherwise, I didn't know how I'd ever get in touch with her unless I ran into her on the mall. I should have asked for her number.

After Leigh and I stowed our bikes, we entered the giant REI that used to house the boilers that had generated electricity for engines on the old Denver railway system. It was a historic building, and the architecture added a certain interesting aspect to the shopping experience there. We ordered coffee from the attached Starbucks and took it into the main store to browse.

"You dig Daria, huh?" Leigh said as she handed me her cup and admired a pair of mirrored sunglasses. She had at least a half dozen pairs exactly like them, but they complemented her style perfectly.

She'd read my mind, though. I hadn't stopped thinking about Daria since we'd met at the street fair. Effortlessly beautiful, she was neither butch nor femme, not that those labels meant anything to me. I'd dated plenty of both in my life and liked them all, but she fell somewhere in between. Interestingly, she gave off a natural sporty vibe, which wasn't my normal type at all. I wasn't very sporty myself, even though I enjoyed riding bikes and hiking. Maybe that could change with someone like Daria. She was smart, too. Brainy women turned me on more than anything else. We didn't talk about what she did for a living, but if I had to guess, I'd say she was a computer person or a scientist. I wondered what her type was and if I fit the description. How could I find out?

"You're overthinking it, aren't you?"

I realized I hadn't answered her question. I feigned indignation. "Overthinking it? Me?" I laughed. "Yeah, of course."

"Yeah, you like her? Or yeah, you're overthinking it?" She picked up a new pair of glasses.

"Both," I said, pretending like the answer didn't scare me to death.

"You like her, but you're trying to talk yourself into thinking it would never work so you don't have to pursue her. Am I right?"

She totally had my number, but I wasn't about to let her know it. "I don't do that."

"Yes, you do."

I sighed. "Yeah, I do. But I don't like that I do it, so there's that." It was true. I didn't want to talk myself out of liking Daria even though it scared me.

"You're talking yourself out of it right now, aren't you? And you'll never look her up, even though the sparks were flying all over the place the entire time."

"They were not."

"Girl, don't even pretend. I haven't seen you this attentive and starry-eyed since your crush on Amelia Longoria in drama class our sophomore year."

"Oh, wow. Amelia. I'd forgotten about her. I always fell for the straight ones back then."

"She plays for our team."

I almost dropped our coffees. "What? How do you know?"

"I ran into her at First Friday last fall. You would have known if you ever went out with us."

I pushed one of my dreads back. "You know I don't dance anymore."

"Right. Except in the privacy of your loft, where you dance your sexy ass off."

I laughed. "Yeah, right." I handed her cup back. "Tell me about Amelia."

"Well, she goes by Mel now, all the hair you longed to run your hands through is shaved, except for a spikey blue mohawk, and all the creamy skin you used to crave is covered in ink."

"Seriously? She was head over heels into...what was his name? Daryll? No, Daniel. The track star she made out with after school every day. I would have thought she'd be married with two point five kids by now."

Leigh shook her head. "Nope. She's a big old lesbo."

I shoulder-bumped her as we made our way to the bike accessories. "She sounds like someone you'd be really into."

"Totally. She caught my eye the second she walked in. I made it halfway across the room with a beer for her when I realized who she was."

I grabbed her arm and laughed. "Oh, crap. Did you hit on her?" I had no jealousy. My crush had been a long time ago. But to think of Leigh taking my high school crush home, I felt a pang of something— failed loyalty? I didn't know, and it didn't matter.

Leigh stared as if I'd offended her. "Hell, no. I don't move in on my best friend's love interests, no matter how long in the past they are. You know that."

I wanted to hug her, so I did. She won the award for the most devoted friend. For all of her womanizing ways, she'd never even come close to moving in on someone I wanted to date. "I do. I know it for certain."

"Good. I did talk to her. She went to some women's college in Kansas and became indoctrinated into Sapphic bliss by her roommate, and she's been on team lesbo ever since. You got part of it right, though. She's been married to her wife for five years and has twin boys. She mentioned you."

A little buzz of excitement lit in my stomach. "What did she say?"

"She said she had a crush on you all through high school but didn't understand it until she started dating women. She said she'd mixed it up with admiration, but the naked dreams were confusing."

I covered my face with my free hand. Oh, the dreams I'd had about her myself.

"Anyway, you look at Daria like you used to look at Amelia. And I don't know what I interrupted right there at the end, but the sparks flying were enough to power downtown. What are you going to do about it? She's a bona fide hottie."

I sighed. I couldn't stop thinking about those sparks. Daria was beyond a hottie, but what *was* I going to do? As I thought about things, my gaze landed on my leg, and it startled me to see it uncovered for everyone to see. I looked around. No one seemed to care. "I don't know. She's beautiful. She's fun and interesting, too."

"But?" Leigh bent to get in my line of sight.

I cocked my eyebrows up. "But nothing. I don't have her number or even her last name."

"Uh-huh." She walked toward the biking department.

"What?" I tried to catch up.

She stopped and stared. "I asked what you're going to do about it."

I didn't like being put on the spot. "What's there to do? I don't have any way to get in contact with her."

Her face clouded with disappointment. "You give up way too easily. Did you try finding her on social media? How many Darias are there in Denver? You said you saw her on the mall. Maybe you can hang out there a little more often and run into her again? It's not like you have nothing to work with here."

"You're describing stuff *you* would do. Plus, you're…" I waved at her. "You're you," I said under my breath and took a sip of coffee.

"What did you just mumble?"

I lowered the cup. "You're you, is what I said. *You* can do those things. Not people like me."

"What do you mean?"

"You…you…I don't know. Look at you. You're confident and intriguing, and you're the whole package. I'm…" I didn't finish. I knew she wouldn't like what I had on my mind.

"You're what?" She stared. "You're *not* the whole package?"

"Something like that." I browsed a rack of silkscreened tees. "Ooh. Sasquatch on a bike. I need this."

She took the tank top from my hand and made me face her. "Phaedra, you are an amazing woman. Please don't let this define you." She glanced down, and I shuffled from foot to spring.

I made a grab for the shirt. I hated talking about my leg. "I don't. I'd rather it not be anything."

Leigh blew out an angry breath, lifting her eyes to the ceiling. "I want to punch Loredona in the throat."

I sighed and started toward the exit without buying anything. Hearing Loredona's name didn't make my heart wither any longer, but I still didn't like hearing it. I considered her my past. "Sometimes I do, too. But she's entitled to her disgust. She had every—"

Angry flashes lit Leigh's eyes as it did any time we discussed my ex. She didn't understand why I hadn't dated since. "No one is entitled to treat you like that."

Shame rose within me. "She's not even a lesbian. She has a husband," I said as if it justified Loredona's behavior. I didn't know why I defended her.

Leigh stomped through the front doors, obviously holding back an avalanche of not-so-nice things to say about Mrs. Loredona Piccelle, for which I was grateful.

I unlocked my bike and got on. "Lunch at the Fish Tail?" My attempt to redirect the conversation fell flatter than a loose violin string.

She didn't answer, but we headed toward our old college dive bar.

"A husband she never told you about," Leigh called as she caught up to me on the bike path. Okay, she'd only held back for a few minutes, and my redirect hadn't worked.

But it was true. She'd never told me about her husband. Or her two little girls, which I had never told anyone about, even Leigh. She did tell me I was the only woman she'd ever been with. I didn't think she'd lied about that.

I met Loredona at work and we became fast friends. She was beautiful, and I was immediately attracted to her, but she was straight, so the attraction was one-way—or so I had thought. Our friendship didn't turn intimate until we'd been hanging out for almost a year. We'd been close, and I thought she'd told me everything. But somehow, she'd never mentioned her family, and I'd never told her about my leg. Mostly because it had never come up but also because I didn't bring it up to anyone. In that, I'd been as guilty as her.

But when she'd started talking about being curious about what it might be like to be with a woman and telling me she might be in love with me, I'd thought she wasn't completely straight. That was when we'd started to fool around a little. Stolen kisses when we'd go out for drinks after work or take lunch. It had been heady. We normally didn't do anything at work, though. I had *some* boundaries.

But one day, she pulled me into a small office we used for interviews. With two chairs, a small table, and a telephone, there was room for little else…except two horny women pressed against a wall. She left the light off, leaving only a thin ribbon of illumination under the door. By then, I was head over heels for her. The first woman I'd really wanted since I'd lost my leg. I thought we'd make out a little. We'd done a lot of that in restaurant bathrooms, dark corners, a couple of times in my car. But in that office, she put my hand under her skirt for the first time, and the next thing I knew, I'd fallen to my knees to put my mouth on her.

We met several times in the tiny office, always standing against the wall, always impatient, always getting each other off through layers of clothing. I taught her what it felt like to have a woman touch her.

I remembered seeing her in meetings, minutes after a dark office rendezvous, admiring the soft, satisfied expression of a woman who'd just orgasmed and feeling smug knowing who'd given it to her. She'd touched me, too, with her hands. She'd been tentative and unsure of herself. I'd found her inexperience endearing. I'd helped her make me come. Eventually, she wanted more time to explore and learn.

I took her to my loft. I hadn't thought it through very well. With the floor-to-ceiling windows, there was always plenty of light. We still hadn't talked about my leg, but I kind of assumed she'd figured it out, having been under my skirt. Still, I hadn't mentioned it, and neither had she. Even so, I almost chickened out when I opened the door to my place.

When we got there, she hadn't wasted any time on small talk or niceties. She took me straight to my bed and pushed me back. The lack of discussion and fast attack kept me from overthinking. I wanted her so badly. I rolled her onto her back, stripped her clothes, and had her screaming my name when she came for the first time. We'd always had to be quiet before, and hearing the ragged growl of my name as she arched beneath me almost made me come, too.

I still remembered the flush on her throat and chest and her beautiful breasts, fully exposed for the first time, heaving as she tried to catch her breath. I watched her from between her legs, drinking her in. Her body was divine. She rose up on her elbows, watching me, and I knew exactly what she wanted. I wanted it, too. More than I could say.

"You still have your clothes on," she said with an amused sparkle in her eye, running a finger along the neckline of my tank top, peering at my bra-encased breasts, licking her lips. My nipples tingled in anticipation of her mouth on them "We need to fix that right away."

My heart was already thumping like a drum in my chest from the excitement of making her come, but it nearly flew out through my throat when she mentioned taking my clothes off. The terror of revealing my leg, in combination with experiencing a height of arousal I'd never even dreamed of, made my center throb.

I climbed up her body, kissing her wonderfully soft, warm skin until I could kiss her lips. I imagined her tongue tracing wet lines along the inner skin of more southern landscapes, and moisture welled within me. When she grabbed the bottom of my top and pulled it over my head, I thought I'd hyperventilate. I'd very nearly forgotten about my worry when she took my bra off and put her mouth around my nipple. My center pulsed again, I rubbed against her thigh, and I tangled my hands in her hair. I barely noticed how she'd pushed my skirt down along with my panties, which were extremely damp. Her fingers tickled down my abdomen and teased through the curls between my legs. I was ready for her when her fingers dipped inside me, and I moaned when they slid back out, spreading the wetness along my clit and very nearly undoing me in my need for release.

"Let's get those shoes off." She kissed my neck and started a trail of kisses down my body.

"No!"

She raised an eyebrow. Her smile told me she hadn't picked up on the terror in my plea. Maybe she thought I had a shoe fetish, who knew? Maybe she thought I didn't want her to stop circling my clit. She moved up again and kissed me hard, thrusting her fingers deep into my need. I spread my legs, and she fucked me hard. Almost too hard, but I wasn't complaining. My release rushed through me, and I came harder than I ever remember coming before or since.

She kissed me long and deep, and I reveled in the taste and feel of her as I tried to catch my breath. She wrapped herself around me, resting her head on my shoulder.

"Why haven't we done this before?" she asked, brushing the end of one of my dreads across her cheek and lips.

"Because you were straight, and then you were figuring things out." I trailed my finger over her shoulder.

"I think I've figured things out now." She laughed and rose to straddle me.

The warm wetness of her sex against my belly made me gasp, and seeing her above me, her breasts swaying and her long hair tousled from my fingers, caused my sex to clench erotically. I ran my hands along her curves, cupping her ass, helping her move against me. She threw her head back and leaned back, grasping my legs, her hands skimming down. I realized what was coming next when she sat up laughing.

"You might like to wear shoes in bed, but we need to get these boots off now." She said it while turning.

I lay there as if paralyzed as she pulled off my boots. They were long boots, nearly to my knees, the only kind of shoes I usually wore since they covered the entire prosthesis. She giggled as she tugged at the first one, which came off with a strong pull. The other one came off more easily, being held on with suction and her being at the perfect angle to pop it right off. I froze when I felt the socket apparatus fall free from my leg. She froze when she noticed the difference in how the boots fell away and maybe the weight from the other boot, which didn't encase several ounces of prosthetic leg. It might have been comedic if it wasn't my greatest nightmare.

Her laugh died in her throat as she swung the boot forward. At some point, I'd covered my face with both hands, and when I dropped them, I watched her face, which lost all expression as she stared at the boot containing my prosthetic leg. I waited for her to speak, hoping for something along the lines of reassurance or even curiosity. But the silence dragged out.

I reached to touch her hand holding the boot, but she shifted off me and lowered the boot and leg to the bed before getting up. I thought her expression showed concern, but I soon found it was anger.

"What's this all about?" she asked, pointing at the boot. She wouldn't look at my leg.

"I lost my lower leg in an accident a few years ago, and I wear a prosthesis?" I was pissed at myself for sounding like a child, and I wanted to cover up with the sheet, but I was lying on it. I berated myself for not telling her sooner.

Confusion knit her brow. "But you don't limp or anything."

"I try not to." And also because I'd practiced and practiced, but that would have sounded defensive. I didn't owe her an explanation, anyway, but that wasn't the reason I didn't try to explain. I didn't try to explain because I was trying not to cry. And I didn't want to cry because I knew it would be an ugly cry. And I was still stupidly hoping she'd find me attractive enough to get past the big surprise. Silly me.

She looked away. "Why didn't you tell me?" Her anger was chilling.

"It never came up. I never thought the time wa—"

"Well, I thought you trusted me." She placed a hand on her hip and brushed her long, dark hair from her face.

"I don't talk about it to anyone. Would it have made a difference if I *had* told you about it?"

She smirked. "Of course it would have made a difference. How do you expect me to feel?"

"How *do* you feel?"

She pulled a hand down her face. "Confused. Angry. You…you have a major disability, and I'm not ready to be a caretaker."

Hold the phone. Disability? Caretaker? Where had that come from? Up until now, she hadn't even suspected. My agility surpassed those I knew who had all of their limbs intact. What the hell did she mean? I never got the chance to say any of it because she dropped a bomb on me.

"I thought I would leave my husband for you, you know." *She started to put her clothes back on.*

Thus I'd discovered she had a husband. I'd found out about the kids a few months later when I'd nearly run into her and her beautiful little family entering the Performing Arts Complex for one of the matinees. She'd seen me but acted like she didn't. Her handsome husband and beautiful kids—a boy and a girl—were adorable in their matching dress-up clothes. Seeing the picture-perfect little family had filled me with guilt. I'd never wanted to be a home-wrecker. Anyway, she'd quit her job the next day.

I'd spent countless hours thinking up the perfect response to her reaction. They ran the gamut from eloquent replies making her want to stay to scathing retorts cutting her to the bone. No matter what, my heart had been broken, along with my confidence and pride. It didn't matter. I'd never gotten the chance to say anything. I'd never spoken to her again.

My memories scoured me raw like they always did when I let them rush over me. Leigh waited patiently for my response.

"No, she never told me about her husband."

We rode the rest of the way to the Fish Tail without talking. When we got there, I took note of how the pain of the memories didn't tear me apart these days. Sure, I felt the familiar stab of old wounds, but the scab hadn't been ripped off, and I didn't feel the sting of regret and shame like I used to. If anything, I felt angry at Loredona for being such a bitch about it all. Oh, well. Her loss.

We dismounted near the side entrance to the Fish Tail and locked our bikes to a metal grate next to the back door. The front of the lesbian bar faced Colfax Avenue, and the front door and windows were painted black. To be honest, I didn't know if the front door even worked. Everyone came in through the back alley where the bouncer sat on a stool next to a beaten-up podium where she vaped and checked IDs. Leigh waved to her as we took off our bike helmets and hung them from our handlebars. I didn't know her. It had been several years since I'd last come here.

Leigh had seemed to move past her anger at Loredona, at least for now. "Anyway, Daria is a nice woman. A *hot* nice woman. And I'll ask you one more time, what are you going to do about it?" She must have picked up a conversation already going on in her mind, one about me but not including me. She did that a lot.

I sighed. A twist of excitement flared in my stomach at Daria's name.

"Give me a few days to think about it?" I said.

The corner of Leigh's mouth turned up. "Fair enough. But I'll be asking you again if I don't hear a plan."

I took a skirt from my backpack and pulled it over my biking shorts. I'd brought it along in case I lost the nerve to have my leg on display. But I put it on now, not because I wanted to cover it up, but because I didn't want to go into a bar in skin-tight shorts.

The bouncer cackled in a rough voice, and a cloud of fruity vape enveloped her head. "I'm used to women removing their clothes around here, not putting them on."

I handed her my ID. At least she hadn't said anything about my leg.

CHAPTER THIRTEEN

Daria

I parked in the narrow alley. There weren't many cars in the few spaces reserved for the bar, and I wondered if we'd have the place to ourselves. From what I remembered, the bar didn't get much business, let alone in mid-afternoon on a beautiful Sunday, and I couldn't imagine many people would want to spend it inside a dark, hole-in-the-wall establishment that served cheap beer and still had fifty-cent pool tables. I hadn't been here in years, but I'd picked it because I'd gone here in my carefree past before Mom and Dad left, and I wanted a taste of how I used to be. So far, the spirit of the carefree times of yore evaded me.

I put my forehead against the steering wheel and peeked at Taryn. "I'm not sure what kind of company I'll be, but a beer sure sounds good."

She peered at the battered brick façade of the alley entrance. I'd taken her to other gay bars, but not this one. It wasn't very nice, and I would not have called it her kind of place. "When you said dive bar, you weren't joking, were you? When I think of gay bars, I think of dancing." She took her ID and some cash from her wallet, put the wallet back in her purse, and hid it under the car seat before she got out.

"This is definitely not a dance club and is very much a dive, but I promise the fish and chips are excellent, and the beer is dirt cheap between three and six every day. At least, it used to be. I haven't been here in I don't know how long."

"This doesn't seem like your kind of scene. I think I like it, though."

I winked. "It's not your scene, either. But thanks for humoring me."

"Hey, when my bestie says she wants to go out for a drink in the middle of the day, and I haven't had to beg her to do it, I'm not gonna get picky about the destination. This is like the old days when we'd blow off classes and go day drinking."

"Don't get too excited, T. I gotta drive home. I might have two."

She flapped a hand dismissively. "They invented a little thing called a car service this century, Dar. It will take you anywhere you want."

I punched her shoulder. I fished my ID from my wallet to show to the woman sitting at the door.

"Did you win?" she asked, glancing at my driver's license.

"Win what?" I asked, confused.

She tilted her head and eyed me up and down, then I remembered I still had my soccer clothes on. I wished I'd at least taken the long socks off and traded my Adidas slides for some flip-flops. Oh well.

I gave her a crooked grin. "We won five to three."

"Congratulations. I guess we're attracting the sporting crowd today. It's a step up from our regulars." She nodded at a couple of bikes locked to the grate next to the door.

I smiled and followed Taryn into the dark interior. At least we weren't going to be the only ones in the bar.

It took a minute for my eyes to adjust. A Melissa Etheridge song played on the jukebox. The place hadn't changed a bit since the last time I'd been there, and nostalgia drifted over me, reminding me of my carefree college days. Under the fried food aromas, it still smelled like cigarettes, even though the law prohibiting smoking in public buildings had been in effect for over a decade. The pool tables were in desperate need of new felt, thin in spots and sporting questionable stains. The beer logo lamps hanging over them were exactly the same, with a few more duct tape strips where errant sticks had hit them. I squinted toward the back wall. I thought I even recognized the bartender slinging drinks from back in the day. She still wore the cowboy hat, jeans, and T-shirt combo, all black.

The place was dead in the gloom. Two women sat at the bar with their backs to us. A young butch took a drink from a mug at a high corner table to our left. Chewing on a red drink straw, she repositioned the white ball on the pool table and set her cue. Looking down the length of the stick, she gave me a nod before sinking the eight ball in the side pocket. I nodded back, and Taryn and I walked to the bar.

"Did I just witness the secret lesbian nod back there?" Taryn whispered.

"You did."

"What does it mean?"

"I'd have to induct you into the sisterhood if I told you." I poked her in the side as I teased her.

She slapped my hand away. "Aside from enjoying the company of men in the conjugal sense, going there with you would be like humping my sister. Guess I'll never know."

We were still laughing when we climbed onto barstools at the opposite end of the bar from the other two women. The bartender, as attractive as I remembered, if not a bit older, tossed a couple of stained beer coasters on the surface before us and leaned forward. Upon closer inspection, it looked as if she'd lived a hard life in the years since.

"What is it you will never know?" the bartender asked, a half-smile tugging up the corner of her mouth.

Taryn shook her head. "Unfortunately, the secret is locked in my friend's head."

"What's the prize if I guess what it is?" She leaned against the bar and winked at Taryn.

Taryn smiled at her with a mischievous glint in her eye. Oh no. That look had gotten us into trouble many times before, but I hadn't seen it in a while.

"I don't know. What sounds fair to you?" Taryn asked.

"How about a kiss?" All bartenders in lesbian bars were smooth. I wondered if Taryn would kiss her if she guessed correctly.

Taryn pursed her lips in thought. "Okay. What do I get if I win, then?" She put her elbow on the bar and rested her chin in her hand.

The bartender cocked an eyebrow and stroked her chin. "A free beer."

It felt like watching an important negotiation.

Taryn slapped the bar. "You've got a deal."

I never thought a free beer would entice Taryn to risk doing something she didn't want to do, especially with the paltry selections offered here. But Taryn had a bit of the feisty in her today. Who knew how far she would be willing to go?

"Do you even know what we were talking about when we came in?" I asked, knowing she couldn't have heard us over the jukebox.

"Sure I do. You wanted to know what Kaitlin meant when she nodded at you two."

Taryn slapped her hands on the bar again. "How could you possibly hear what I said?"

The bartender folded her arms across her chest. "It's loud as fuck in here. I learned to read lips so I don't mess up the orders."

I laughed so hard I nearly peed my pants. Taryn had to kiss the bartender now. This was the best thing ever.

Taryn pointed at her. "Not fair. You have an advantage."

The bartender shrugged as if to say she couldn't help it while I continued to laugh. She crossed her arms and tucked her fingers into her armpits. "First, I don't make bets unless I'm sure I'll win. Second, it's not cheating because I chose to use one of my God-given gifts." She ran her hands down her sides and hooked her thumbs on the large silver buckle gleaming from her belt, implying that she possessed other additional God-given gifts she could employ if she chose.

Taryn winked and wagged her finger. "Point taken."

The bartender winked back. "Don't you want to know what it means?"

Taryn sighed. "I need to know now."

"The nod can mean a few things. The usual is an acknowledgment from one lesbian to another, letting her know she's not alone in the world, and if needed, she'll have her back. Kaitlin stands up for her sisters. Today, it meant she'll help your friend take care of you if anything comes up."

Taryn glared at me incredulously. "I don't need taking care of."

I knew it, but that was just how the butch code worked.

"I believe you." The bartender crossed her arms again.

Taryn took a deep breath and slid off her barstool. "I guess I owe you a kiss, then."

It was impressive how well she took her loss. The furthest from gay of anyone I knew, she'd never even flirted with another woman, let alone kissed one, but it looked like she was prepared to honor the bet. I couldn't help but feel a little weird about it.

The bartender poured two beers and put them on the bar. "These are on me. You're beautiful, but I don't kiss straight women." She nodded at me. Uh-oh. "I'll take a kiss from your cute friend, though."

My mouth dropped open. How did I get roped into this? "No offense, but this is between you and Taryn."

I expected Taryn to jump in to save me. After all, she'd been the instigator. But she just stood there, amused and maybe a little relieved.

"Did I hear someone is giving away kisses?"

Recognizing the voice and wondering if my constant thinking about Phaedra had somehow manifested her in this dank and dingy bar,

I leaned forward to find none other than Phaedra and Leigh sitting on barstools near the end. A surge of excitement exploded in my stomach.

"I won a kiss fair and square," the bartender said.

Leigh took a sip of beer. "I heard most of the exchange, and I would have to agree."

"Then you know the bet is between my friend Taryn and…what's your name?" I asked the bartender.

"Rocky."

"The bet is between Rocky and Taryn," I said, hoping Phaedra understood I had nothing to do with this. Because now I didn't care so much about whether I had to kiss a stranger but about not wanting to give Phaedra the wrong idea. What that idea might be, I wasn't sure, but I didn't want her to see me kissing another woman.

What? Had I just thought that? Even in my head, I got flustered around Phaedra. "I'm an innocent bystander."

Phaedra crooked her finger as if she wanted me to come to her. Of course, I did. What choice did I have? When I got to her side, she leaned close. "Do you want to kiss the bartender?" She faced me so Rocky couldn't read her lips.

I tried to be discreet, too, since I didn't want to piss anyone off. "Definitely not."

Phaedra smiled, putting her arm around my waist. "I'm sorry, Rocky. I'm too jealous to let you kiss my girl."

Rocky tilted her cowboy hat farther back on her head. "She's not your girl. You didn't even acknowledge each other when they walked in."

Phaedra laughed, and it sounded like music in my ears. "It's a thing we do. We pretend to be strangers meeting in a bar. It spices things up. Right, babe?"

I nodded, loving the warmth of her arm wrapped possessively around my waist.

Rocky chuckled. "And I suppose you expect me to believe these two are bumping uglies, too?" She motioned between Leigh and Taryn.

The mischief sparked in Taryn's eyes again, and I wondered what she thought about doing this time, but Leigh cut her off. "The role-playing kink is their thing. Taryn and I are meeting for the first time."

"Well, I guess she can have the kiss I'm owed," Rocky said, gesturing toward Phaedra. "You've been an entertaining group on a dead Sunday afternoon. This round is on me."

Phaedra focused on me, and everything else in the room receded.

Excitement tickled my belly, and heat encircled my waist where her arm rested. The hypnotic pull from last night returned, threaded with an electric current hanging in the air. I vaguely noticed Leigh ask Taryn to play pool, leaving us alone. Even Rocky left us to pour Kaitlin a fresh beer.

Phaedra's eyes drifted to my lips. I wanted nothing more than to find out if hers were as soft and as warm as they looked. I gazed into her eyes. The brown irises held tiny green flecks, and her unwavering gaze pierced my natural reserve. I shifted within the circle of her arm. An undeniable pull, like a tractor beam, had me in its grip as I drifted closer. Finally, our lips touched, and I closed my eyes. Her mouth proved as soft and as warm as I thought it'd be, maybe more. No kiss had ever affected me like this. Probably because it happened in slow motion, allowing me to acknowledge every sensation. And there were countless sensations happening in every inch of my body, especially the parts touching hers. Tingles of awareness charged throughout me as if liquid energy flowed through my veins. I hadn't even had a sip of beer yet, but I felt drunk.

When our lips parted, I had to catch my breath, and when I opened my eyes, I heard Phaedra take a deep breath, too. Wow. I wanted to kiss her again and never stop.

To my dismay, her arm dropped from my waist, releasing me, but she left her hand on my hip. I was so turned on, I didn't know what to do with myself.

I cleared my throat and scanned the room, trying to get ahold of myself. Taryn racked balls on one of the tables, and Leigh stood next to her, probably asking how she knew Phaedra. My mind was on one thing, though, and my eyes pulled back to Phaedra's lips. I was in so much trouble.

"What next?" she asked, her mouth turned up in a half-smile.

"Do you want to play pool?" I had other options on my mind, but none of them were appropriate.

She smiled, making me want to kiss her again. "Sure."

"I need to visit the restroom first, but I'll be right back," I said, backing up before turning. I felt a little floaty.

When I got to the bathroom door, I snuck another peek at Phaedra and saw her standing next to the stool with her hands on the bar and her head tilted back as if she was studying the ceiling. Even from here, I could see her smile. Had she been as affected by the kiss as me? I hoped so. When she shifted her weight, her skirt hiked up a bit, and something caught my eye. At first, I thought it might be the stool, but then it occurred that it might be a running prosthetic. Yes. Definitely. My aunt, who ran marathons, had one like it, although Phaedra's appeared newer. Interesting. She didn't move like she wore one. The detail made me like her even more. Such a beautiful and talented woman, rocking her challenge with grace. I couldn't wait to get to know her better.

I went into the bathroom before she caught me staring, only to be greeted by my own goofy smile in the mirror.

CHAPTER FOURTEEN

Phaedra

I unlocked my bike while Leigh took her time finding her key in her backpack. I kept an eye on the door, afraid Daria would come out and catch me making my pathetic getaway. What had I been thinking? I shook my head as I wrapped the cable around the U-lock and stowed it in the pocket of my hydration pack. Maybe I should have asked about what I hadn't been thinking. I was practically planning to follow Daria into the bathroom when I'd hopped off the barstool and nearly face-planted when the toe of my prosthetic got caught on a loop of frayed carpet. I'd forgotten about my leg. Daria couldn't have seen it in the shadows, but there was no way she'd miss it when we moved to the pool tables, where it wouldn't take eagle eyes to see there was no shoe where my right foot should be. I needed more time to tell her.

I straddled my bike. "Hurry."

Leigh stored her lock. "Why are you in such a rush? You and Daria were certainly getting cozy a few minutes ago. I thought we might have to call the fire department on you two. What's the deal?"

I rolled my eyes and squeezed my brake handles. I didn't know how to answer.

Leigh zipped up her backpack. "Are you seriously freaking out over a little kiss? A hot kiss, but it wasn't like she asked you to marry her. You were saving her from having to kiss Rocky."

I kept my eyes on the door as I tightened the knot of the bandana holding my dreads back, and Leigh finally got onto her bike. "I don't know what came over me. I should never have kissed her. It's never going to go anywhere." Well, at least not today. Maybe after we got to know each other. Hopefully, her friend believed the story I gave about an emergency call from work. She'd tell Daria when she came back. I groaned at the stupidity of it. Why couldn't I have waited the two or three minutes to tell her in person? I was a terrible liar. She was going to hate me.

We rode back to my loft. It was a short trip, but we didn't talk as we flew through the streets, keeping an eye on the traffic. I would have rather been out in the country or on a bike trail, but the Fish Tail was downtown. The ride gave me the opportunity to think about why I wanted to run away.

That kiss.

Wow.

It had been a long time since a kiss had affected me like that. Like I'd been reduced to nerve endings and raw emotions. It had been a long time since I'd kissed anyone period. But, oh my Lord, Daria knew how to kiss. Vibrations were still coursing through my body. I was glad Leigh was next to me, as distracted as I was about that kiss.

We arrived at my building faster than I thought possible, and Leigh and I got on the elevator with our bikes. She was shooting looks at me as if she knew what was going on in my head. But the joke was on her. There was no way she knew. No one could.

"What?" I asked.

She turned to study the floor numbers changing above the doors. "Nothing."

"I know what you're thinking." I could play this game.

"Uh-huh?"

"You think I'm being stupid."

"You're putting words in my mouth."

"But you're thinking it."

"No, I'm not."

"What are you thinking, then?"

"I'm thinking you're going to have a hard time running away from this one."

Whoa. The sting of truth hit me right across the face. I didn't expect that. But it was exactly what I'd done. I didn't want to give her the satisfaction of seeing how on target she was, though. "I'm not running away."

She gestured at our bikes. "Okay. Riding away."

I shook my head. "You don't know how it is."

"You're right. I don't. But I know you like her. I'm pretty sure she likes you, too."

As high school as it sounded, hearing her say she thought Daria liked me sent a shiver down my back. I tried to ignore it. "Which makes it worse."

The elevator stopped at my floor, and we rolled our bikes toward my door.

"You're going to have to deal with it someday."

I dropped my head as I stabbed the key into my lock. "I know. But not right now."

CHAPTER FIFTEEN

Daria

Taryn and I found a bench under a tree a little way up from where I'd seen Phaedra perform the other day. With perfect temperatures and sunshine galore, lunchtime on the mall bustled with tourists, the usual crowds of buskers and transients, and hordes of business people trying to grab a bite outside their office walls. I scanned everyone who walked by in the hope of catching sight of Phaedra, even though I'd never seen her perform during lunch.

Taryn opened her bag and pulled out a sandwich. "I haven't had a peanut butter and jelly sandwich since my mom made them for me in grade school. Tell me again why we decided to start bringing our own lunches."

"I made the suggestion when they screwed up your order again last week."

"Uh-huh." She peeled her sandwich apart and examined the contents.

I nodded at her food. "You know you can make any kind of sandwich you want, which is the glory of bringing a homemade lunch." I smugly pulled out the grilled cheese Marnie had made me. What a huge surprise to get out of the shower and smell food cooking. Marnie always ate Cap'n Crunch Crunch Berries for breakfast. *Always.* At first, I'd thought it might be one of the neighbors cooking. But when I went out to get a cup of coffee, instead of seeing her scrolling the news on her phone, there she'd been, standing next to the stove with spatula at the ready, frying the sandwich.

"This is unexpected," I'd said.

"I heard you talking to Taryn on the phone about taking your lunch to work. I thought I'd make us both lunch today." She'd flashed her happiest smile. The one she wore when she gave me a birthday present or a very rare surprise, since surprises were definitely not something she liked herself.

"I love it."

She'd bounced on her toes, a sign of her absolute joy. My heart had swelled with absolute love.

"You said you enjoyed the grilled cheese sandwich I made you Saturday night."

"Hugs," I'd said, facing her. I usually had to announce a hug before giving it, so she wouldn't stiffen up.

"Thirty-seven seconds," she'd said, her eyes never leaving the pan.

So I'd waited.

Precisely thirty-seven seconds later, she'd turned off the burner and dropped the perfectly browned sandwich onto a plate before she'd turned and hugged me.

Now on the bench next to Taryn, I took a bite. Not quite as good cold, but it was still delicious. Marnie sure learned fast. I glanced at Taryn. "I'd offer you half of mine, but I'm selfish. You know, you can make BLATs with no tomato at home."

"I forgot we'd agreed to bring our lunches until the last minute. PB and J was all I could think of." She took an unenthusiastic bite.

I laughed and handed her the other half of my sandwich and accepted the half of PB and J and went back to scanning the people on the mall.

"You're looking for her, aren't you?"

"Who?"

"You know exactly who I'm talking about."

I slumped. "Yeah. I just want to know why she left so suddenly yesterday."

"I told you. She said she got an emergency call from work."

I chewed and continued trying not to take it personally, which proved difficult since the last thing we'd done was kiss. She'd even agreed to play pool. I couldn't imagine how I could have offended her or driven her off in the brief moments I'd spent in the bathroom.

"She's a musician. What kind of emergency crops up for musicians requiring running off at the ring of a phone?"

"Can you call her?" Taryn asked.

"I don't have her number. I don't even know her last name." I could go to the show she'd invited me to on Wednesday, but she'd invited me before the whole kiss and disappearing act. Would she want me to show up?

I scanned the crowds again, and I didn't see Phaedra, but I didn't expect to. Another figure caught my eye, however. A short woman in a black dress and shawl on the other side of the mall, walking away. I wanted to point her out to Taryn, but she vanished behind a group of people walking the opposite direction. Madame Eugenie. She reminded me of my reading, and I remembered the Tower card the younger Madame Eugenie had flipped over. She'd said it signified change. I felt it all around me now. Things were changing. I was changing, I had no doubt.

"Daria?"

I sat up at the unfamiliar voice. A very well-dressed woman who resembled the school president in *D.E.B.S.* stood before me. Appearing as if she were there on official business, she held out a piece of paper, and I imagined a half dozen Secret Service snipers watching through their sights while she waited for a response.

She seemed to be waiting patiently for a response. Which I gave. Impolitely. "Do I know you?" I regretted being so snotty. My bad mood over possibly repulsing Phaedra was no excuse to be rude. "I mean, have we met?"

She smiled and laughed. "Hopefully soon. You're as gorgeous as she said you are." She glanced at her hand holding the slip of paper. "I thought I would give you this in hope that you will use it to put her out of her misery, one way or another."

This was interesting. I hesitated to take it, convinced she was handing something lethal to me. "I'm not sure I follow."

"I've said too much already."

Could she sound more like a spy? I looked around us for the snipers. Or, more likely—and I wasn't sure I liked this idea much better—cameras. With today's obsession with reality television, it wouldn't have surprised me to find we were being filmed. Could they do it without getting a release first? I imagined coming across a video of myself on Buzzfeed with my face blurred out, being ridiculed for my natural response to a random prank.

What the hell, I could play along. I cleared my throat and leaned forward before whispering, "I understand. Your secret is safe with me. I won't let you down."

She smiled as I took the paper. "I knew you were special. I trust you to be the kind of person who can see through someone's insecurities."

She winked and turned away, walking down the street and disappearing behind the building on the corner.

"What the hell just happened?" Taryn said.

I'd almost forgotten she'd seen the whole thing. What a weird conversation.

"I have no idea," I said, staring at the corner of the building where the woman had disappeared. I half expected someone to approach us to tell us we were being filmed. I got ready for it, whatever happened.

"What did she give you?"

I read the scrap of paper as I took the last bite of my sandwich. She'd given me a business card with a phone number on the back. I turned it over. The front featured a colorful but professional design for Calamity Graphics. I recognized the logo from a building a block away with the company name emblazoned across the top. More interesting was the name printed below it. Phaedra Jean-Julian, EVP Marketing and Sales.

I couldn't swallow the food in my mouth, and I almost had to spit it out before I choked. I managed to force it down and looked for the mystery woman. Okay. I hadn't been punk'd, but some sort of divine intervention had happened, and it had given me what I desired most in the world: another chance with Phaedra.

Chapter Sixteen

Phaedra

Barb leaned against the door frame, crossing her arms. She looked almost as done with this day as me, and we still had half of it to go. I'd come to work tired and cranky, and things only went downhill from there, even though I tried my hardest for the opposite. I hadn't gotten much sleep last night because of my cowardice with Daria, and like always, little annoyances kept cropping up, making it hard to keep a positive attitude.

I lifted my hands above my head and stretched, whacking my head against the 3D sign I'd put on the credenza behind my desk after what had surely been a failed pitch during the last meeting. The pitch had been to one of our most difficult clients, and the meeting had stretched from the scheduled ninety minutes to almost three hours, forcing me to reschedule two other meetings. And she'd made us agree to an unscheduled second session after lunch to discuss where we had gone wrong. I had an hour and a half to decompress.

"Fucking hell," I hissed, rubbing my head and restraining myself from pushing the stupid sign to the floor. I scowled at Barb. "Is there a thing where you can fire your client? Because I think I want to."

"Believe me, I'm this close." She held her manicured thumb and forefinger barely apart.

"You won't."

"I might."

"You won't."

She slumped. "I know."

"Do you want me to?" I stood, waiting for her to give me the go-ahead, and I almost thought she'd let me. But she just rested her head against the door.

"As much as it would amuse me no end to kick that vapid snatch to the curb, I can't. Astrid Mercer is a decision maker on the Performing Arts Center contract we're about to close, and she refers a lot of people to us. It's too big to risk."

Despite my onerous mood, I stifled a giggle. It always amused me when Barb used such vulgar language. I was no prude by any means. But hearing a woman who usually held herself with grace and composure say such a thing, well, it was funny to me. She'd be back in less than an hour to apologize not only for using such a lurid word, but for saying it about a client.

"Let me know if you change your mind," I said.

"I won't, but if she snaps her fingers at Lou or Cherie one more time and demands a Brown Palace macaron *she doesn't even eat,* or something just as ludicrous, I don't know if I can contain myself. Privilege is so unattractive sometimes. The worst thing is, she doesn't even recognize it. Her upbringing made her exactly who she is."

"You're not like that," I said.

She blanched. I wished I hadn't said it. She never liked to be reminded of her wealth. Astrid's riches were nothing compared to hers. Barb gave away more money to charity in a single year than Astrid's net worth. I only knew because it was public knowledge, and I'd looked it up out of curiosity when she'd asked me to come work with her. She'd never have offered up such information. She was one of the humblest people I'd ever known. It was amazing what kind of information you could find about super wealthy people on the internet. I never told her I'd checked her out, but she must have known I wouldn't have walked into this job without knowing what I was getting into.

"I used to be." Her eyes grew unfocused as she spoke, as if she was remembering back to a painful period in her life. She shook herself. "But let's just say I had my eyes opened for me."

That was how it always went when her past came up in conversation. She and I were pretty close, but she never talked about it to me, and I never pressed. It didn't matter to me anyway. I was very curious about the eye-opening thing, though. She'd mentioned it a couple of times before but had said nothing more. I'd read that her family had started to amass their fortune generations ago in shipping and making excellent business decisions since then, increasing their wealth exponentially in the last several decades. Barb was the last surviving heir, and it was all hers. She had people running her various companies, including managing her massive charitable contributions, and for a week each quarter, she flew to New York to attend meetings, but she focused the majority of her time and effort on Calamity Graphics. Aside from the charity aspect and Calamity, I had the feeling that little of all the other stuff mattered to her.

I sighed. "We still have this afternoon with her. Hopefully, she'll have run the designs by her people and will have a decision for us."

"Right." She took a few steps into my office and rested a hand on my arm. "I'm glad we have each other."

"And that's why you pay me the big bucks."

"You deserve so much more, my lovely. Let's grab one of those chai lattes you love and come back and eat some of the lunch Ms. High and Mighty didn't touch."

I didn't really want to go anywhere. The whole ordeal with Astrid Mercer had drained me, even though it kept my mind off the cowardly exit I'd made the day before. I was exhausted. I hadn't slept well, and I'd toggled back and forth from mentally reliving that kiss to emotionally flagellating myself about running out, which didn't help. But I never turned down a chai latte. I needed the comfort of the warm beverage because even as it grew warmer as we moved further into summer, chai lattes were meant to be consumed hot.

Barb and I made our way downstairs and were conspiring about how to manage the various ways Astrid Mercer might try to make our lives miserable later in the afternoon when we rounded a corner onto the mall, and I laid eyes on the last person I'd expected to see that day: Daria, eating lunch with her friend Taryn.

I backed several steps around the corner and slammed against the building, out of sight. I didn't intend to be dramatic with the body slamming. It was mostly due to me tripping over my skirt and the less than flexible dexterity of my booted prosthetic. If the building hadn't been there, I would have fallen on my ass. Barb just watched me freak out. If I wasn't so exhausted, I would have laughed hysterically at the expression on her face.

She started as if I'd lost my mind. "What has gotten into you?"

I waved her over. "Come here," I whispered, though Daria and her friend were easily fifty feet away. Even in my current state, just seeing her made my body tighten with desire.

As Barb approached, she glanced over her shoulder. "Did I miss something? What or whom are you hiding from?"

I told her all about yesterday, the CliffsNotes of the story.

Her eyes twinkled with amusement. "I knew there was more to

your mood than Astrid Mercer." She peeked around the corner. The enormous smile she wore when she met my eyes again made me feel better. "She's very cute. Why don't you go talk to her? Clear things up."

I pressed into the rough marble of the building's façade. "I can't."

She took my hand and gently pulled. "Come on."

I held my place. "I can't. I don't know what to say. I need some time to think, to make sure I don't come off as the total jackass I really am."

She dropped my hand. "You may be a jackass, which I agree with after hearing your story, but you are a sweet and kind jackass, and she will certainly submit to those charms. She'd be a fool not to."

"You only say those things because you know me. She only knows what she's seen, and I acted like a world-class jerk yesterday, running off without saying anything."

She studied the ground for a moment and then looked up with a gleam in her eyes. "Okay, then. Let's go get our coffee and conspire about how you can fix this. The shop is across the street, and she's not facing it, so we can move by undetected. And if she's still there when we're done, you can pretend you simply bumped into each other and explain everything then."

"No way."

She crossed her arms. "Okay, I'll go pick up our drinks. I had my heart set on a latte. What are they called again?"

"A chai latte."

She rolled her eyes. "I know it's a chai latte. But you like the spicy kind. What are they called? Burmese Chai?"

"Bhakti Chai." My eye was twitching now. I just wanted to get out of there.

She shook her head. "I'll never remember. I don't have my purse. Give me something to write on. One of your cards."

I pulled my card case from my pocket, an embossed silver thing she'd given to me after I'd pulled a bent card from the crumbs of protein bars and escaped Altoids at the bottom of my purse and had given it to a potential client we'd met in line at a falafel cart during local business appreciation day. Opportunities came at the oddest moments, she'd said, and we needed to be prepared. She took out a card and unsnapped the tiny silver pen from the clip on the inside. "This pen is so adorable. Whoever gave it to you has impeccable taste." She winked. "Bhakti has an H in it, right?"

"Yes." I spelled it for her.

"Perfect," she said, handing me back the case and the pen. "I'll be back in a few minutes."

"Thank you." I said as she strode away. "Extra spicy and extra hot. Please. And thank you. I'm going back to the office now."

"Yes. It's probably best," she said, shooing me away as if *I* was the one acting weird.

Seriously, if we didn't have the meeting with Astrid Mercer in less than an hour, I'd have written off the rest of the day and gone home.

CHAPTER SEVENTEEN

Daria

My heart was in my throat. Like, I seriously could feel it beating inside my throat, and I worried about it choking me.

When Taryn and I got back to the office after lunch, I had to cancel the weekly staff meeting I'd scheduled for one thirty. After the mystery woman had given me Phaedra's phone number, I knew I wouldn't focus on anything else until I called her. The thing was, did she even want me to call? Had *she* sent the woman to me to give me the card? How did she know where I'd be? Or had the woman done it on her own? If so, how did the woman know who I was or where I'd be, and how did she even factor into how I knew Phaedra? The bizarre exchange on the mall had given me little information. Mystery settled over me like a cloud.

I heard the older Madamee Eugenie's voice from the first tarot card reading. "You're on a railroad track…you have two paths…there's the Two of Pentacles…balance…or the Two of Cups…connection… everyone has multiple paths." Hadn't she said she saw me choosing the right path? But which one? Madamee Eugenie's raspy voice echoed in my mind: "There's music and dancing. Color and laughter. Good things. Love." I remembered watching Phaedra playing on the mall.

I picked up the phone and dialed the number on the back of the card.

CHAPTER EIGHTEEN

Phaedra

One thirty-five, and Astrid Mercer was five minutes late. The meeting was the last thing I wanted to do, so I secretly thanked her for the extra time. I sipped the chai latte Barb had brought back, and it helped me relax. Chai made everything better. I spun my chair to review the metal sign behind my desk. I thought it perfect, clever, but Astrid had scoffed at it and called it "rustic hillbilly shit." Her exact words. After so many years of working with her, I'd gotten past taking anything she said personally, but it still frustrated me to work so hard on a campaign only to have it torn apart in such a cold and unfriendly manner. We'd only shown her one mock-up of the sign we had planned out, but she didn't give us the chance to finish the pitch, let alone discuss the finer details. If she had, she might have liked it.

As the president of the University of Denver Alumni Association, Astrid chose Calamity Graphics to do the signage for a themed fundraising dinner. She'd been thrilled with our initial pitch, *The Wizard of Oz*, which had landed us the campaign. She'd once said the classic movie was one of her favorites. There *was* a resemblance between her and the Wicked Witch of the West. I was so bad. I laughed as I sipped my chai.

Astrid wasn't the primary thing on my mind. She should have been, but she wasn't. Daria had looked pretty in the two and half seconds I'd seen her sitting on the bench. She'd looked adorable in a business suit. She'd looked good in a soccer uniform, too. Hell, she looked good in anything, I imagined. God, I felt like such a coward for running out on her and then almost injuring myself by avoiding her today. What the hell was wrong with me? I was surprised Barb hadn't brought up my insane behavior when she got back with our drinks.

I had to stop obsessing about this woman. I'd probably destroyed any chances I had with her by leaving the bar without saying good-bye.

Okay.

I had to get ready for the impromptu meeting with Astrid, who was now ten minutes late.

Back to the pitch. What had happened, and where had we gone wrong? In this morning's meeting, we'd revealed our ideas for the actual artwork for the event. The sign, an example of our favorite design, was intentionally rustic. A simple arrow with marquee lights around the edges with the words "Follow Your Heart" written to appear as if it had been dripped on with an oil can. The idea was to hang it around the Tin Man's neck so it pointed toward the donation table. There would be interactive character actors stationed around the room, standing on a yellow brick road, with signs around their necks: a wooden sign for the scarecrow with burned lettering saying "Feed Future Minds"; a purple velvet sign for the Cowardly Lion featuring "Giving Takes Courage"; and a ruby-red, gem-encrusted sign around Dorothy's neck saying "Never Forget Where You Come From." The signs would each have tap-to-pay terminals in them, and while the old-school alumni could whip out their checkbooks to show their generosity, the younger grads could simply transfer funds with the wave of their smartphone or credit card after selecting the money transfer application of their choice.

But we'd barely had a chance to talk about any of it because Astrid had taken one look at the arrow and declared her hatred because it might as well come from the wall of a greasy diner. "Besides," she'd said, "it's supposed to be 'if I only had a heart,' not 'follow your heart.'"

I shook my head and stared at the sign. She didn't get it. Out of all the concepts we'd batted around, it was the one I liked best. It made sense in context with the event. In our business, the customer was always right, though—even if they were mean and tactless. Maybe I'd keep the sign. Hadn't Madamee Eugenie used those exact words during my reading? "Follow your heart." But I'd sent the design to the art department the week before last, several days before my reading, and it was just a coincidence she'd used the same words. Or was it?

The faint sound of my cell phone interrupted my thoughts. I checked my watch. One forty-five. Still no buzz from the front desk announcing Astrid's arrival. I pulled my phone out of my bag, didn't recognize the number, so I sent the call to voice mail. The last thing I needed was to be in the middle of a personal call when Astrid decided to show up. I'd never hear the end of it if I wasn't already in the room when she entered.

I stared at the sign and took another sip of my chai. I loved Barb. She knew how to calm me down.

The phone rang again. It was the same number. Whoever it was, was persistent. I ignored it. They'd leave a message if it was important.

"I like the signs concept," Ralphie said from behind me.

I lowered my phone into my lap and spun my chair to face the door. "Yeah. Me, too."

"Did Mercer approve the concept?"

I didn't want to squash his enthusiasm. The sign was one of his first projects. He'd have to get used to picky and harsh customers, but for this one, I could temper the feedback a little. "We're still working with her on it. We didn't have her sold on it this morning, but I'm waiting for her to show for a follow-up meeting." It wasn't over until it was over. And if she still hated it, we had a dozen other ideas to show her. She would pick one of them. She always did.

Ralphie flashed his enthusiastic smile. "I know you'll sell it. It's perfect."

I thanked him as he pushed off from the door, and I downed the rest of the chai, grimacing at the gritty dredges but enjoying the flare of ginger on my tongue.

My phone rang again. The same number. I put my earbuds in and answered, knowing I could hang up if it was a robocall or political fundraiser or any other unsolicited caller who didn't deserve my time.

"You've reached a private and registered no-call number. I hope this isn't a telemarketer or robocall. Okay, go."

There was no response.

"Hasta la vista, criminal." I pulled out my earbuds and lowered the phone, but I heard a tiny voice a millisecond before disconnecting. Was it wishful thinking that I thought it was Daria's voice?

I put the buds back in my ear. "Hello?"

"Hi. It's Daria. Daria Fleming. We met at the street fair and again at…at the Fish Tail?"

I smiled at the phone. She was so cute, and she sounded nervous. Did she really think I needed reminding of where we'd met? I had a last name, though, *and* her number. My stomach filled with a chaotic excitement. "Hi, Daria."

"Hey." I could hear the smile in her voice. When she didn't speak again, I wondered how she'd gotten my number, and then I remembered how I'd ghosted her yesterday, and I started to panic because I still didn't have an excuse. My brain started to go in about a million directions all at once in a sort of short circuit madness. I heard her take a deep breath. "A woman with the most subtle streak of pink in her otherwise blond and perfectly coiffed hair approached me on the mall today and gave me your number. Do you know anything about that?"

She'd described Barb perfectly. Women would kill for her hair.

I dropped my head into my hands. "That was Barb."

I heard her take another deep breath. "At first, I thought it was a joke. She was so *mysterious*. But she gave me your card, and I was relieved because I didn't have a way of contacting you, and I wanted to know if you were okay."

"Oh." One syllable sounds were all I could manage. How could I explain without telling her what happened and coming off as a complete fool and possibly scaring her off?

The blue light on my office phone blinked, and a buzz sounded. The front desk. Shit. Astrid was here. I needed to get to the conference room. I checked my watch again. It was one fifty-nine.

"I can hear the phone ringing," Daria said. "I should let you go."

"It's okay," I managed to get out. Screw Astrid. She was late. Let her wait a minute or two.

Daria sighed, and it sounded like relief. "I thought about going to your show this Wednesday, but you left so suddenly yesterday. I have to admit I thought the phone call was an excuse. It's probably just my insecurity. But anyway, I worried you had second thoughts about what happened at the bar, and you bailed, using the call as an excuse. Then that lady gave me your card, and here I am, calling you. Um. Shit. You're probably very busy, and I'm prattling on like an idiot. I should have asked you first…is this a good time?"

"Um, yeah. It's good." Good Lord. My brain was broken. I couldn't think of anything to say, except that I felt like an idiot for running away, and I wasn't about to get into why.

I heard a big a sigh. "You're probably busy, and I sound like a crazy person."

"You're fine. Totally fine." I'd finally found some words, but I was far from my normal eloquent self.

"Sorry for all the calls." She sounded relieved. "I chickened out on leaving messages. But I couldn't just *not* leave one. Anyway, the short and skinny of it is, do you want to have coffee with me after work tonight? I can give you time to think it over. You have my number. You can call me later to let me know."

She was talking so fast, I could feel her nervousness through the phone.

"I'd love to." I didn't need to think it over. I wanted to see her again.

"Really?" She sounded surprised, and I felt bad for making her doubt herself. "Your building is two blocks from me, and we can meet at Café Café. Have you been there? It's a cute place on the mall. I love their chai."

I peered at the empty cup on my desk from Café Café. "I mean it. I'd love to. I'm glad you called." I couldn't help the smile plastered on my face. I dropped my head back against my chair. "I go there all the time. What time?"

"Perfect." She sounded excited, which made *me* excited. "How about after work? Say, five fifteen?"

"Five fifteen works great," I said, wondering how I could wait that long.

When we hung up, the dark gloom hovering over me all day finally lifted. I'd see Daria in three hours. I spun my chair and caught sight of the sign behind my desk. The marquee lights were on. I must have hit the switch. I turned it off and laughed.

"What's so funny?"

I spun around again. Barb was standing in my office, probably to find out why I wasn't in the meeting with Astrid Mercer, and I honestly didn't care. Well, I cared about giving Barb stress, but I'd had enough of Astrid Mercer for the day. I had an assignation with Daria in a few hours. It made Astrid's mean behavior appear insignificant in comparison. I didn't care about being late to the meeting. She'd find something to be nasty about regardless of my being in the room when she arrived or not, and right now, I didn't care.

I picked up the alumni campaign folder and rounded my desk to follow Barb to the meeting. Poor Lou and Cherie. They were alone with that evil woman.

"Put the folder down. We're done with Astrid Mercer for today." Barb took the file from my hand and tossed it on my desk, then led me out of my office by the elbow. "I was never so relieved to get a message from the front desk canceling a meeting in my life." I was confused, but she kept on talking. "Neither of us ate lunch today. I'm starving. Plus, I need to confess something to you. You may want to box my ears."

I knew her so well. She felt guilty for giving Daria my number. Hell, I was glad she did. But I would let her squirm a little before I let her off the hook. Or maybe I wouldn't. It depended on why Mercer canceled the meeting. A shadow tried to creep into my good mood, but it was easy to push away. I was going to see Daria soon.

Ralphie met us in the hall and gave us a double thumbs-up. "I just heard. I knew she'd love the signs and actors. Another ace served up by the dream team." He put up his hand for a high five, which we returned, and walked past us with a smile.

This day had gone from shit to awesome, and the best part was still to come.

Chapter Nineteen

Daria

I checked my watch again. Four thirty. Time crept by when it usually sped at the end of the day. I guessed the difference was that I had something to look forward to after work.

My phone rang with a call from the front desk, and I almost didn't answer. Calls from the front desk usually meant more work. Whatever it was could wait until morning. Something told me to pick up, though. I sighed as I reached for the phone. "This is Daria."

"Hey, Daria. You have a Marnie Fleming here to see you. Says she's your sister, but she doesn't look a thing like you." Abby laughed at her own little joke.

I couldn't remember the last time Marnie had come to my office all the way downtown. I started to worry. "I'll be right there."

I found her studying the pictures on the wall when I got off the elevator on the fifteenth floor, the company lobby. McSweeney and Price had the fifteenth through twenty-third floors of the Grimwald Plaza building.

I came around without touching her, so I wouldn't startle her. "Hey, Marn. I wasn't expecting you. Is everything okay?"

She smiled and opened her arms so I could hug her, and I stepped in for the quick embrace. I realized it had been a long time since we'd hugged or even touched, and here we were, hugging for the second time in one day. I realized I'd missed it.

She stepped back and hooked her thumb toward the receptionist. "She didn't believe I'm your sister. I showed her my identification."

I tried to hold back a laugh. "Abby's joking."

I was in a business suit, and Marnie was in her version of work clothes, which consisted of nice jeans and T-shirt, but even so, she had more than a passing resemblance to me. I knew it threw people off, especially when they knew us and how absolutely different our personalities were.

"Oh, I get it." She laughed. She had a good sense of humor but didn't display it often, and she always missed sarcasm. "Everything's fine. But I have something I'd like to talk to you about, and I wanted to get to it sooner rather than later. I was talking to Sam today and—"

"Sorry to interrupt," I said.

She chomped her mouth closed and tilted her head. Her response looked comical, but it was something my parents had trained her to do. Sometimes, when she got hyperfocused and started talking, she'd keep going until she got out every word, and sometimes, it took a while. She didn't pick up on social cues and would even talk over a person as if she didn't hear them if they tried to cut her off. But if you said, "Sorry to interrupt," she knew she needed to stop and listen.

"Do you want to go to my office to talk?"

She nodded and smiled again. "I haven't seen your office in a while. Is it still on the seventeenth floor?" She had a phenomenal memory.

"I'm on the twenty-third floor now. It's been about three years since you were here last, right?"

"Three years, seven months, and twenty-two days." We waited for the elevator. "They changed the art. There were photos by Ansel Adams before. Now there are Monet prints. I preferred the Ansel Adams work."

"Me, too," I said.

She pointed at the ceiling and shrugged. "Better music, though."

I had to agree.

We boarded the elevator, and she watched the floor numbers change above the doors. I wondered if she was counting the seconds to calculate the mean climb speed between floors. It was something she did. The first time she'd ridden on a high-rise elevator, she'd offhandedly announced the mean climb speed for the ascent had been a little slower compared to the descent speed. The ease with which she'd come up with that information by simply counting the seconds between start and end of the elevator motion relative to how many floors we'd traveled had been amazing, especially since she'd been only four at the time. But when she'd casually stated that if the elevator brakes happened to fail and the car was on the top floor and carrying exactly half the weight capacity and assuming the elevator weighed six thousand pounds by itself, it would take less than four seconds to fall to the first floor, leaving no survivors.

My parents had merely looked at each other. A second or two later, she'd corrected herself, saying the air compression in the elevator shaft beneath the car would actually slow the rate of descent, increasing the likelihood of survival, especially since there were numerous backup systems. I'd only been seven at the time, but even now, as an adult, I thought about it almost every time I boarded an elevator, and I'd never had a moment of worry, at least as far as elevator safety went.

There'd been plenty of what I'd learned to call danger-facts thrown at me from my sister over the years. Most terrifying of all were the food-related ones. Because of them, I didn't eat any sort of processed meat. Ever. And no one should get me started on food trucks. All of this passed through my mind in the time it took the elevator to arrive on the twenty-second floor. Funny how memories worked.

When we got off the elevator and walked to my office, Marnie's head swiveled from side to side as she took in the cubicles and offices. It must have looked incredibly bright and spartan compared to her office. The developers liked to keep the lights dim, and there were huge monitors everywhere displaying games. People spoke over low, dark-colored cubicle walls covered with gaming posters. In comparison, our office seemed sedate, with bright florescent lights and tall cubicle walls. It was even quieter than usual because it was the end of the day. It was probably a nice change for Marnie, as I knew she wore noise-canceling headphones most of the day at her office so she could focus on her game testing work.

Her eyes zeroed in on me as soon as we entered my office and sat in two of the four chairs encircling the planning table. She picked up the conversation exactly where she'd left off. "And I invited Sam for dinner sometime. He asked if the invitation was only for him, but I couldn't tell him because he has four kids, and we have the two barstools and the couch, which seats three comfortably, leaving some people standing. He said his table seats twelve, and we are welcome to come to his house instead."

Hold the phone. Sam had four kids? "How old are Sam's kids, and do they have a mother?" I asked.

She looked at me as if I'd asked her if fish swam. "Of course they have a mother. Science hasn't progressed *that* far. Her name is

Melody, and she's Sam's first wife. The oldest are twins, fraternal, not monozygotic, aged seventeen, both male, named Kyle and Richard. Sam calls them Sam Two and Sam Three. The others are not twins, aged fifteen and thirteen, both male, named Liam and Michael. Sam calls them Sam Four and—"

"Let me guess, Sam Five?" This Sam guy came off as a real character and kind of fun, but I wondered if Marnie knew what she was getting herself into with a person I now imagined as a middle-aged gamer with four teenage sons and at least two ex-wives, since she referred to the boys' mother as his *first* wife. On the other hand, I wondered if Sam knew what *he* was getting into, semi-dating my awesome sister, who happened to be smack dab in the middle of the autism scale. His intentions had better be fucking noble. If he turned out to be some jerk—

Marnie interrupted my thoughts just as I was getting ready to plan an intervention before even meeting the guy. "No. He calls him Sam My Man."

I cleared my throat. "How many times has Sam been married?"

"Once."

"But you said his first wife."

"That's what he calls her. My first wife, which she is."

My friend Eric referred to his ex-wife's new husband as his husband-in-law. People were strange. "Tell Sam we'll be happy to come to dinner tomorrow." I looked forward to meeting SamBot420.

"Okay." She stood to leave.

I consulted my watch. Five o'clock. My stomach fluttered because I would see Phaedra in fifteen minutes. Oh. But what to do about Marnie? The flutters turned into a free fall. It wouldn't be right to send her home by herself when she'd come all the way here to see me. But the thought of introducing Marnie to Phaedra scared the crap out of me. For a lot of reasons. But now was as good a time as any. I mean, if Phaedra didn't like Marnie, as much as I would hate it, it would be a deal breaker, right? Getting it over with sooner rather than later was best. Still scary, but it had to happen sometime.

"Hey, I'm meeting a friend for a quick cup of coffee before I head home. Do you want to come meet her?"

She followed me to the elevators. "Sure, but do you think caffeine this late in the day is a good idea?"

Not the response I expected, but okay. "I think you'll like her."

We got on the elevator, and as the door closed, she elbowed me in the side and grinned. "Branching out already, huh?"

She was full of surprises today.

❖

The first thing I saw when we entered Café Café was Phaedra sitting at a table near the back. Everything about her drew me to her. She seemed to get more beautiful every time I saw her, and my lips tingled at the thought of the kiss we'd shared the day before. A faint feeling of disappointment that we weren't alone floated through me. I wanted nothing more than to kiss her again. There would be no repeat or even discussion of it today with Marnie around, but any time with Phaedra was better than no time with her. My heart rate sped up as I approached her.

She looked preoccupied, staring into her cup, but when she spotted us, her eyes locked onto mine, treating me to a brilliant smile, exuding warmth, welcome, and something else. Desire? The last one probably fell under the category of wishful thinking, but just the thought of her wanting me like I wanted her filled me with excitement. She stood when I approached, giving me a long hug where her cheek rested briefly against mine, and her hands spread against my back, letting me feel her softness. The hug was over all too soon, and her eyes flicked to Marnie, who was a step behind me.

She leaned to the side a bit to get a better look at her. "You have a twin sister?"

I stood between them out of habit. Introducing Marnie to new people usually went well, but occasionally, she had issues with the casual contact that came with greetings. I didn't know how many times I had to explain why Marnie refused to shake a hand or return a hug, but more often than not, things went just fine.

I put my hand on Phaedra's shoulder. She wore a tank, and her skin was warm under my palm. It felt more intimate than I intended, but that was probably because I enjoyed it more than I should have. "Phaedra, this is Marnie, my younger sister." I turned. "Marnie, this is Phaedra, my new friend."

Marnie held her hand out, surprising me and giving me hope that it meant good things. Her making an overture to someone didn't happen often and only when she had already met them and liked them.

But then again, Marnie had liked Lisa when she'd first met her. It wasn't until Lisa started spending more time at our apartment that Marnie displayed stress. But that was a long time ago. I needed to stop thinking about it.

Phaedra shook her hand, and we all sat. "Do you mind if I ask the age difference between you?"

Marnie beat me to the answer. "Three years, one month, and seven days. My birthday is April third at twelve thirty p.m., and Dar's is February twenty-fourth, also at twelve thirty p.m."

"You were both born at twelve thirty?"

"Just a coincidence," Marnie said. "How many siblings do you have?"

Oh, boy. I knew where this was headed. When Marnie liked someone, she tended to grill them. While I was interested in the answers, I tried to think of how I could distract her. I'd rather get to know Phaedra in a more casual way.

"Actually, I don't have any. I always wanted one, but it was only my mom and me, and now it's just me."

"It's just the two of us, too," Marnie said.

"Are your parents…" Phaedra let the question dangle and raised her eyebrows.

I was confused at first, and then I realized it sounded like Marnie had implied that our parents were no longer alive. "Oh, they're alive and kicking," I said. "They moved to California for their jobs. They're teachers. But right now, they're on sabbatical working in Central America on their sociology research. Last time we talked to them, they were getting ready to go deep into the Amazon. Apparently, they think they're Indiana Jones."

"Wow, intense. Are you worried?"

I glanced at Marnie, who didn't appear affected by the question. She worried constantly about our parents.

"They're very resourceful," I said. "It's a bit disconcerting to not hear from them for long periods of time, but they know what they're doing, and they always give us a call when they get back to a phone." I wasn't about to lay a bunch of personal concerns on the table when I barely knew her. Something told me she'd want to know, though. "How about your parents?"

"My mom passed a few years ago, and my dad died before I really knew him. It's only me now, since I don't have any siblings, and I never knew any of my family in Haiti."

I sensed sadness in her voice, and I wanted to comfort her, but Marnie chimed in before I could. "I'll bet you miss them."

It was so unexpected. Where did this come from? She rarely sympathized with others. It just wasn't in her toolkit. Since this wasn't the first time she'd done something unexpected recently, it kind of knocked me back for a few seconds, as if the fabric of our reality was being re-spun. With all of this whirling in my head, I felt like an observer to the conversation. I watched them talk and tried to reconcile what was shifting within me.

"I do. Especially my mom. She and I were complicated, but we were pretty close."

"Complicated?" Marnie asked, and I gave Phaedra a look that said I was sorry for the inquisition even though I was intrigued more than anything else. She smiled as if she didn't care, and I thought I could fall in love with her for it.

"Yeah. Complicated in the sense of me not taking her old-school superstitions seriously, and she never got comfortable with me being a lesbian."

Marnie's face lit up. "Hey, Daria's a lesbian, too!"

"Oh, really?" Phaedra was about to take a sip of her drink, so her mouth was covered, but I saw amusement fill her eyes. She glanced at me and winked.

"Totally." Marnie didn't seem to notice the wink as a look of reflection settled over her face. "I'm not into the whole label thing, but if I had to pick, I'd say I'm pansexual. Gender and sexual orientation don't matter to me as much as kindness and intelligence. Anyway, you and Daria have something in common."

Her statement floored me. What was all this talk lately about asexual and pansexual labels? The subject didn't bother me at all, not even that it was Marnie bringing it up. But she'd never brought any of it up before, and I wondered if it had anything to do with the thing with SamBot. I tried to find something to say when she stood.

"I'll get us coffee. What would you like, Phaedra? I know Daria will have a decaf drip, since it's so late in the afternoon."

Used to her way of changing subjects, I wasn't surprised by the abrupt switch. What did surprise me was her query about what we wanted so she could order. Her actions were normally driven by internal stimulus, and it wasn't her way to consider others when she performed a task for herself, such as ordering coffee. But she'd reached outside of herself just now in a typical, everyday gesture. I didn't expect how such a simple gesture would affect me. I was used to taking care of her, not the other way around. Something had changed in her, and I'd missed it. But I liked it.

"Thanks for asking, Marnie, but I ordered a chai before you got here." Phaedra took a sip and smiled her dazzling smile.

Marnie smiled back. "You're very pretty."

Phaedra looked taken aback by the unexpected compliment, but she recovered quickly. "Thank you."

Marnie nodded. "You're welcome."

"I'll think I'll have a chai, too," I said.

Marnie lowed her head and eyed me with a questioning gaze, but I just smiled. I turned to Phaedra as Marnie walked to the counter. "She knows caffeine will keep me up all night."

Phaedra leaned toward me, and when she did, our hands were next to each other on the table, and she hooked our pinkies together. "Your sister is so cute, taking care of you. So you're a lesbian, huh?"

"Surprise." Our heads were close, and I could smell the spicy ginger scent of chai on her breath. I stared at her lips, and before I knew it, they were pressed against mine. It was a quick kiss, but oh so nice, and laughter bubbled up inside me. It took a second before I thought to check to see if Marnie had seen.

Phaedra moved even closer when I turned back. "I couldn't wait to kiss you. And don't worry, she didn't see." And she kissed me again. This time, she lingered, and her tongue glided across my lips. I might have whimpered when she sat back and took another sip of coffee. The twinkle in her eye over the rim of her cup indicated she'd heard it.

"I'd like to do a little more of that," she said.

God, the way she looked at me melted my brain. I wanted to grab her hand and take her anywhere where we could kiss for hours. "Me, too."

"I'm glad you brought your sister. I don't think I have a whole lot of willpower when you're around. It might be good to get to know each other a little bit first. After all, I only recently learned you have a last name."

I had to agree. The desire to kiss her again was powerful. If Marnie hadn't been there, I might have made a bit of a spectacle with the amount of PDA I was willing to participate in at Café Café. Instead, when Marnie came back with her coffee and my chai, we sat around the table and got to know each other. Marnie expressed special interest in Phaedra's playing the violin. One of the games she'd worked on contained a violin soundtrack, and it was awesome to watch her and Phaedra bond over styles of music. The more I got to know Phaedra, the more attractive she became on far more levels than just the physical, which, for the record, already knocked me out. I was especially impressed with how at ease she seemed with her leg. Now that I knew about it, I noticed she unconsciously rubbed it, but she never mentioned it. It reminded me of Marnie, who was well aware of who she was, but without discussing it, she expected people to treat her like they would anyone else. And they did.

After we finished our coffee, we lingered outside.

"I'm glad you had time to meet," I said to Phaedra.

"I'm glad you called," she said.

Marnie held out her hand. "I hope I get to see you again, Phaedra. I'm glad Daria decided to branch out a little bit."

Phaedra smiled but quirked an eyebrow at me. "The pleasure has been all mine," she said taking Marnie's hand. "Is it okay to hug you? I'm a hugger."

"Sure," said Marnie, letting go of her hand and holding out her arms. "But I've had pleasure today, too, so it's not completely all yours."

Phaedra laughed and gave her a quick hug. It impressed me, the ease with which both of them managed that everyday transaction, minor as it was. Phaedra picked up on things quickly, it seemed, and asked first and hadn't been too abrupt in her movements, which kept Marnie relaxed. Phaedra had a natural ease with people, and I admired that.

She turned to me next. "Is it okay if I hug you, too?"

"I'd be offended if you didn't." I wrapped my arms around her, and all the tingles from the day before raced through me again. I let my hands rest on the bare skin of her shoulders and forced myself not to caress it and make the hug into anything more than a friendly good-bye, even though a lot more than friendly feelings surged through me right then.

I leaned back to see into her eyes, and it took everything in me not to kiss her right there. I think she wrestled with the same thing from the way she bit her lip and the way her eyes bounced from my eyes to my lips as if she was trying to decide what to do. I snuck a glance at Marnie, who had her back to us as she walked toward one of the outdoor pianos installed on the mall. The skateboarder kid was leaning against it in conversation with the man Phaedra had been talking to the first time I'd seen her.

Taking advantage of Marnie's inattention, I stole a kiss. I couldn't get enough of her lips and tongue. She cupped my face, and I held her tight. I might have kissed her forever if I hadn't become aware of the music. Reluctantly, I stepped back, needing a little distance to calm my racing libido. I almost laughed when I noticed Phaedra breathing hard and fanning herself.

"Holy shit," I said before I could filter myself.

"My sentiments exactly," she said in a husky voice.

I glanced toward the piano, where Marnie was talking to the man and the boy. I caught one of Phaedra's hands, and we went to join them.

We arrived in time to hear Marnie ask, "What do you do when it rains?"

"There are places that will take most of us in, but we also know some spots where it stays dry."

Sometimes, Marnie came off as more direct than people were comfortable with, and I tensed up a bit, wondering where the conversation would lead.

The boy jutted his chin. "When it gets bad outside, I go back to my mom's and hope she's in between boyfriends. She usually sticks to weed, then, and she's nicer. Otherwise, I stay away. I don't want to end up like her."

His voice hadn't fully changed, and I pegged him at maybe fifteen. Too young to be on the street. Too young to be worrying about a safe place to sleep. Too young to already know his mother wasn't a good role model.

Phaedra sat next to the man, who was picking out a tune I didn't recognize on the keys, but she added her own melody, and it sounded nice. He moved his hands to the left, and she took over the right side of the keyboard and started singing a song I'd never heard. I'd seen things like this in YouTube videos but always suspected they were staged because who really did that kind of thing? But the song sounded great, and my attraction to Phaedra grew deeper with her versatility as a musician. It struck me that music wasn't even her full-time job, but with all of her talent, it probably should have been. Whatever she did at the graphics design company couldn't be nearly as important as what she did with her voice and instruments. What an amazing woman.

While I watched Phaedra play, Marnie took her wallet from her backpack, removed some cash, and split it in half, handing some to the kid and some to the old man. After a moment, she gestured to me and tilted her head toward the train station. She wanted to leave. Phaedra saw, too, said good night to the man she called Taco Bill and the boy she called Q, and we walked together.

"It was kind of you to give Bill and Q money, Marnie," Phaedra said.

"I thought maybe they could rent a room or something when it rains."

When we arrived at Union Station, Phaedra said she had rehearsal with her band a few blocks away, but when we offered to walk with her, she waved us off, saying she'd walked there for years on her own, so we said good-bye, and I spent the train ride home thinking about kissing her.

CHAPTER TWENTY

Phaedra

I looked forward to the exercise as I slipped into the bottoms of my gi and tucked my white tank into them before shrugging into the top, wrapping it around me, and fastening my new yellow belt. I wasn't fooling myself; the yellow belt was more about putting in the time rather than skill, but I was still proud of having advanced. Considering how close I'd come to not even coming in the first day to talking to the sensei about how one would *theoretically* do judo if one *theoretically* wore a prosthetic, advancing in belts felt like a pretty big accomplishment. I was already trying to figure out how I could spend more time in the dojo so I could get my orange belt faster. One day a week in class was not enough time for me, even though I had precious little free time as it was.

I wrapped extra bandages around my lower leg and the socket of my blade to help keep it in place. Last week, while grappling, my opponent had been a little overzealous, and the suction had given. Luckily, I had been able to pop it back in by just following through on the move, getting my feet back under me, and pushing my body weight into it. My opponent probably never even knew what happened, but the potential of what could have happened made me nervous. The last thing I wanted was for my leg to go flying off and traumatize the little ones in my class. Hell, it would probably traumatize *me*, but I knew it was inevitable with the amount of body contact judo required.

I tried to be positive about the incident. I had to, otherwise I'd never step outside of my comfort zone again and change my perspective. I had to think of issues that came up due to my leg as opportunities rather than challenges. Kind of like choosing to participate in full-contact activities when you have strap-on appendages. I laughed out loud at where my mind went as soon as I thought the word "strap-on." It had been a long, long time since I'd wandered in that direction. A thrill spread through my body, and I thought of kissing Daria. I had to pry myself from my memories when I realized I'd stopped getting ready and was staring into space. There was a good possibility that a faint moan might have escaped my throat. I glanced around, relieved to be alone. I slammed my locker closed and started for the mats. Maybe the locker room at my dojo wasn't the most appropriate place to get semi-aroused, but I was glad to know I wasn't dead in that regard like I'd thought I was.

I was so damn into her.

There was something about her. She had confidence, but she was sensitive. She listened when someone talked, like she wanted to know what you were all about. She didn't just listen to what you said, but how you said it, too. Being around her was an experience of sensations. And her kisses…oh, damn, her kisses. Those were on another level completely. I couldn't even try to describe what they did to me. Like, putting words around them would make them less than what they were.

But, oh my. Those lips. And what would it be like to be touched by her?

Clapping in the gym made me realize I was daydreaming. What had gotten into me? I'd lost track of everything for a few minutes. I took a few deep breaths and proceeded through the locker room door. Most of the other students were already warming up.

I had it bad. Really bad.

Telling her about my leg had to happen sooner rather than later. I needed to get it out there before we inched past the point of no return. I already knew it would hurt like hell if she decided she wasn't into a woman who worried about terrifying her grappling opponents by losing her leg during a basic hip throw. A chuckle rolled through my chest when I imagined it. At least I could laugh about it.

CHAPTER TWENTY-ONE

Daria

"Did you type in the correct address?" I asked Marnie as I pulled up to a guard booth in front of a gate.

Marnie double-checked the address on her phone. "I did."

"Did SamBot give you instructions on what to tell the guard?"

"He asked for the license plate, so I snapped a picture and sent it to him in the garage before we took off."

Sure enough, the guard opened the gate and waved us through.

My eyes nearly popped out of my head when Google navigation directed us through the main entrance of an exclusive Cherry Hills neighborhood. I looked left and right as we drove past ginormous houses on huge manicured lots. If I'd been asked to guess where SamBot lived before we arrived here, I was embarrassed to say I would have said Aurora, Parker, or another one of the many other blue-collar suburbs of Denver. This information forced me to throw out all the scenarios I'd imagined where SamBot sat in a dark basement, chatting up my sister as they stalked alien beings in the latest online multiplayer game. Not in a million years would I have pictured him living in a sprawling mansion with acreage and next-door neighbors who might play for the Broncos.

"This is totally not what I expected." As I drove, I leaned forward and gazed up at a house fashioned like an Italian villa. The next appeared to be a replica of one of the castles in medieval Europe. Not the kind with delicate spires and gabled turrets but the ones with humongous blocks of granite and chunky wooden beams. I expected bridges with massive iron chains over brackish moats. What was it with rich people and their penchant for garish architectural décor?

Google Maps had us pull up a long driveway to a tastefully

appointed ranch-style home with a nearby barn surrounded by pasture. The large house and land were impeccably maintained, but it still seemed homey.

"This is SamBot420's house, huh?"

Marnie shut off the navigation. "His name isn't really SamBot420. It's just Sam. SamBot420 is his gamer handle."

I snickered. She was so serious sometimes. "I figured as much. I'll call him Sam to his face."

She nodded, grasping the wine we'd brought. I turned off the car, and we got out. I turned in the direction of rhythmic thudding and the rattle of a chain to see a tall boy shooting hoops on a court near the barn.

A man who looked like an older version of the kid came from the barn and approached us as we walked toward the front door.

"Glad you're here, Marnie! And this must be Daria," he called as he approached.

Marnie handed him the wine, and he extended his other hand to me.

"Hi, Sam," I said, shaking his hand. "Marnie has told me a lot about you."

"Same here," he said, walking us toward the house. "Your sister loves you something fierce. She speaks of you often."

The information hit me in the feels. It never occurred to me that Marnie talked about me at work. She didn't do small talk, and I'd always thought it was out of sight, out of mind for Marnie. I didn't take it personally. It was just how Marnie's mind worked.

"I hope it's good stuff," I joked and winced inwardly. Had I just channeled my dad?

Marnie stopped on the front porch and touched my arm. "I wouldn't say bad things about you, Dar."

"I know. It's a figure of speech. It wasn't very funny."

"Oh, a joke." She smiled.

Sam smiled during our little exchange, taking it in. Maybe he understood my sister better than I gave him credit for.

"Well, I hope you're hungry," he said, opening the massive front door. "I asked Marnie what you two like to eat, and she sent me a very detailed list. We should have something you'll like."

Oh God, I thought, stepping into a large foyer. *I hope he doesn't think I'm finicky.* I didn't eat crustaceans, couldn't stand goat cheese, and I wasn't much of a red meat eater, but I was good with most everything else. I'd even choke down the aforementioned items if someone prepared them for me unknowingly. I glanced at Marnie, but she was gawking at the house. "I'm not picky. I'm sure whatever you made is perfect."

He winked. "Marnie mentioned grilled cheese is your favorite. But we have Impossible burgers and sliced veggies from the grill. I've whipped up my special cowboy baked beans. Our kiddos like to cook, and my oldest boy tried his hand at Gruyère mac and cheese. Our youngest made a fruit and cheese plate. I can't attest to either yet, but if the past is an indication of the future, they'll both be delicious."

"It all sounds great." I liked him more by the minute. "What do you do at the company?"

He laughed. "As little as possible."

"Not true," Marnie said. "You do everything."

It occurred to me then that SamBot was *the* Sam from Bottoms Up Gaming. Samuel Bottoms. We'd been invited to dinner at the house of one of the most successful game designers in the world, and all this time, I'd assumed him to be a tester like Marnie.

"Wait. You're Samuel Bottoms. *The* Samuel Bottoms." I was so uncool. At least my voice wasn't as shrill with excitement as it could have been.

He laughed again. "I could deny it, but I'd be lying. You sound surprised. Marnie did tell you we know each other from work, didn't she?"

"She did. But I assumed you were one of her testing coworkers." I didn't want to admit that Marnie very rarely spoke about her coworkers, and this was the first time she'd ever socialized with one outside of work. Boy, and when she decided to socialize, she picked the top dog.

When she'd first started working, my parents and I had tried to get her to talk about work life, but she'd always been less than enthusiastic about telling us about anything other than the work. I didn't want to say that the people she worked with weren't important to her, but realistically, it was probably true. She operated on a hyperfocused level, making it easy for her to block out almost everything around her. In fact, in the first few days, she'd stayed there, completely head down, doing her tasks past the time everyone else went home. My mom had bought her a special watch and set alarms to make sure she took lunch and left at a reasonable hour. After a while, she'd settled into her routine and the alarms weren't as necessary, but even now, when her routine was disrupted at work, I could tell because she wouldn't come home until late, and only then because I'd call her to check in.

Sam dropped an arm over Marnie's shoulders, and I was blown away when she didn't stiffen or shrug away. She seemed to enjoy it. "Marnie's doing a great job leading the design team."

Marnie nodded.

"Wait. What?" I asked before I thought better of it. My astonishment overshadowed my manners. "You lead the design team now?"

Sam turned to Marnie. "You didn't tell your sister about your promotion?"

She shrugged, but she wore an expression I'd never seen before: pride. She was proud of herself. Even as a child, I'd never seen her like this. She always just tackled things and moved on to the next. But this was obviously something she found pride in. My heart swelled at this new development. I wanted to jump up and down in excitement for her.

I grabbed her hands and squeezed, and she actually squeezed back. "You were promoted, Marnie? Congratulations."

Sam chuckled. "She's knocking it out of the ballpark, too. Her team loves her."

"She has a team?" Really? Marnie had great social skills when she was up for it, but management? Even I sometimes struggled with a team reporting to me. Teams tested their managers constantly. I found it hard to think about Marnie dealing with personnel issues and things requiring nuanced communication.

Sam stood behind her and squeezed her shoulders like a proud father. "Four managers and twenty-nine developers. We provided a little sensitivity training in the beginning, you know, to help everyone understand how to work with her since she'd be managing them, but I have to say, it's worked out extremely well. It turns out that when people are forced to specifically express what's on their minds and discuss expectations instead of letting everyone guess, we have a lot less misunderstandings. And the setting boundaries thing is a no-brainer. Her team is running like a well-oiled machine. She's helping other managers do the same in their own departments, and they're there for her when she has a situation that needs a specialized touch. It's actually created a distributed management structure at the company that is enhancing our employee development process. It's kind of unbelievable."

An element of pride was evident in his words. More than that, I saw Marnie in a new light, and this new perspective made me almost giddy until I realized I'd been underestimating my sister, which brought a wave of guilt with it. What else was I underestimating?

In typical Marnie style, as if all this praise meant little to her, she moved farther into the front room, which was outfitted almost as a command center with big, wall-mounted monitors, leather chairs specialized for gaming comfort, and a wall of shelves outfitted with gaming towers with blinking lights, making me think of spaceships and advanced military technology. It made Marnie's gaming setup look miniscule in comparison. I saw another trip to Best Buy in our future.

A tall woman who might have been a model from an outdoorsy catalog came into the room. She stood next to Sam and wound her arm around his waist. "I thought I heard voices." She had a warm smile.

Sam squeezed her to his side and put a hand on my shoulder. He was obviously a demonstrative man, but he exuded a safe and nonthreatening energy. I liked it. He gestured toward me. "Melody, this is Marnie's sister Daria. Daria, this is my wife Melody."

"It's nice to meet you." I shook her outstretched hand. Wife? As in current wife, not ex-wife? It appeared another of my perceptions had been drastically off, and I tried not to let it show in my expression.

Melody nodded. "You two could be twins."

"We get told that a lot," I said.

Melody withdrew her arm from around Sam's waist and clapped. "Who wants a drink? I made a batch of my specialty whiskey sours, but we have other drinks, including beer, wine, and nonalcoholic." She looked expectantly between me and Marnie, who was still geeking out over the gaming gear.

"Whiskey sour for me," Sam said, lifting his eyebrows. "If you like whiskey, you need to try Mel's special mix. It's perfection."

"I guess I'll have to try it, then," I told Melody, who was taking count on her fingers. Her smile in response told me I'd made a friend.

"I'll take a whiskey sour," a voice said from behind me, and the tall boy we'd seen shooting baskets on the driveway walked in.

"So, a Coke for Sam Two." Melody smirked at her son and held up a finger on her other hand. "How about you, Marnie?"

"Beer sounds good to me, Mel, please." Marnie approached us with a controller in her hand. "Heck-almighty, Sam. You have the X214. It's totally pre-beta. Hawk hasn't even opened the vault on them yet."

Sam's face lit up. "I have three of them. They asked us to test them on Sphere."

Her mouth dropped open. "How'd they hear about Sphere?"

I had no idea what they were talking about, but I'd heard about Sphere, the game Marnie was working on, and everyone knew Hawk. They were the makers of the high-end controllers Marnie drooled over at Best Buy. Some of their gaming computers were more expensive than the car I drove.

Sam rocked on his heels. "It's my job to work with other companies to make sure we're compatible with new tech. I'd tell you how the conversations went, but then I'd have to kill you."

Marnie shook her head as she examined the controller. "I know you're kidding, Sam. You don't like blood."

Sam winked at me. Even when completely at ease, Marnie was so literal. And he totally got it. "Yeah, that's the only reason why I wouldn't kill you."

I kind of fell in love with him right then. He got my sister.

Dinner turned out to be fun, but the glimpse into Marnie's life away from me was amazing. I'd never seen her interact with someone outside of our combined life. We'd only ever done things together with people we both knew. But this was different. Marnie and Sam used a whole work language I didn't know. And this language came with shortcuts and knowledge of one another that I didn't know Marnie was capable of. But when I thought about it, she and I had our own language, too. Slowly, it dawned on me that in my role of big sister and protector, I'd restricted my perception of Marnie into an almost one-dimensional person when she was anything but. This revelation struck me like a shot, and not the fun kind.

CHAPTER TWENTY-TWO

Phaedra

Nine thirty, and I was beat. I'd almost skipped a shower, but an hour and a half of judo required bathing in my book. I didn't regret it, either. There was something about hot water and sore muscles that went together.

I wrapped a towel around me, grabbed my crutch, and made my way to the bed. Tonight was going to be an early one. I didn't care if I'd intended on working on the Mercer account for a couple of hours. I was tired. Too tired to even put pajamas on, I slipped into bed and tossed the towel onto my desk chair. Trance made his way up the bed and curled up on the other pillow.

"Alexa, bedroom lights off, please." The AI turned off the lights, and I wondered why I continued to say "please" and "thank you" to a piece of computerized technology. Actually, I knew why. My mother. She might not have mothered me in a traditional way, but she'd sure instilled manners in me. There had been hell to pay for a forgotten "yes, ma'am" when I was growing up.

My pillow felt like a cloud under my weary head, and I was just about to drift off when my cell phone rang. If it hadn't been by my bed, I would have ignored it. But I picked it up to turn off the ringer and saw Daria's name. All of the drowsiness fled my body as I answered the phone.

"Is it too late to call?" she asked after we'd said hello.

"Not at all." I wanted to tell her it was never too late for her.

I heard her sigh. "I almost hung up, but I couldn't help myself. I just wanted to call."

"I'm glad you did."

There was a pause, and I almost thought the call had dropped, but then she spoke again.

"I really don't have a reason. I just wanted to talk to you."

The simple statement melted my heart. It was so sincere. "You don't need a reason." I shifted to get more comfortable and became aware that I was completely naked. I wondered what she'd say if she knew. Would it embarrass her or delight her?

"I had a good time at coffee yesterday."

"Me, too. I enjoyed getting to know you better. Your sister is sweet, too. Don't tell her, but you're my favorite, though."

She laughed. "That's a relief. She showed up at my office, and I didn't want to make her go home alone, so…"

"I'm glad you brought her. Do you two live together?"

"She's my roommate."

"It's cool that you two are so close."

"Yeah. She's easy to get along with. I won't bring her next time, though."

She wanted to see me again! "Oh, you want a next time?"

"Definitely." There was another pause, but this time, I could hear her breathing. "Maybe somewhere quieter."

"So we can do more kissing?" I couldn't believe I said it. Just thinking about it made my insides tremble.

"I can't stop thinking about those kisses. You're really good at it, by the way."

"I was thinking the same about you," I said with a smile. Her kisses made me feel things all over my body, and remembering them made me very aware of how naked I was.

"I'm glad we both think so. It has to be a good sign." I could hear the smile in her voice.

"Maybe we can have lunch together sometime?"

"I'd like that. I'll let you go now, though. It's late, but I'm glad I got to hear your voice."

We hung up, and I couldn't stop smiling. And I was wide awake. And totally nude. And completely turned on thinking about kissing her. There was only one way I knew of to deal with that, so I took matters into my own hands.

CHAPTER TWENTY-THREE

Daria

A flood of delicious scents assailed my senses when I opened the tall glass door to Pho House. I'd never been here, but Taryn said it was awesome, and when Phaedra texted to ask if I wanted to have lunch with her there, I had to say yes. I would have said yes if she'd asked me to meet her at a lobster bar. I must have it bad for her if I'd choke down a huge oceanic insect just for her.

Phaedra's smile knocked me out from across the dining room. I wonder if she'd been watching the door. I threaded through the tables and stood next to the table where she sat. "Hi."

Was it me, or did the intensity of her smile go up about a thousand watts?

She kept on smiling and motioned to a chair. "Do you want to sit?"

I kind of scrambled with the chair. Damn. I'd been standing there like a weirdo, staring at her and thinking about our call the night before.

"Sorry I'm a couple minutes late. Taryn, my friend, felt the need to interrogate me about going to lunch with you. I may have walked out on her mid-sentence."

"You're fine. I sat down seconds before you came in. Does Taryn interrogate you often?"

"All. The. Time. In fact, she's already demanded a full recount of this lunch when I get back."

"Taryn is a work friend?"

"We met in college, but we work together now. We were recruited at the same job fair when we graduated and have been working at McSweeney and Price ever since."

"Right, you told me you were an accountant when we were at the street fair. Is she one, too?"

"Yep. Accountants tend to run in pods."

"Really?"

"I'm kidding." I rested my hand on hers and was about to take it away when she put her hand atop it, holding it in place. Her hands were warm and soft, and the touch became a focal point, sending warmth all through me.

"Was it your dream to be an accountant?"

"Are you judging my profession?" I joked, but my mind was still on her hand.

"Not at all. I'm just wondering who you are, Daria Fleming."

That was a good question, and although she probably didn't mean it to be a query that scoured my very soul, it was a startling reminder of how I'd recently realized that I'd basically just let life happen to me. I wasn't about to lay all of that on her over what was supposed to be a getting to know each other better lunch date, so I tried to keep it light. "I love details. I like finding ways to be more efficient. I like order. Numbers also tell stories, so believe it or not, there is a creative element to it that appeals to me."

"I never thought about it like that."

"Intriguing, right?" I said with a straight face before I burst out laughing. "What about you? Have you always wanted to be a graphic artist?"

"I've always wanted to be a professional singer and performer, actually."

"You mean more than what you already do with Washtub Whiskey?"

"Yeah. I'd love to cut an album and tour. You know, live the rock and roll thing?"

"I've seen you perform. You're amazing. You could totally do it."

"I almost had it once. Seven years ago, a record label was scouting me."

"What happened?"

"An accident laid me up for a while, and when I got better, I had a hard time picking up the pieces. By the time I did, the label had already moved on." She shrugged as if she'd accepted how things had worked out, but it made me sad.

"That totally sucks. You're so talented."

She tilted her head in a way that told me she had accepted what had happened. "I'm happy with how things worked out. I love working with Barb. She's been very generous. And I still play."

She traced her fingers across the top of my hand. It felt amazing. I watched her fingers and imagined them touching other parts of my body.

"Daria."

When I lifted my gaze to her face, it was just her and me sitting there, staring at one another.

"I meant what I said last night. I can't stop thinking about kissing you," she said, reminding every nerve in my body about the kisses I'd been thinking about, too.

"What can I get you ladies?"

The server's voice broke through my awareness, and I noticed the menu lying on the table. Phaedra ordered something, and I told him to make it two because I had no idea what I wanted, and I didn't want to figure it out right then. When the server left, I realized I was still holding Phaedra's hand, and I started giggling.

She joined in. "You know, I would never have pegged you as a giggler."

I tried to stop, but having it called out made me giggle even more. "It's an embarrassing habit."

"It's cute."

"I have no idea what I ordered," I said, a little embarrassed.

Her expression told me she had an idea why and she found it amusing. "Vegetable soup. Tofu, veggies, a few beans, and noodles."

"You distract me." I threaded our fingers together. The giggles had stopped, and I was back to thinking about kissing her again.

"I do?"

I nodded. "Big time."

"Well, it's mutual. You distract me big time, too."

"I like that."

Phaedra smiled, and this time, her nose wrinkled, and her eyes sparkled. It was the smile of pure happiness, and I liked it. I liked it even more because I was the cause of it. But her expression changed, and insecurity clouded her eyes when she let them drop to our intertwined fingers. She cleared her throat. "Hey…"

"Hey, what?" I asked when she didn't continue.

"I have something I want to tell you. It might not be a big thing, or maybe it is a big thing, but since I like you, and I want to spend more time with you—"

I couldn't help it, I had to say, "You do? Because I do, too."

Her shoulders, which had crept up to her ears while she talked, almost as if she was trying to shrink into herself, relaxed, and the little girl smile returned. Not as bright as the first one but just as pretty. "I'm glad. I'd hoped…but I didn't want to expect it…but anyway…"

I stroked the back of her hand. "You don't need to be nervous with me."

"I am."

"Don't be. Whatever you need to say, you can say it. I'm not a scary person."

She laughed. "You're probably the least scary person I know."

The server came back with our food, set it on the table, and the scents of basil, onions, and ginger wafted between us. We took careful sips of the hot soup, and I knew I'd found a new favorite thing.

"You like it?" she asked.

"I love it," I said taking another sip. "You were going to tell me something?"

She sat back in her chair, stirring her soup. "Yeah. I hoped you'd forget." She sighed and sat forward. "It has to do with the accident I told you about a few minutes ago. The thing is, I wear a prosthetic leg. I lost my leg below the knee and wear long skirts to disguise it, but I wanted to tell you before things went any further, so you'd have a chance to, well…you know…you could—"

"I already knew." Had others found her leg a problem? I couldn't imagine someone not wanting to be with her because of it.

"What?" She stopped stirring her soup and stared at me. I wondered if I'd said something I shouldn't have.

"I saw it the day at the Fish Tail."

"You did?"

I put down my spoon. "I did. And even though it shouldn't even be a thing, I want you to know it doesn't bother me, if you're worried about it. Like I said, it shouldn't even be a thing. I like all of you, including your badass hardware."

She looked as if she didn't know what to do with the information. "Oh."

"What happened? Do you mind me asking?"

She looked relieved and shocked all at once, and I wanted to do serious damage to whoever had made her feel like she wasn't perfect the way she was.

"I was walking home one day after work in the cold and slush. A man in a walker was having a hard time navigating some of the accumulated ice near a crosswalk, and I kind of jogged over to help him, and I slipped. I banged my leg against the light post. It hurt, but I didn't think much of it. I got up and continued helping him across the street. When I got home, I changed from my wet pants, and I discovered a cut above the ankle. I cleaned it up and thought nothing more of it. But the next morning, when I got up to get ready for work, I couldn't even stand, and the wound was swollen and angry. I went to my doctor, who said it was infected, and she sent me straight to the emergency room. I don't remember much of anything after I arrived there because I had a fever and was really out of it, but when I finally came to, the doctors told me they had to amputate my leg a little below the knee to remove the necrotized parts and to prevent the aggressive sepsis from spreading."

"How bad was the cut?" I grimaced, imagining a terrible wound.

"Not much more than a scratch."

"Crazy. You lost part of your leg because of an infection?"

"It was a particularly aggressive form of staph. It took hold and spread quickly. I'm lucky to be alive. When the sepsis started, the doctors flooded me with antibiotics and kept me on them for months afterward."

She recounted the experience in a matter-of-fact way, but I couldn't help but imagine how scary it must have been for her to wake up in a hospital bed with part of her leg missing. I reached for her hand, which was in a fist on the table. "I can't even imagine. I'm sorry you went through all of that."

She squeezed my hand. "Thanks. So now I wear a prosthetic." She shrugged as if it wasn't a big deal, but I got the impression she was studying me closely and analyzing my reaction. I wondered again who had disappointed her, leaving her to think others would walk away from her because of it.

"You're amazing, and if you were worried I'd want to take a pass on whatever is happening between us because of it, you don't need to be."

She squeezed my hand, and the dazzling smile I'd seen when I'd first entered the restaurant reappeared.

Chapter Twenty-four

Phaedra

The dressing room was more than crowded. The five of us were sharing it with the headlining band, Nick's Army, and even though the four of them would have the room to themselves while we were doing our set, they'd joined us as if it was a big party or something. Normally, I didn't mind. Getting hyped up for a show was fun, and I liked them. We'd played with them a couple of times, and they were always a kick. But tonight, I had other things on my mind. Namely Daria. She was always on my mind these days. But ever since lunch earlier in the day, when I'd told her about my leg, I'd become even more preoccupied with her.

I couldn't believe I'd gotten up the courage to tell her, but after coffee with her on Monday and realizing I was starting to really like her—like, really, *really* like her—I found it more important than ever to tell her. I couldn't wait until it was too late again. I couldn't go through that again. And even though I'd gone over a million ways to tell her in my head, none of them sounded right. I still hadn't figured out how to tell her when I'd asked her to lunch. I just knew I had to. When we got there, I'd nearly chickened out at the last minute, but she was sweet, telling me she wasn't a scary person. But I already knew that. In fact, she was so *not* scary, it was scary.

But when she'd said she already knew about my leg, I didn't expect it. It had never occurred to me it had been visible at the bar. They kept it dark on purpose to mask the decade's worth of wear and tear. Or maybe it was to cover the wear and tear of the clientele. It didn't matter. She'd seen it, and she didn't care. Now I was sorry I hadn't stuck around. I'd have saved myself a ton of worry.

The dressing room was getting warm. I'd gotten ready before coming down to the Royal Standish, and with everyone in the room,

I left and wandered to the side of the stage to look out at the audience, which was slowly filling the standing-room-only venue. The place held about five hundred people, and between Washtub Whiskey and Nick's Army, the place was sold out. I scanned the audience and didn't see Daria. I wasn't worried, though. We still had twenty minutes until we went on.

CHAPTER TWENTY-FIVE

Daria

A huge crowd milled in front of the venue when the Lyft driver dropped me off into a sweet-smelling cloud of vape. I'd never heard of the headlining band, but the crowd consisted of people about my age and dressed like me, in jeans and T-shirts, to my relief. I wasn't much of a concertgoer, and I'd briefly panicked about the appropriate dress for the show. Interestingly enough, Marnie had calmed me down when I mentioned my insecurity on my way out the door. She and Courtney from the soccer team had been sitting on the couch playing an online game, and she didn't even look away from the screen when she said, "Who cares what they think? As long as Phaedra likes what she sees."

She'd sounded like our mother and was probably only reciting one of Mom's favorite responses. Marnie usually didn't care about what others thought of her. It made sense, though, and she was right. Either way, it held me over until I got to the venue.

After I arrived, however, another set of insecurities threatened to derail my confidence. I wasn't sure how having my name at the door worked. Did I go up to will call? Or did I wait in the door line that wound around the block? I decided to check will call first, since there was only one person in line. I was glad I did, too, because the woman behind the window told me to go right up to the door, skipping the line, and they would let me right in. I was a little self-conscious about the stares I received, but I also enjoyed the little thrill of bypassing the line because I knew someone in the band.

Nostalgia took hold of me as soon as I walked in. The last time I'd been here was in college. I'd always liked the old-time atmosphere of the place, with the worn red carpet, gilt sconces, and shiny gold wallpaper with velvet designs. The dim preshow lighting was enough for me to make my way up the short flight of stairs and through the open showroom doors. I scanned the place from the back. The entire lower section was already filled, and the sections behind the front were filling up fast. I recognized some faces from the street fair.

As much as I wanted to be right up front, I didn't want to deal with making my way through the dense crowd. I made my way to the bar and was lucky to find an empty stool. As soon as I made my order, the lights went down, and the house music stopped. When the spotlights came on, there was Phaedra, right in front, standing behind the mic stand and holding her violin against her leg and her bow in the other hand, her radiant smile beaming a hot path into my chest. She was so fucking beautiful. I think my heart stopped for a second as I took her in. My hands even began to sweat. I took a sip of beer because I didn't know what else to do.

The crowd roared when she lifted her violin and tucked it under her chin. It was about then that she saw me, and when her eyes locked on mine, I was lost.

Chapter Twenty-six

Phaedra

Could Daria be any sexier? I'd only caught a quick peek at her before the stage lights kicked on, and I lost sight of her in the glare. But, sweet Jesus, what I'd seen was pure perfection. She made a simple pair of jeans and a leather jacket into living sex. Good thing music was as natural as breathing to me, otherwise I might have been in trouble, what with my mind on her instead of the set we'd just started.

I forced myself to rein in my libido and concentrate on the show even as I struggled to see all the way to the bar, but I couldn't see past the edge of the stage with the lights on. That was when I realized I was actually standing on the edge, having danced my way there. And I was *still* dancing. The realization nearly caused me to trip forward, so I pivoted and made my way back a few feet. Heloise, Ty, and Jennifer were watching me with huge smiles on their faces, and Leigh caught my eye and winked. They were as surprised as me, by the expressions on their faces. I hadn't planned on dancing at this gig. I never planned on dancing. Maybe it was because Leigh had talked me into wearing the spring. The old joy filled me, making me fly about the stage. I didn't care about the crowd seeing it. I'd never imagined I'd dance publicly again, but here I was. Whatever had come over me, the crowd was into it, and it was amazing.

After the long musical intro, I went back to the mic stand to sing because I wasn't wearing a cheek mic. Having to stay in one place allowed me to reflect on the last few minutes, and a hint of anxiety tried to sneak in. But all I had to do was scan the audience to see they were having a great time and that no one was staring at my fucked-up leg. Glee flowed through me again, and I threw myself into the performance, deciding to do all my overthinking later.

The show ended too soon, and the response from the crowd was amazing. As usual, I had a post-performance high pulsing throughout my body, only this time, there was an element of anticipation to it. When the lights came up, there was Daria, all sexy, back by the bar, beaming at me. I pointed at her and motioned toward the steps to the side stage. She put her hand on her chest with a questioning look on her face, as if I might have been signaling to someone else. I laughed and nodded. The band and I took another bow and walked off stage, where all four of them surrounded me, asking me about the dancing. In fact, the entire band was on a high almost as intense as mine. There was nothing like nailing a performance. Few things were as intensely satisfying.

Speaking of intensity, it took me a minute to untangle from the hugs and astonished chatter. I made my way to the side stage door, and there was Daria, standing at the top of the steps. I moved the curtains back and pulled her backstage with me.

"You were amazing!"

She gave me a quick hug and pulled away, but I held on, even though I was a bit damp from sweat. The house music was back on and a little loud. It didn't require me to speak directly into her ear, but I used it as an excuse to hold her for a little longer.

"Thanks for coming. Sorry about the sweat, but you feel good," I said.

She squeezed me tighter and put her cheek against mine. "You do, too."

Her voice was low, and the vibration moved well beyond my ear and into other parts of my body.

"Phay! Get your ass back here. The guys from Nick's Army want to do a preshow shot with us before they go on," Leigh called from deeper within the side stage gloom.

I let go of Daria. "Come on." I took her hand and pulled her toward the greenroom.

The room was crowded with both bands and a few other people, some of whom I knew, most of whom I did not. The energy in the room was off the charts, and a shirtless, tatted-up guy I recognized as the drummer from the other band poured shots of Jack into red plastic cups. What was it with guy bands and Jack? I accepted my cup and took another, handing it to Daria. She sniffed it and raised an eyebrow.

"You don't have to if you don't want to," I said.

"Are you kidding? It might be a work night, but how often will I be in this situation?"

Her eyes were bright, and I liked the way she kept them on me. I hoped the answer to her question was often.

When everyone had a drink, Nick, the lead singer of the other band, draped an arm over Ty's shoulder and lifted his cup. Ty's grin indicated she enjoyed his attention. "When Nick's Army gets big, we're taking you ladies on the road with us." He raised his cup even higher. "To an A-plus fucking performance by Washtub Whiskey. I hope you don't make us look like shit in comparison. Boys, we're gonna have to rock the house tonight."

Acknowledgment by the headlining band always felt good. I didn't know how many times we'd been told we'd exceeded expectations from the bands we opened for. They always expected local bands to be passable but nothing great, and I always expected the bands we opened for to be a dime a dozen. Lots of bands toured through Denver, and we'd opened for more than I could count, but this was the third time we'd played for Nick's Army, so they must have requested us from our management company. They were definitely not one of the dime-a-dozen bands. I raised my cup and tapped it to Daria's. The whiskey burned my throat on the way down, and I laughed at the grimace Daria pulled when she tossed her shot back. She wiped her mouth with the back of her hand and exhaled a trembling breath.

"Good stuff." Her eyes watered.

I laughed. "No, it's not."

She shook her head vigorously. "It's awful."

I couldn't help it, I hugged her and laughed. She hugged me back and buried her face in my neck. She shook with laughter as I became single-mindedly aware of her face pressed into my skin. A rush of tingles spread through me.

"Is it warm in here, or is it the whiskey?" she asked.

"It's a little of both. Come on." I took her hand, and we left the greenroom where Nick was setting up another round of shots. The guys were ramping up to be in a good mood when they hit the stage in a few minutes.

We threaded through the narrow backstage hallway to the back of the building. The door to the alley was open, and I pulled Daria out into the cool night air. A single weak light worked hard to illuminate the space between the buildings, and no one else was around, although I smelled the fading scent of a recently smoked cigarette.

The sweat I'd worked up from our performance had mostly dried, but it was enough to make me shiver as we moved from the warmth of the building. Daria slipped her leather jacket off and draped it over my shoulders. It was warm from the heat of her body, and it smelled like her. I hugged it to me.

"Thanks."

"Thank you."

"For what?"

"For this," she said, raising her arms and spinning in the alley. She appeared young and carefree. I had a feeling she didn't let this side of herself out very often, and it touched me.

When she stopped spinning, I moved closer. "Are you having fun?"

The muffled sound of the MC introducing Nick's Army floated out the door, followed by applause, and music began to pulse.

She laughed and stepped toward me until we were nearly touching. "I am." Her voice was soft, and her eyes sparkled in the dim light. They were large and infinitely dark. I couldn't tear my eyes away from them, not even when she put her hand on my cheek and stepped even closer, bringing our bodies together. Anticipation twitched in my stomach and need flared in my chest. I wrapped my arms around her waist. We were going to kiss. Her lips were inches from mine. Our previous kisses had been fun or stolen. People had been around, preventing me from giving in completely. But here we were, darkness all around, and all I could see was her. All I could feel was her. All I wanted was her. I lowered my head to meet her lips, letting the excitement course through me.

"I don't know how they can even perform after a bottle and a half of that shit." Heloise's voice echoed from the doorway.

Daria and I froze, our lips centimeters apart.

I recognized Jenn's braying laugh. "Says the queen of Fireball shots."

"*Former* queen of Fireball shots," Heloise countered.

I gazed into Daria's eyes. We hadn't moved apart, but her expression asked if we should, or maybe she hoped they weren't headed outside. I didn't know. I grabbed her hand and pulled her behind our gig van, which was parked along the brick wall of the building opposite.

Just in time, too, because I heard Jenn, Ty, and Heloise tromp out into the alley.

The narrow space between the wall and the van was only wide enough for the passenger door to open halfway. Daria stood with her back against the cold wall, and I leaned into her. The laugh that caught in my throat during our getaway died when I noticed Daria's hand land on my ass in our hurried attempt to hide. Now we were pressed against each other in the darkness of the narrow space, panting to catch our breath, and she pulled me against her. My heart raced, and it wasn't all because of the rush not to be seen. I was sure she felt it beating between us. Impatience seized me, and I kissed her. I had to. Her mouth was so close, our bodies were touching, and my mind went blank for everything except my desire for hungry, urgent kisses. The time for tentative exploration was over. I needed to taste her, feel her, know her.

Daria's hand pressed against my ass, grabbing my skirt as she caressed my throat and the back of my neck. She stroked the base of my skull, and I was about to explode as her tongue slipped between my lips and traced along the sensitive edge inside before her mouth opened and deepened our kiss. The beat of my heart spread to the rest of my body. Every nerve ending was on fire.

I trailed kisses across her jaw as she threw her head back, and I licked the inches to her ear and sucked on the soft skin of her earlobe, spending moments there before I moved my mouth to her neck and skimmed my teeth over the taut flesh of her exposed throat. As I explored the skin of her neck, I stroked her sides, slowing down to appreciate the soft curves of the sides of her round, firm breasts. She squeezed my ass even more tightly. My lips explored lower down her chest until I was kissing the warm skin at the lowest point of her V-neck shirt, pushing it down to taste the skin between her breasts. Oh my God. I wanted to touch her everywhere. I wanted it with an intensity so pure, I ached. Moving the T-shirt aside, I found one of her silk-covered nipples with my lips, circling it with my tongue before I nibbled it lightly with my teeth, extracting a quiet moan from her. The sound and vibration made my lips tingle, ramping up the burn of my desire, and as I tongued her silk-covered nipple, I dipped my hands down to the waist of her jeans, inching the hem of her shirt up, and I swept my fingers along the warm softness of her lower back.

As my lips explored her chest, her hands traveled under the heavy warmth of the borrowed leather jacket, up my arms and across my shoulders, leaving a trail of heat across my skin. As she squirmed with the ministrations of my mouth upon her nipple, she pushed her hands down the back of my tank top, and then dragged them back up, her short nails scratching lines of fire as they moved. My clit pulsed. I had no intention of fucking her in the alley when I'd pulled her out here, but right now, it seemed like an excellent idea.

CHAPTER TWENTY-SEVEN

Daria

"Come here," I whispered hoarsely, pulling Phaedra up to kiss her on the mouth. When her lips released my nipple, I was both relieved and absolutely frustrated. Had she continued for another minute, I'd have come. The throb between my legs was insistent, though, and when her mouth fell on mine again, the sensations of her tongue in my mouth increased the intensity.

I grabbed her shoulders and reversed our positions, pushing her against the wall. My action was sudden, and she stumbled a little, but I held her tight and steadied her, my leg coming to rest between her legs.

"I'm sorry," I mumbled against her mouth when I kissed her again, running my fingers along the undersides of her breasts.

"I'm not," she said without breaking the kiss. Her hips ground against my leg, and even through our clothes, the heat between her legs was like fire. Her arms wrapped around me, and her hands moved into the back of my jeans, under my underwear, cupping my ass. The motion made the pants tighter around my waist, pulling the crotch of my jeans against me, and the friction of the seam against my clit sent frissons of sensation through my body. I succumbed to my need and rocked against it for a moment, ready to come. I gasped for breath, pulling my lips from hers and burying my head against her shoulder, the coiling tension pulling in, readying for the ultimate explosion.

That was when a car door creaked open and the lights in the van flashed on.

We froze, but my orgasm continued, and I forced myself not to make a sound or move at all. This muted the overall effect of the climax, which pounded through my center for a mere second before it trailed off suddenly, leaving my body extremely sensitive and literally aching for more. I wasn't sure if Phaedra even knew.

The voices we'd hidden from hadn't stopped talking during all of this, even though I hadn't paid attention to anything they'd said. But now the sweet scent of marijuana wafted through the alley. Our position near the rear of the van and away from the windows kept us hidden…unless someone decided to get in through the passenger door, when they'd surely see us. By now I didn't care.

"Why?" I whimpered.

Phaedra leaned her head against mine. "Heloise swapped booze for pot about a year ago." Her whisper was a low vibration against my ear, eliciting a shiver. She pulled her hands from the back of my jeans and rubbed my arms. "Are you cold?"

I kissed her ear. "Just the opposite."

"Hey. You guys seen Phaedra?" I recognized Leigh's voice. I imagined her leaning out the open back door of the venue, calling to the others.

"Not since she left the greenroom with her hot new girlfriend," one of the others said. They thought I was hot?

"I'll bet they're tucked behind some equipment somewhere in there getting high on each other," another voice said, clearly holding in smoke. Her response was followed by a cough and a laugh. Probably Heloise.

"Cool," Leigh said. "You guys should watch this band. They're pretty good."

"Sure. Let's get back inside," one of them said.

The door to the van slammed closed, the lights went out, and the sounds of footsteps trailed away.

I lifted my head from Phaedra's shoulder, and she started shaking against me. When I met her eyes, they were streaming tears, and my heart dropped until I figured out it was from suppressed laughter. I started to laugh, too. In a minute, both of us were wiping away tears.

When we'd caught our breath, Phaedra laid a hand against my cheek. "I was about a second away from coming when they got into the van."

"Me, too." In fact, I was still swollen and sore, needing more.

She kissed me hard, pulling me to her, rocketing my heart rate again, inflaming my still-burning desire. I felt the movements of her tongue in my mouth as if they were stroking my throbbing clit. When she pulled her head back, the laughter in her eyes was replaced by a carnal focus.

"You want to take this somewhere else?"

I said yes with another kiss.

CHAPTER TWENTY-EIGHT

Phaedra

I barely paid attention to the Lyft ride back to my place or unlocking the door to my loft, but the trip in the elevator up to my floor was etched in my brain because Daria nearly had me screaming when she lifted my tank, pushed my bra up, and sucked on my nipples. It was all I could do to hold the handrail while she had her way with my breasts, which, by the way, I never knew could be that sensitive. She discovered a whole new erogenous zone. Every move, every touch, every lick sent electric shocks straight to my core.

We fumbled all over ourselves on our way to my bed, unwilling to disengage our lips, but shedding clothing along the way. When the back of Daria's legs hit the bed, and we tumbled into my unmade bedding, Daria was in her bra and jeans, and I was only clothed from the waist down. I rose onto my knees, straddling Daria, and gazed down upon her, seeing her nearly naked torso in the moonlight streaming through the windows.

"God, you're gorgeous," she said, tracing the edges of my areola so lightly, it was like a feather grazing my skin. "You're like a beautiful photograph in a glossy magazine, selling sex and expensive perfume."

She laughed and rolled me over until she was on top, my legs dangling over the side of the bed. "How cheesy and sincere. I like that about you."

She kissed my neck, sucking on it but not hard enough to leave a mark. I wouldn't have cared if she did. Then she sat up, straddling me, unlatched her bra, and teased it from her shoulders and down her arms, tossing it aside. She cupped her breasts, caressing them, and I wished my hands were handling the pale flesh. I brushed up and down her sides, slid my fingers under the waistband of her jeans, and brought them to the button, which I undid with a flick of my fingers before lowering the zipper. Daria leaned down and kissed me deeply before rolling off and pushing her jeans and panties down her legs. She struggled with her boots for a moment, but once she got those off, she removed her jeans and lay naked beside me on the dark sheets, her skin glowing in the light from the windows, a contrast of silver and black. I rolled onto my side and took her in, my heart pounding and anticipation stealing my breath away.

Not all of it was from the erotic tension building inside me.

She rolled onto her side, facing me, and placed a hand on my cheek. "Are you okay? You look so serious all of a sudden."

I sighed, and it came out shaky. I nuzzled her hand. I didn't know how to tell her how I didn't have any experience with the mechanics of undressing with my prosthetic while making love. A flash of being in this very bed with Loredona, seeing her expression when she'd first seen my leg invaded my thoughts. I squeezed my eyes shut against the unwanted vision. This was nothing like that time, but I wasn't sure how to proceed without making it weird.

Daria removed her hand from my cheek and rolled me to my back, and I finally opened my eyes. She stood by the side of the bed, between my legs, watching me. She lifted my skirt, and I covered my eyes with my hands.

"Is this okay?" she asked. Her hands were warm along my thighs.

I nodded, but I left my hands over my face.

She moved her hands higher, lightly kneading my thighs, brushing along my hips, hooking her fingers into the waistline of my string bikinis.

"How about this?" Her voice was low, the timbre making the skin along my hairline tingle.

I nodded again.

Her fingers inched along the waist of my panties, the back of her hand grazing my pubic hair. I wanted to spread my legs in an invitation to explore further, but I was still too self-conscious, so aware of my prosthetic, I couldn't move. I lay there, still, while my breathing grew heavier.

She pulled her fingers out and ran her hands over my front, along the creases of my legs, and between them, gently pushing them apart. Warm air passed over the sensitive skin of my inner thighs, and a soft pressure pushed against my center, over the silk of my panties. I lifted one of my hands and peered down, seeing the top of her head over my bunched-up skirt, between my legs. I gasped as her lips moved against the fabric, my clit throbbing with the pressure. She skimmed her fingers along my inner thighs—up, down, back up—grazing the edge of the fabric between my legs, her mouth still moving against my clit.

I spread my legs, loving what she was doing, hoping she'd remove my panties soon and put her tongue where I needed it the most. As she grazed my clit through the silk with her teeth, I anticipated the sensation of her warm tongue stroking the same aching need. When she moved the fabric to the side and skimmed her tongue through my wet folds, my hips shot up.

"Yes," I hissed as I fisted the sheets.

Her tongue played with my sensitive flesh while she held the fabric to one side with one hand, and the other wrapped around my thigh. She drove her tongue deep inside me as she ran her thumb across my clit. The pulses preceding my orgasm started to flutter deep within me. I wanted her inside me. I rocked my hips, and she brought her mouth to my clit again, this time wrapping her lips around it and gently sucking. I was on the edge, about to tumble over, but I held back, imagining her filling me with her fingers. I needed her inside me. I reached down and started pushing my panties down. Daria stopped what she was doing to ease them all the way over my legs and off.

"I need you inside, Daria," I moaned, lifting myself up to my elbows.

She looked up at me with a sexy smile before she lowered her head to my center while stroking my wet folds with her fingers. She eased into me with one and then two fingers while she sucked my clit. I dropped back to the mattress, and my hips rose in time with the thrusts of her hand. I buried my fingers in her hair and pressed her to me as my climax surged and then exploded, forcing waves of brilliant sensation throughout my body. My muscles fluttered around her fingers while she gently licked me, fingers no longer thrusting but gently rubbing the sweet spot at the front just inside me, until another rush of liquid spilled from me and another climax rocked straight through me.

I threw my head back and sucked in air, all of my limbs tense until I released them with the last waves of pleasure washing through me. Daria kissed my inner thighs and rested her head on my leg. The warm puffs of her breath drifted against my sensitive folds, causing deep throbs in my body. I ran my fingers through her hair.

She arose, but I was too overwhelmed to open my eyes. She eased my skirt off and climbed into bed beside me, sliding her arm under my neck and pulling me to her, cradling me against her.

"It's okay. Let me hold you." She kissed my eyes and my lips and rested my head on her shoulder. It was a dream to be close to her, skin on skin, her legs entwined with mine.

I wondered why she told me it was okay, and then I realized I was shaking. Shaking so hard the entire bed was vibrating. And it was because I was holding in my tears. As soon as I realized it, the tears escaped, coursing hot down my face, and a sob erupted from my throat.

"Oh, baby. It's okay. I'm here. I've got you."

Daria kissed my tears and held me tight. She pulled the sheets over us and scooted us up until we were lying on the pillows.

"I'm sorry," I mumbled against her chest as soon as my throat relaxed enough to speak. I tried to wipe the snot from my nose discreetly, but she handed me something to use. I noticed it was her T-shirt because I could smell her on it, and I laughed sheepishly.

"Are you okay?" she asked.

The truth was, I felt great. What the hell had all the tears been about, then? I took a deep breath. "Aside from being utterly humiliated at crying after sex? Yeah. I'm more than okay. You were amazing. Perfect. Beyond perfect."

She lifted my chin to kiss me gently, almost reverently. I rested my hand between her breasts, and her heart was hammering beneath it. She let out a big breath when she pulled away. "I'm glad."

"I'm sorry. I've never cried after sex before. Ever."

"Don't be sorry."

I trailed my fingers up and down her arm. "But it must have concerned you."

"Well, I guess it did. A little. But when you let me hold you, I thought it was probably just a response of some sort. People joke about crying after sex. So it must happen."

"It's our secret, though. Okay? My street cred will be ruined if it gets out."

I must have sounded serious because she looked worried.

"I'm kidding." I gave her a quick kiss and was happy to see her smile. I kissed her again, and the kiss quickly grew heated before I pulled away. "You were absolutely amazing. My body is still rocked by what you did to me."

"Same here," she said, nuzzling my neck.

I stroked her satin-soft hair, burying my nose in it, getting lost in the smell of shampoo and musk, with my scent tangled in there, too, which turned me on. I pressed closer to her, and that was when I noticed my prosthetic was off. And I had my leg wrapped around hers as if we did that all the time.

She shifted closer. She didn't seem to notice my leg, or if she did, she didn't care. "What is it? You tensed up."

I gazed into her eyes, unsure of what to say.

She stroked the side of my face. "You need to tell me, or I'm going to be all anxious thinking that you're maybe regretting being here with me."

Her words and her ease with her insecurity were the perfect antidotes to my tension, and I relaxed. I captured the hand she used to stroke my face and kissed it. My smell on her fingers filled my senses, arousing me again. "I'm definitely not regretting being with you. You're a goddess."

"It was something, though."

"Um, yeah." I took a deep breath. "I noticed I don't have my prosthetic on."

"Oh. I kinda accidentally popped it off when you wrapped your legs around me when you came." She cocked her arm up and held her hand with two fingers out, in an almost crude gesture mimicking sex, except is wasn't as crude as it was hilarious. "My elbow went up, and your leg came down, and I think I hit it in the exact right spot, because it sort of fell off, bounced down my back, and hit the floor. I think it landed on the rug or on my jeans, but I was a little preoccupied with… are you afraid it might be damaged? Let me get—"

She tried to get up, and I pulled her down. "It's fine. It's pretty much indestructible."

"Are you sure?"

"I'm absolutely sure. It would take a lot to damage it. Besides, it's insured."

She lay over me, propping herself up with her arms, her body pressing down on me. I was aware of the erotic way her breasts pressed against mine and how her thigh pressed between mine. But her expression was what grabbed my attention. It went from animated to something soft, then to dark and passionate in a matter of milliseconds, each change causing a new sensation in my chest, but the last one caused my center to clench. She kissed me, and it was my turn to rock her world.

CHAPTER TWENTY-NINE

Daria

The quiet of Phaedra's loft was peaceful. Chill night air came through the open windows, and I could hear the distant rush of the cars on the highway, but the streets below had gone silent. Her face was a study in beauty as I watched her sleep, curled on her side, her hands tucked under her chin. Her tiny snores were adorable. I didn't want to wake her, but more importantly, I didn't want to be the kind of person who skulked off in the middle of the night, leaving the other person wondering if they'd ever see them again. Hopefully, Phaedra knew better, but still, I wasn't about to take off without making sure she knew I'd had the best night of my life.

I kissed her temple, brushing my lips across her face and then kissed the corner of her mouth. "Hey, beautiful. Wake up for a few seconds." I brushed a stray dreadlock back and ran my hand down her bare arm. She smiled and reached for me without opening her eyes.

"Come 'ere." She sighed when her hand met empty mattress. Her eyes fluttered open. "Why are you leaning over the bed like a stalker? Come over here." She pulled weakly at me, barely awake.

"I have to go."

"Go where?"

"Home."

Her eyes blinked open.

"Oh."

She sounded disappointed. I was, too. But I had to be home when Marnie woke up. It would throw her entire routine off if I wasn't there to do my half of the morning ritual. It hadn't occurred to me to tell her I might stay out this late, let alone all night. We hadn't made a list. It was also a work day, so there was no telling how that would go because she'd know she needed to be at work, and she'd definitely go, but in what condition? I had to go.

I leaned down and kissed Phaedra. "I wish I could stay. It took everything in me to get out of bed."

"And you kiss me and stand there like that and expect me to let you leave?" I was fully dressed, with the exception of a shirt.

"I was hoping you'd let me borrow a T-shirt or something."

"Oh, yeah." She covered her face with her hand. "I got snot all over yours last night."

"Which I didn't mind at all, except I need another shirt to wear home unless you want me to stay here, shirtless," I offered, only half joking.

She snickered. "My ploy appears to be working. You're trapped here, never to leave. You might as well get back in bed." Her sleepy softness was replaced with playful friskiness. She pulled me down and pinned me down, her dark eyes captivating me before she kissed me. I was lost, though, when her hand crept down my body and into the front of my pants.

Several minutes later, I tried to catch my breath, and Phaedra lay beside me doing the same, both of us recovering from orgasms. It hadn't taken much to take me over the edge where she was concerned. A simple look or touch sent my pulse racing.

I ran my fingers across her flat stomach, circling her naval. "May I please borrow a shirt?"

She blew out a breath. "I had hopes of making you forget your foolish thoughts of leaving." She joked but not really.

"I'm sorry. There's nothing I'd rather do than stay here with you, but I have to take care of Rowdy, and Marnie expects me to be there when she wakes up." I *was* sorry, too. Mostly for myself. I relished sleeping with Phaedra. I loved the way she molded to me after we finished making love and how she fit against me as we slept. The last thing I wanted to do was to leave her in the predawn light, but I had to.

CHAPTER THIRTY

Phaedra

My phone vibrated on my desk, and a shiver went up my spine when Daria's name flashed across the screen. I had a meeting in fifteen minutes that I was barely ready for, but I wasn't about to ignore Daria's call. I was as tired as I'd ever been after getting little sleep last night, but my body sprang to erotic attention as I remembered all the things Daria and I had done to keep us up.

"Hey, sexy," I said. I squeezed my thighs together, and my center clenched.

"Hey, yourself." Daria's voice was low and sultry, and I wondered what she was doing and where she was. I imagined her in her office with the door closed, feet kicked up on the corner of her desk. I loved her in business suits. She always appeared put together, hip, and professional, the perfect combo for anyone who thought powerful women in business attire were sexy—like I did. "I called to hear your voice and find out how you're doing today."

I leaned forward and rested my head on my hand. I was pretty sure the smile on my face was as goofy as hell. "I'm a tired unit. Someone kept me up all night."

"All night, huh?"

"Well, most of the night, until she skulked home in the wee hours of the morning, leaving me all worn out and lonely."

Daria laughed, and I was relieved because I hadn't meant for my teasing to sound as real as it came out. "She must be crazy to leave someone like you in bed, all naked and lonely. You might need to have a talk with her."

"Oh, I plan to. I just need to figure out when I can see her again.

Would it come across as too needy to ask her to go to lunch with me today? Is it too soon?"

"It's not. In fact, I think it's a little aloof, if you ask me, which you did. And me, being an expert at these things, thinks you should *not* wait for lunch and ask her to coffee. Right now."

"Well, I'm glad you called, then. I would have completely flubbed it up. I better call her and ask her to meet me at Café Café."

"How about at your office?"

"But Café Café is between our offices. She'd have to backtrack."

"I'm…I mean, *she* is already at your building."

My heart rate went up. She was close. I stood and walked to the door of my office. "You are? I mean, she is?"

"Yep."

I was about to ask her where she was when I opened the door, and there she stood, cell to her ear, looking delicious in her business suit.

I grabbed her hand and pulled her into my office. The windows on either side of the doorway were frosted glass, but anyone passing by could make out shadows, so I pressed her against the solid door and kissed her. It wasn't a sweet kiss, either. It was deep and greedy, and it reminded me of all of the physical and emotional energy we'd exchanged hours before. Every inch of my body was taking part in the kiss, and from the way she kissed me back, I could tell she wasn't holding anything back, either.

After an immeasurable amount of time—because who had the kind of resolve to tell time when they were being kissed senseless by a goddess—I pulled back enough to get lost in her eyes.

"Hi."

"Hi."

We stared at each other, and it wasn't uncomfortable or weird. I loved to watch her eyes. They were as expressive as hell, and right now, they were telling me she was just as affected by our kiss as I was. It was hard to think of anything other than how fucking good she felt in my arms.

She lifted an eyebrow. "So?"

I smiled back. "So."

"About that coffee."

I laughed and dropped my head to her shoulder. "Oh, yeah. I remember there was something about coffee."

"I think we should go. It's too dangerous to stay here much longer."

"Dangerous?" I knew exactly what she meant, but I wanted to hear her say it.

"There is a huge possibility that I will have your clothes off and you bent over the desk very quickly if we don't move to somewhere more public in the next two to three minutes."

I wanted to test her theory. I wanted it so bad, I could almost taste her. But we were at work. I'd been there once. I wasn't going back. I reached for the doorknob.

"Before you open the door, you should fix this," she said, running her thumb along the edge of my bottom lip. She didn't wear lipstick, but I did, and she had it all over her mouth.

"Oh, yeah." I backed to my desk and grabbed a couple of tissues. I handed one to her and wiped my mouth with the other before applying a fresh coat. I checked myself in the small mirror I kept in a drawer. There was definitely a gleam in my eye, but otherwise, I was passable. Daria still stood with her back to the office door, watching my every move, and was gorgeous, as usual.

"Ready to go?" I asked, trying to talk myself out of kissing her again.

I was losing the debate while she regarded me with a stare that clearly communicated she wouldn't mind if we had to do the lipstick fix one more time, when there was a knock on the door. I laughed when Daria jumped, and the door started to inch open.

Barb popped her head in. "I came to find out what's holding you up."

"Holding me up?" I asked, clueless.

She stepped in and noticed Daria, who had moved into the corner. She gave me a sly smile and then nodded at Daria. "Who do we have here?"

"Hi again." Daria held out her hand, cool as cool could be. "I'm Daria from the bench on the mall the other day. I don't believe I caught your name."

"Barb. It's nice to meet you again." She took her hand, eyes shifting from me to Daria. They were both so poised, unlike me, shifting from foot to foot. "I guess I should have anticipated seeing you again. I see you made the call."

Daria smiled, unfiltered, and I knew Barb would figure out what had transpired in such a short amount of time. If she did, she didn't show it, though.

"Thank you for the information."

The polite chatter and the underlying things *not* being said were causing me anxiety. I wanted to get going. I walked closer to the door in an effort to guide them both into the hall.

"You said you were looking for me?" I asked.

"Yes. We were going to discuss the Mercer account."

"Right now?"

"Actually, about ten minutes ago."

I backed up and tapped the keyboard to my laptop to wake it up. Sure enough, a calendar reminder flashed in the corner of the screen. "Shit." I'd forgotten about the meeting.

"You had other things on your mind." Barb chuckled and glanced between me and Daria. "Well, you get a pass since it's usually *you* holding *me* to my schedule. We can move it to the afternoon, if you're free. She's not due back here for another few days."

"Yes, please. I'm sorry. I was distracted." I couldn't help glancing at Daria, and Barb caught it. She caught everything. She'd make me tell her everything as soon as I got back from coffee break.

"Enjoy the coffee. Take an extra-long break, Phaedra. You deserve it."

Barb left my office, and I let my shoulders relax. When I blew out a breath, Daria was laughing silently. I couldn't help but laugh with her.

"That was awesome," she said, clearing her throat to regain her composure. "She totally has you figured out. Is it a good thing or a bad thing?"

"Normally, it's a good thing." I pinched the fabric of her suit jacket and pulled her out of the office before my mood changed once again and I had to attack her with more kisses.

After we ordered our drinks and took a seat at a table near the back of Café Café, I caught Daria watching me. It reminded me of a few hours ago when I'd caught her staring as I slept. Her expression had been so soft, so open, so rapt, as if she'd forgotten to apply her protective filter. It was profound to be the subject of someone's unfettered adoration, especially hers, because she looked how I felt every time I gazed at her.

I leaned forward, resting my chin on my hands. "About you leaving this morning. Was everything okay when you got home?"

She paused before she answered. Was it my question? Was it something else? "Everything was fine. Marnie had a friend spend the night. It was out of character for her."

"Marnie's three years younger than you?"

She nodded. "She's twenty-five."

A sip of chai told me it was still too hot to drink. I rubbed my lip where it burned. It wasn't too bad, and I liked how Daria licked her lip in solidarity. "Was this a *friend* friend or a *special* friend?"

"She's a *friend* friend. She plays on our soccer team. We've both known her for a few years. She and Marnie have always been super friendly, but I've never seen Marnie attracted to anyone. She says she's pansexual, but I don't *really* know how she identifies. She might be ace for all I know."

"Ace?"

"Asexual."

"I know what ace is. I guess I just thought most people identified one way or another by twenty-five, at least for the moment they're in, since some people are fluid." I worried that I sounded like an idiot. I'd never known anyone who was ace before, but I supported whatever people wanted to call themselves. They knew better than I did. "But it makes sense if she hasn't been involved with someone before. Or even if she has." I needed to shut up and tried another sip just to burn myself again.

She bit her lip, seeming not to notice my fluster. "Marnie's a little different. I'm not sure if you picked up on it when we met the other day after work."

I had picked up on it, but it wasn't extreme, whatever her difference was. "She was charming, if not a little reserved."

Daria smiled, her eyes glimmering in the subtle light. She spun her cup between her hands. "Charming and reserved are a great way to put it. She has autism. She's right smack dab in the middle of the spectrum, so it's not pronounced, but it does pose a few challenges for her."

"Makes sense. I noticed she was fairly literal and didn't join in when we joked around, but she was laser focused on the music Taco Bill was playing and the conversation they were having when we walked up. I wasn't sure if it was just social awkwardness or something else."

"She's actually pretty socially stable. She has her moments, but generally, she's good at removing herself from anything overstimulating or overwhelming. She has an amazing shutdown talent. She'll seem like she's right there next to you, but in reality, her mind is a million miles away. Nothing gets through to her then."

"Nothing?"

"Well, mostly nothing. I can usually get her to reengage by asking her about her work or one of her favorite movies. Soccer is always a good topic, too. She follows all of the teams in FIFA."

"You love her quite a bit, don't you?"

She appeared confused by the question. "She's my sister."

I took her hand. "I meant that it's evident how much you care about her by the way you talk about her."

Her expression softened. I wondered if she had some unresolved questions or issues about her relationship with her sister. I knew how hard it was to love someone you were supposed to love when they actively pushed you away. An image of my mother came to mind. She'd died two years before my accident but had never been a great parent. Sure, she'd tried, but in the sense of trying to control me. In other ways, she wasn't present. I'd always had to figure out where I would get food, how to clothe myself, and how to deal with bill collectors when they came around the house. My mom had been a hard worker, but she'd had different priorities, and I wasn't one of them, although I knew without a doubt that she'd loved me.

When she'd found out I was a lesbian, though, she wouldn't have it. She'd all but turned her back on me, telling me that in Haiti, they killed folks for having what she'd called unnatural relations. In some ways, I wished she had kept her back turned. It would have been easier. Instead, she'd tried to mother me, belatedly, even while she'd continued to berate me about my lesbianism. Maybe she was why I had never tried to hide it, to show her I couldn't be bullied to change. It was interesting how hard I'd tried to hide my disability.

All of those inner thoughts flashed through my mind in the space of seconds, but I didn't think Daria caught on to it.

"Yeah, Marnie and I are pretty different."

"You look like you could be twins."

Daria smiled. "She's beautiful, and I take it as a compliment." Pink tinged her cheeks as she took a sip.

"But she doesn't compare to you. No offense to Marnie, but she doesn't have the shine you do."

"I wasn't fishing for a compliment. Besides, when the word 'gorgeous' was invented, you were who they had in mind."

"Nope. Nope. Nope." I held up my hands. "You don't get to deflect my compliment like that. You need to acknowledge your own beauty and bask in my praise."

"So demanding."

I laughed. "You have no idea."

CHAPTER THIRTY-ONE

Daria

If asked to make a choice, I would have had to say I liked indoor soccer better than outdoor. It was faster paced, and everyone got more ball time. But as a midfielder, holy hell, it wore me out with the constant running. With only five minutes left to the half, I was glad when Harper signaled for me to sub out.

I slapped Harper's hand as she entered the field, and I went back to the bench, wiping the sweat from my face and neck with the bottom of my shirt. Courtney handed me my water bottle, and I took a long drink. It was a tight game. We were evenly matched for once. Normally, our team dominated the indoor leagues, but this game had us playing all out.

We'd been together for several years, and most of us had played in college. Courtney had even gone pro on the women's circuit for a while, until her mom got sick, and she came home to take care of her. The other team was newer, but some of their players really knew how to handle the ball. One woman in particular had a precision kick, landing the ball exactly where she wanted it to go with ease. I would have been more impressed with her skills if she wasn't so arrogant, puffing out her chest and goading our team with crappy comments any time she made a great play, which was often.

"Who's number twelve?" I asked Courtney. Out with a pulled hamstring, I could tell it was killing her not to be on the field.

"I've never seen her before. She's new."

"I heard someone say she moved here from Argentina," Sibyl said. Sybil had been subbed out before me, and we were watching together. She was stretching her quads, which reminded me to do the same. It wasn't good for our muscles to go from constant running to leaning. I kicked my foot back, grabbed it, and pulled it to my butt. Every muscle in my leg and hip felt the stretch, and not all the aches were from the game. Erotic images from last night with Phaedra ran through my mind. As much as I loved this game, I would rather have been with her right now. But she was at rehearsal, and I'd made a commitment to the team. It wouldn't be fair to leave them short players, which meant fewer sub outs.

A whistle blew, and at first, I thought it was the end of the half, but the clock still had three minutes on it when I checked. That was when I noticed the ref had called a foul on number twelve while I'd been distracted with thoughts of Phaedra.

"What happened?" I asked.

"Holding. She pulled the back of Marnie's jersey."

The ref placed the ball on the turf before Marnie for a direct free kick and backed the opposition ten yards from the ball. Marnie surveyed the field where the players were jockeying for an opening. I knew what she'd do; we'd practiced this play ad nauseam. And sure enough, Marnie kicked it toward the goal but a little short, and Harper headed it into the goal. It was beautiful. One of the opposing players patted Harper on the shoulder and then ran to Marnie to do the same, but instead of touching her, she stopped short and congratulated her. Most of the players in our league were aware of Marnie's dislike of being touched, and they were good about it. Marnie, who was deeply focused like she usually was during our games, didn't acknowledge it. She simply took her spot on the field for the kickoff, as did most of the other players.

Number twelve, however, approached her. "Hey! Someone was talking to you, freak." I could hear now that they were on the center line, and anger rushed through me.

Marnie didn't react or even acknowledge number twelve. She was watching the ball.

Number twelve went offsides and stood directly in front of Marnie, who simply moved so she could see the ball again. Most of the people on the field were now watching, and one of the opposing players tried to bring number twelve back to their side, but she wouldn't move. She merely stood before Marnie, talking low. I was frustrated I couldn't hear.

"Ladies," the ref shouted, "I'm close to calling delay of game."

Number twelve continued saying things I couldn't hear, backing toward her side of the field, and the players started running when the whistle blew. Our team got the ball and took it toward the goal. Marnie received the ball and, using the wall, dribbled past two of the opposing players. Her control always amazed me. She was just about to take a shot on goal when a blur flew at her feet, knocking the ball away and whacking her feet out from under her. She fell hard onto the turf. The whistle blew, sounding the end of the half, and a red card was pulled on number twelve, who had performed an illegal slide tackle.

Our entire team swarmed onto the field, and I beat everyone to Marnie, who was trying to stand. I gave her my hand, and she popped up, but she grimaced when she tried to put weight on her right foot.

Courtney wrapped an arm under Marnie's arm, helping her. "How bad does it hurt?" she asked.

"I don't think I can stand on it," said Marnie, testing it again.

"Do you think it's broken?" I asked.

She rotated her ankle and leaned on it. "I don't think so. The more I move it around, the less it hurts. I think it's okay." She took a few steps. Courtney removed her arm, and Marnie's limp disappeared as she walked it off.

"What was that B-I-T-C-H thinking?" Courtney was glaring at the other team's bench where number twelve was in her sports bra, swapping her jersey for a T-shirt. The red card meant she had to leave the field. She'd probably be suspended from playing for at least two or three games. I hoped she'd be asked to leave the team. Our league wasn't into her kind of play.

Several of the players on the opposing team as well as the ref were standing with us while we made sure Marnie was okay. Shel, the captain of the other team, put a hand on my shoulder. "I'm really sorry. Trust me, I'm going to deal with it. I'm glad Marnie's okay."

Courtney pushed into the group. "What's twelve's deal, anyway? She can't pull crap like that." I'd never seen Courtney so fired up. I guess it was founded, but I expected it from Harper, not Courtney.

Marnie was standing to the side, and several players on Shel's team were trying to apologize for number twelve, but I could tell it overwhelmed her. They meant well, but they didn't know that their concern caused her even more anxiety. Her hand was in a fist, hitting her thigh. Her eyes were flicking back and forth along the ground. She was definitely in the rumble stage, and I wasn't sure how close she was to meltdown or shutdown. Either scenario was never good. Not because of the possibility of a scene. I couldn't have cared less about that. I was more worried about the more lasting effect it would have on Marnie. It could take months to get her back to an even keel after she went in either direction. For a person who typically didn't care what people thought, she had a tendency to obsess about the effects of her meltdowns and shutdowns. Fortunately, it had been a couple of years since her last incident.

I leaned toward Shel. "Can you call your team together? I think Marnie needs some space."

Shel glanced at the small group and trotted over, telling her team to meet at the bench. Shel was good people.

I ran back to the bench and grabbed Marnie's water bottle and towel. I was taking it to her when I noticed she and Courtney were sitting on the turf. Courtney didn't touch her, but she leaned toward her, making an effort to get into her line of sight. I caught my breath when Marnie engaged eye contact with Courtney. Aside from our mom and dad, I was the only one Marnie would respond to when she was agitated.

The fifteen minutes between halves went by far too quickly, but fortunately, Courtney got Marnie off the field and onto the bench before the second half began. As interested as I was in how Courtney had dealt with the situation, I left them alone. Both to limit the number of people Marnie dealt with, even if one of them was me, and because we needed the players with two of ours currently unavailable. And also, part of me was relieved to know someone else could help Marnie through a crisis. She deserved to have more than just me to rely on. And yes, a big part of it was selfish. Thanks to Taryn's constant stream of unwanted yet sage advice, I was getting used to admitting to the fact that I'd taken on a huge responsibility in being my sister's support system.

Even so, I would be lying if I said I didn't feel a few mixed emotions at not being the one to help her. So I threw myself into the rest of the game, which we won.

After the game, I was mulling over my feelings about someone else being able to calm down my sister, when Marnie and I pulled into the parking garage at our apartment. She had been a little pensive after everything, but mostly, she was acting like her old self by the end of the game. If I hadn't seen the slide tackle and its aftermath, I wouldn't have suspected anything had even happened.

Marnie was scrolling through her phone. "Hey, Dar, do you mind if Courtney comes over?"

It was eight thirty. Not late, but it was a Thursday night, and we both had work in the morning. But I'd been thinking about going over to Phaedra's house anyway.

"She can come over. You're both grown-ups. You don't need to ask my permission to have friends visit."

"I wasn't technically asking permission. I asked if you minded. That's called being considerate."

Her response was unexpected, and I didn't think it was shitty as much as literal. It was unexpected because her comment implied that she was taking my feelings into consideration. She might have been repeating something she'd heard someone else say, too, which she often did in her way of trying to relate. She picked up on what people said even when she didn't pick up on their nonverbal cues. Either way, the comment made sense in the moment.

When we got upstairs, Courtney was already waiting. She must have followed us from the game. She and Marnie went into Marnie's room, and I took a shower.

I had a text when I got out of the shower, and a flutter of excitement flashed through me when Phaedra's name showed on the screen.

What are you doing right now?

Just got back from a soccer game. Now I'm standing in a towel, reading your text.

Picture?

I giggled, seriously giggled. What was I becoming? *No way. You'll probably sell it to the tabloids.*

My phone rang, and I grinned when I answered it.

"I'm not sending you a picture."

"Come on," she whined, and I came close to giving in.

"I'm too worried about hackers." Still in my towel, I wandered to the kitchen and poured myself a glass of water.

"Then come over here and show me in person. You have me all worked up. I need to see you."

I sagged against the counter. I wanted to with every fiber in my body, some fibers more than others. She wasn't the only one getting all worked up. I'd been in a near-constant state of arousal ever since I'd left her house that morning. The kisses in her office had only driven the arousal higher. "I would love to come over. You don't know how badly. But I can't. I need to stay with Marnie tonight."

I heard her sigh of disappointment, and I hated being the cause of it. I was disappointed, too. I was about to tell her as much when Marnie, holding a couple beers, tapped me on the shoulder.

"Can you hold on a minute, Phaedra?" I asked. I put my hand over the mic. "What's up, Mar?"

"Sorry. I was listening. You can go over to Phaedra's tonight if you want. Courtney can stay with me."

"She stayed last night. Are you sure she wants to stay again tonight?"

"She likes getting out of her house. Her mom has a night nurse now, which gives her more flexibility."

"Thanks, Marnie. I'll only be a couple of hours."

Marnie's cheeks grew pink. "Stay the night if you want. It's okay."

CHAPTER THIRTY-TWO

Phaedra

I placed the coffee cup on the bedside table, leaned my crutch against the bed, and whispered into Daria's ear. "Wake up, beautiful." I was rewarded with two warm arms wrapping around me, pulling me down. I settled against her under the covers and basked in the warm softness of her sleep-pliant body and the way our skin felt when we moved against each other. A low pulse started to hum inside me. I couldn't believe I wanted her again after having made love with her for most of the night. With only a couple of hours' sleep, I was aware of muscles I'd forgotten I had.

I'd already been exhausted from the previous night's exploits and had every intention of going to bed early, but as I was about to lie down, I'd called Daria. I'd only wanted to hear her voice, or so I'd told myself as I picked up the phone. I hadn't expected to ask her to come over. It had just slipped out. I might have even whined a little. I honestly didn't know where I even found the energy, but as soon as she'd arrived with her hair still wet from her after-soccer shower, a flood of desire had taken over. I didn't know how many times we'd made love last night. We'd never really stopped, actually, once we started, not until deep into the night, when the sounds of the city had muted themselves and the energy of the streets was tucked in for the few hours before the morning. I wasn't sure I'd say we even went to sleep, so much as sleep claimed us.

Daria hadn't responded to the alarm she'd set for 5:00 a.m. I'd shut it off for her and had gone to make her coffee. I'd already known I'd be a tired unit at work today, but I was counting on the residual energy of good sex to keep me going.

"I don't want to leave this spot." Her sleepy voice rumbled against my neck, eliciting a delightful shiver down my back.

I didn't want her to leave, either. But she'd made me promise the night before to not let her sleep in. "You said you have to feed Rowdy and make lunches."

"Right. I have to be a good sister and dog mama." She yawned and stretched as I ran my hands up and down the taut muscles of her torso. She spread her legs. "Mmm. A little lower, please."

I moved my hand between her legs and stroked the wet heat I found there. She was swollen and soft as I explored the dips and contours, sliding over and through her folds. I pushed a couple fingers inside, and she spread her legs even farther.

Her eyes were closed, and her mouth was open a little, her breathing getting heavier. "Do the thing where you hook your finger— oh! God. Just like that."

The muscles inside her sucked at my fingers as her torso and legs contracted in a sensual dance. Watching her body respond to me was fucking erotic as hell. I rubbed her clit with my thumb as I pulled out and then back in again, diving deep to hit the spot she loved. She came fast and hard and didn't take time to recover before she was inside me, taking me to the same heights. I broke our kiss and screamed her name into her mouth when the body quake pounded through me, leaving me gasping and twitching beneath her.

Oh, I wanted to fall asleep right there, under the weight of her body, but I couldn't let her lounge after I came. She'd told me she had to leave early, and as tempted as I was to lure her to stay, I didn't want to be the person to get in the way of her responsibilities.

I pushed her off me, albeit gently. I wasn't a dick. "Drink your coffee, gorgeous. You need to get going."

She sat up in bed and took a sip of her coffee while I sat up and retied my robe. Her eyes twinkled over the rim of her cup. "Are you trying to get rid of me?"

"I'm trying to make sure you aren't late. I can't have you saving excuses to turn me down when I want you to come over again. Which will be soon. Real soon."

"Oh. I see. You have ulterior motives."

The moment was sublime, casual and comfortable, yet new; her sitting against the headboard, the sheet draped over her lap, me in my robe, sitting next to her cross-legged, facing her while we talked.

Her body was a study in artful perfection, and I took her in while we spoke. Maybe that was why it came as a shock when her hand came to rest where my leg ended and the rest of my shin should have been. I didn't think she did it on purpose. She'd been caressing me, and her hand absently settled there. I loved her touch, but I had to fight to not move away. Incidental touches during sex were one thing, but this was different. I felt exposed. It was hard enough to let her see my leg, but touching it was almost too much.

She must have sensed my stress. "Is this okay?"

I cleared my throat, pausing to find the right answer. I considered brushing it off, but I didn't want to minimize the weight of the moment for me. "It's weird." She went to move her hand, but I put my hand over hers.

"Weird? Tell me what you're thinking."

"I'm thinking I feel…vulnerable. No one's ever seen me like this, let alone touched it. I mean, except for doctors."

She put her cup on the end table and sat up, facing me, her hand still on my leg. I was breathless when she bent to kiss the scar, the touch of her lips against my skin sending tremors all through me.

"You're beautiful. Every part of you."

It was the second time I'd cried in front of her, and I thought this time, she began to heal me.

Chapter Thirty-three

Daria

My legs were feeling the effect of too little sleep and more exercise than usual as I trudged up the stairs to the apartment. The sun had been up for almost half an hour already, and the city was still relatively quiet at 6:00 a.m., before the hustle and bustle started with people on their way to work. I couldn't suppress a yawn. I wished I was still in bed with Phaedra.

The apartment was quiet and still when I entered, which I expected, since we usually didn't get up until 6:30. I heard Rowdy's collar shake in my room, then a thud as his weight hit the carpet. A couple seconds later, he slowly walked into the living room, pausing to stretch into a downward dog before trotting over. I picked him up and kissed his little nose.

"You probably need to go out, huh, buddy?" His little butt shook in my arms, and he licked my chin. I wondered if Marnie had remembered to take him out the night before since I hadn't been here at bedtime.

"I'll take him." Marnie came out of her room in a *Ms. Pac-Man* T-shirt and some *Ren and Stimpy* boxers. Her hair was sticking out in every direction, revealing the little girl she used to be. She stepped into a pair of flip-flops near the door and grabbed Rowdy's leash. When I put him down, he eagerly ran to her, knowing the leash meant outside even though it was usually me who took him in the morning.

"Thanks, Mar."

Courtney came out of Marnie's room wearing the same clothes she'd been wearing the night before. I hoped she hadn't slept in them. It would be like Marnie not to offer her a T-shirt to sleep in or something. I should have talked to her, but how often would this kind of thing come up?

"Morning, Daria," Courtney said, plopping onto one of the barstools.

"You can sleep in, Courtney," Marnie said, putting on Rowdy's leash.

Courtney yawned and rubbed her eyes. "But everyone is already up."

"I'm going right back to bed after I finish walking Rowdy."

"Don't you have to get ready for work?" I asked.

"We get today off since the Fourth of July falls on a Saturday this year," Marnie said. "I wondered why you came back so early."

I consulted the calendar on my phone. She was right. Today was a holiday, and I could have stayed in bed. With Phaedra. A total missed opportunity. How had I forgotten about the holiday? I knew how. I'd been distracted yesterday. People had probably even mentioned it, excited by the three-day weekend, but I'd had my head in the clouds, not to mention sleep deprivation.

I walked toward my room. "I must have spaced. I'm sorry I disrupted everyone's sleeping in."

"No worries," said Marnie with her hand on the doorknob. "I'll jump into bed when I get back up."

Courtney smiled sheepishly and pointed back toward Marnie's room. "Sweet. I'm gonna just go back now, then."

"Do you need something to sleep in?" I asked. "Sleeping in your clothes can't be comfortable."

Courtney glanced at Marnie and blushed. "I'm fine. Marnie took care of it." She backed into Marnie's room. Strange.

Sometimes, Courtney was a little odd.

Part of me wanted to head back to Phaedra's place since I had nowhere else to be, but I was tired and needed a shower.

CHAPTER THIRTY-FOUR

Phaedra

Dropping my laptop onto the couch, I tried not to pay attention to my bed. The pull to take a nap controlled every tired cell in my body. It wasn't even funny. I was glad I'd changed the sheets and made it already. Otherwise, it would have been impossible to not fall back into it and spend all day thinking and dreaming about being with Daria.

Trance jumped onto my lap as I moved my laptop and pushed his furry black head into my hand.

"Are you feeling a little left out? Is that what this is about?" I asked while giving him a good scratching, eliciting a loud purr. He was such a friendly cat when he knew someone, but he'd been hiding the last couple of nights while Daria had been here. I stood up with him in one arm, pulled my crutch under my other arm, and went into the kitchen. His excitement made him squirmy because he was good at reading my mind, and he knew I was going to guilt treat him. He jumped from my arm onto the counter and eagerly paced as I spilled some liver treats onto the granite.

Leaning against the counter with my head propped in my hands, I watched him devour the smelly little treats and tried to ignore the silent call of my bed.

A vibration by my elbow startled me until I realized it was my phone with an unknown number displayed on the screen. Normally, I let those calls go to voice mail for screening, but because I was close to losing the battle in favor of a nap, I chose to answer. Maybe talking to someone would shake away some of the lethargy.

"Hello?" I stifled a yawn.

"Is this Phaedra?"

"It depends on who I'm talking to."

"That's fair enough. This is Nick Tanner."

His voice sounded familiar. "Hi, Nick Tanner. How do I know you?"

An easy chuckle rolled across the line. "We've played a few shows together. Most recently a few days ago at a funky venue on Broadway. You were the kickass singer from the opening group, and I was the scrapper who tried not to suck from the follow-up band."

It dawned on me who it was. "Oh. *The* Nick from Nick's Army." I laughed. "You're definitely not a scrapper. How's it going?"

"It's going well. We're in Nashville today. It's where most of us are from, and we have a great fan base here. We're looking forward to playing later."

"Sounds great. You guys were awesome the other night." He didn't need to know I'd only listened for a few minutes from the alley. They'd been good. That was all that mattered.

He chuckled. "I wasn't sure you got a chance to listen. You were pretty focused on your girlfriend."

The mention of Daria as my girlfriend made my stomach flutter. Was she my girlfriend? We hadn't talked about it. I thought I'd like it if she was, though. He was waiting for a response, so I searched for something noncommittal. "Well, you know…"

"I hope you don't mind me calling you directly. Normally, I would have my booking agent call yours, but I wanted to talk to you."

"Okay," I said for lack of anything else to say since I didn't know where he was going with this.

"Well, first off, I think you have an awesome stage presence. Wickedly sexy. Wait. I just sounded like a skeevy dick, didn't I?" I wasn't about to answer him. It would be fun listening to him try to unbury himself. "What's another word? Shit, I should have figured out what I wanted to say before I called. Anyway…dynamic! Yeah, that's it. You're dynamic with the dancing and playing and singing. You had the crowd eating out of your hand. They were enthralled, couldn't keep their eyes off you. You're also the real deal, super talented. Between you and your drummer, you two have a certain cool energy. It really resonates, you know?"

"Thanks. I appreciate it." It was nice to hear, but it also made me self-conscious. There was a little annoyance about him ignoring most of the band, too. We were a tight group. Without them, I'd probably be relegated to playing alone in my loft.

"It's true. There's something about you I can't even describe. It's intense, very, very intense."

He sounded sincere, and I was flattered. "Thanks, Nick."

He blew out a breath. "I have a proposition for you."

"Oh yeah?" I wondered if he was going to ask us to open for him again when they came through town. He'd said something to that effect when he did the toast at the gig. Or maybe he was going to ask us to go on a mini-tour with them. But he was right, his booking agent would have called mine.

"Yeah. I know this is going to sound weird, but I want to sort of join our bands together."

Totally not what I'd expected. Did I hear him correctly? "Join them together? Like into one band?"

He made a humming sound as if I was close but not quite. "Well, kind of."

I wasn't sure I understood. "Tell me more."

"I'd like you and your drummer to join us." He sounded relieved that I hadn't already shut him down. "I think your stage presence and sound would bring something great to ours. Right now, we're doing pretty good. Our demo is getting picked up on radio stations, mostly in college towns. We got some great feedback from the satellite radio people. They love the music, but it's too close to a lot of what they're already playing, and they want something a little different. They mentioned adding some other strings and maybe some percussion, but their main focus was to hear what we sounded like if we added a female lead. And that's the main reason for my call."

"But you're the lead of Nick's Army."

"I'd still be the male lead, but we'd have two. I think we'd sound great together. We could even change the name a little. Maybe something like Nick and Phaedra's Army. But we can figure it out later. I just wanted to pitch the idea to find out if you're even interested."

"Wow. I'm not sure what to say." There was too much to think about. I couldn't give him an answer so soon. I had to talk to the others.

"You don't have to agree to anything yet. The next step would be to meet up, play some music together, and make sure we sound as good as I think we will. The four of us have to finish this tour, and we're booked up through the end of August. But maybe we could get together to play and talk about it then?"

I was relieved to have some time to think it over. I had a job to think about, along with the rest of my band. I wondered what Leigh would think. Actually, I already knew. She'd be all in. It wasn't like Leigh and I couldn't continue to perform with Washtub Whiskey. Musicians did this kind of thing all the time, right?

"Have you talked to Leigh?" I asked.

"I wanted to talk to you first. You're the deciding factor. She's super cool, but without you, it wouldn't matter. You're the full package we need."

Chapter Thirty-five

Daria

I sat up against my headboard and traced the shape of a heart over a pyramid tattoo on the inside of Phaedra's forearm. My room was dark with the curtains closed against the midmorning sunlight. Her dark skin was lighter there, but still in the shadows, and the ink lines were difficult to discern unless you were looking for them. I hadn't noticed them the first few times we'd been intimate together, but then again, I'd been distracted by other parts of her luscious body. Now that I was aware of it, I found the artwork undeniably sexy.

I couldn't get enough of touching her soft skin.

"Does this tattoo have a specific meaning?"

Phaedra opened her eyes, still basking in postcoital languor, her head in my lap as I played with her hair and ran my fingers over her skin.

She stretched like a sated cat before she studied the marking. "It's the symbol of Maman Brigitte, a very powerful loa my mother used to call on for healing. I got it when she was sick. It didn't help, but it made my mother happy. She liked that I was showing respect for her faith."

"What's a loa? A saint or a god or something?"

She shrugged. "Pretty much."

"What religion?"

She cleared her throat. "Vodou."

I blinked. "Did you say voodoo?"

She spelled it out. I'd never met someone who practiced voodoo or Vodou. "It's the same, but voodoo, the way you probably think about it, is mostly associated with bad spirits and hoodoo. Am I right?" I nodded, feeling a little called out on my judgment, but there was no sign that she was offended. "Vodou does practice magic, but it's more about a conglomeration of African religious practices. Very spiritual. Very steeped in magic. Very in tune with nature. Very superstitious."

"You said your mother practiced it? Do you?"

"I don't practice any kind of spirituality. My mom sort of turned me off to all of it. I wouldn't say she practiced it, either, as much as she believed in it and thought it had powers over her and the world around her. The superstitious part of it played a big part in her life and the way she saw the world." She rubbed the tattoo. "I'd always liked that Maman Brigitte was a dancer, too."

"It fits you, then," I said as I played with her hair.

Talking about magic and superstition summoned thoughts of Madame Eugenie. She popped into my head a lot, especially in light of my unexpected relationship with Phaedra, which happened almost immediately after my reading. Somehow, the old woman had known. It occurred to me that I definitely wasn't in a rut anymore. I kind of attributed it to having met Phaedra. I didn't want to tell her, though, at least not right now. We'd only been seeing each other for a couple of weeks, and I had no idea if it would freak her out. I was enjoying our time together too much to risk it.

"Have you ever noticed the psychic's shop on 16th Street, down near Union Station?" I asked. It was out of my mouth before I could stop it.

"Madamee Eugenie's?"

Goose bumps rose across my skin. "You know it?"

"I went there once to get my cards read."

My heart started beating a little faster. "I did, too. I think…and don't think I'm a freak, okay? But I think the old woman predicted us getting together like this."

"Like this? Sexually?" Her expression was innocent, but the sparkle in her eye was anything but. And it made me less nervous about talking about it.

I tickled her, and she grabbed my hands. "Romantically, you pervert." I laughed.

She kissed my fingers and let go of my hands. "She did? The old woman or the younger one?"

"The old woman. She gave me a flash reading. She told me when the planets go direct, I'd feel better. I was intrigued, so I let her give me a reading."

"Mercury retrograde is over today, by the way. Do you feel better?"

I traced her eyebrows and the edges of her lips. "Much better."

"Have you ever had a full reading?"

I nodded. "A few days later, I went back and had one with the younger one, which supported the old woman's prediction but in a more ambiguous way. The old woman told me she saw connection and romance in my future." I didn't mention that she also said she saw love. A flutter filled my stomach at the thought. It was way too soon to be thinking about love, yet I was. I wasn't about to say it aloud, though. "She also mentioned music and dancing. It seems we were meant to be together."

Phaedra's dark eyes held my gaze. I could almost see her thoughts dancing in their depths, but she only smiled.

"What?" I asked.

"I think the old woman is a ghost."

I laughed. "No way. You're just trying to scare me."

She kissed my palm. "I'm serious. I catch sight of her sometimes. But when I look again, she's always gone."

"You're creeping me out." I'd seen her, too, since my reading. But she never disappeared, more like walked away. I didn't think about it much because her shop was near where I worked. Still, Phaedra's comment and the whole Vodou thing spooked me.

She rubbed my arms. "You have goose bumps. Don't think about it. I'm probably wrong." Her words were not convincing.

"I hope so." I played along but couldn't help a shiver.

A knock on my bedroom door made me jump. "Daria. Rowdy needs to go out."

I giggled, embarrassed by my nerves. "Okay, Marnie. I'll be out in a minute."

Phaedra's brows furrowed with questions. I got off the bed, bending to kiss her as I got up.

"We have a routine. She feeds Rowdy, and I walk him in the morning and after work. I feed him, and she walks him before bed."

"Not to be a dick about it, but can't she take him out for you this once? She's only playing a game, and you're, well, you're naked, and I'd say somewhat indisposed."

I pulled a pair of sweatpants on. "Change is hard for her. I'd rather introduce changes to our routine one at a time."

"I'm a change, aren't I?"

I smiled at her. "Yeah. So far, so good, though. She didn't like my last girlfriend coming over here, and it was a bit of a nightmare." I pulled a T-shirt over my head.

"What happened?" she asked.

I stood next to the door, but I wished I was still in bed with her, not talking about an ex-girlfriend. "I don't know. At first, Marnie was fine, but very quickly, things got tense. Marnie started stimming any time Lisa came over, and she totally ignored her, but her agitation lasted for hours even after Lisa left. It was uncomfortable for all of us, and I have no idea what kind of stuff was going on inside Marnie's head because she'd shut down when I asked."

Phaedra sat up, pulling the sheet up over her breasts. She was beautiful wrapped up in my bedding. "What's stimming?"

"It's short for self-stimulation, when someone does repetitive movements like rocking or shaking their hands. They think it helps to soothe a person with autism when they get overwhelmed. Marnie only does it when she's stressed. When it's really bad, she hums, too. Right before Lisa and I broke up, she was humming a lot."

"Was the relationship strained, thus Marnie's stress? Or did Marnie's stress cause the relationship to become strained?"

"Marnie's stress caused the breakup. I still don't know what the exact trigger was. I suspect it was the interruption of our daily routine."

"I totally get it." She smiled and lay back into the pillows. "You should probably take care of Rowdy. I'll be here when you get back."

"Promise?"

"Promise, and I'll be thinking of doing delicious things to you while you're gone."

A pulse of desire rocked my center. "Will you be doing delicious things to yourself while you're thinking of doing delicious things to me?"

Phaedra winked. "I'll let you know when you get back."

CHAPTER THIRTY-SIX

Phaedra

Whole Foods was busy for a Wednesday night. Actually, it was always busy. I liked coming here, though. It was just down the street from my place, and I often came in to get something to eat from the hot food bar. It saved me from eating my own cooking since I was a miserable cook. I wasn't here to get dinner, though. I'd promised Daria I'd bring a salad when she'd invited me to dinner at her place with her and Marnie. I was excited by the invitation. Normally, I didn't get to see Daria until around 9:00 p.m.

I'd been spending most of my free time with her lately and was enjoying it. While I'd gone to her house in the late evening a few times, more often than not, she came over to mine. She'd explained that Marnie required a steady schedule, but from what I could tell, Marnie seemed pretty chill to me. I totally respected how Daria wanted to maintain her sister's schedule. She was the expert, after all, and we usually waited until after dinner before we got together. It worked for me because I often had judo, rehearsal, or gigs after work. And when I didn't have that stuff, I usually caught up on work. Because Marnie played online games after dinner, it was easier for Daria to leave then.

A few times, I'd joked to Leigh about going home to meet my booty call, but nothing about Daria felt like a booty call. When she came over, she spent the night, only leaving a little early to get ready for work. On the weekends, she slept in, and we spent some of the day together. I liked our time together, and it fit our busy lives.

I'd picked out the salad kit I'd promised as well as a variety of ice cream macarons and was headed to the checkout when I spied a display of custom chocolates. The candies were fun, a bunch of heart-shaped pieces in different flavors. You could fill a small pink box and tie it up with a purple ribbon. I thought it would be a nice little present to bring to say thanks for making dinner, so I made a box and picked up a small vase filled with lavender to go with it. The lavender reminded me a little of my mother, who'd believed lavender oil cured all ills, physical and emotional. I loved the smell, and I hoped Daria would, too.

"Someone has a hot date."

I turned toward the familiar voice, and Leigh was standing next to me with a six-pack of beer and a loaf of bread.

"I kind of do. I'm going to dinner at Daria's."

She nodded at the box of chocolates and grinned. "Sounds cozy."

"Her sister will be there, but yeah."

The grin became a leer, which I hadn't seen on her in a while. "Is her sister hot?"

I tipped my head to the side as we got into the self-checkout lane. "She could be Daria's twin, actually."

Leigh's eyebrows shot up, but she waved the loaf of bread. "Bad habit. I don't know why I'm even asking. I'm on my way to meet Morgan. We're going to a potluck at one of her friend's house up in Highlands."

I sometimes missed the old womanizing Leigh. Oh, the stories she used to tell about the women she met. But I quite preferred the settled down Leigh because it meant she was happy. It reminded me that I still hadn't met the woman responsible. "How's it going with Morgan, and when do I get to meet her?" I started to scan my groceries.

Leigh's eyes got all soft. She didn't need to say. I could already tell. "I can't wait for you to meet her. Things are going good. We're taking it slow, which is weird for me, but she said she doesn't want it to hurt too much if it doesn't work out. I honestly don't get it, but I respect it. So slow it is."

"Slow can be good."

She winked. "Says the woman I haven't seen except for gigs and rehearsals in over two weeks."

"Aw." I placed the last grocery into my reusable bag and hugged her. "Are you saying I'm neglecting you?"

She laughed and pushed me away. "You're a fool. But, yes. Let's plan something soon. You bring Daria, and I'll bring Morgan."

"Deal. I'll text you with some times, and we'll get together soon."

CHAPTER THIRTY-SEVEN

Daria

There was a kind of tired that even coffee didn't help. That was the kind of tired I was. I was staring at a spreadsheet and had been for a while, but if someone had asked what was on it or what I was supposed to be doing with it, I couldn't have said. All I wanted to do was lay my head on my desk and rest my eyes. Better yet, I could climb under my desk and curl up for a bit. I was seriously considering the last option when my door, open a crack, swung open the rest of the way.

"Hey, zombie lady. Let's go to lunch." Taryn's voice should have startled me, but I was so zoned out, it seemed as if it came from a distance. But I sat up and smiled. I might have been tired, but I was in a good mood. I was always in a good mood these days.

"You saved my reputation. I'm pretty sure I was about to start snoring with my eyes open."

"I couldn't tell, what with your glassy eyes and the drool hanging from your mouth," she said with a smirk.

I wiped my mouth. There was no drool. "You lie."

"Only about the slobber. Now, let's go get some food, and you can tell me the latest about your sex life. Scott's still up in Wyoming, and I need to be reminded that sex is something real and not something I made up."

The fog of drowsiness lifted, thank goodness. I needed this interruption. I shut down my laptop and grabbed my wallet. I hadn't had time to make my lunch this morning, and Marnie had been asleep when I'd left, which was odd, but she'd been stepping outside of her routine a little more lately, and I wasn't about to question it lest I send her back to her previous rigid enforcement and mess up the time I was able to spend with Phaedra. She'd said she was fine when I'd knocked on her door, so I'd told her good-bye and headed out.

"Spare my sleep-deprived mind. I don't need visions of you and Scott engaging in unholy acts giving me nightmares. How about I keep my sex life to myself, and you do the same?"

"But I *want* to hear about yours."

I pushed her out my door and led her down the hall. "Let's get out of the office before someone hears what a pervert you are."

Taryn straightened her collar, shook her hair out, and frowned. "How's this?"

"Better." I giggled.

We headed to our favorite sandwich shop where I ordered a grilled cheese, and Taryn ordered her usual BLAT without the T. Of course, they put the T on it, but instead of complaining, she simply took the tomato off when we sat on our regular bench and poked her elbow into my side. She had a one-track mind, tomatoes be damned.

"Spill it. How's this thing with Phaedra going? Don't skimp on the details, either."

"I don't even know where to start. It's great."

"Then start with the sex. I know you're getting it on. You have a ditzy glow."

I paused with my sandwich halfway to my mouth and narrowed my eyes. "A ditzy glow?"

"You know, all smiley, daydreamy, that kind of thing."

I forgot about my sandwich for a second. "Yeah. I really like her, Taryn."

"I can tell. I haven't seen you this way in…ever. I kind of like this look on you." She sounded kind of gushy, and it made me smile. "You haven't mentioned Marnie having any problems with you dating Phaedra. It's been about a month. I take it things are going well?"

I'd been playing everything by ear with respect to Marnie and Phaedra, and so far, things were good. I sometimes worried that things would go the other way, but not often. And not in a pins and needles it was inevitable sort of way but in a just being aware sort of way. It felt way different than it had been with Lisa. "Marnie likes her."

"Excellent. Does she sleep over?"

I swallowed a bite. "She has, yes. But she usually leaves early to maintain Marnie's routine. I stay at her place more often than not. I go over after dinner and come home early in the morning to get ready for work."

Taryn pointed at me. "That explains the lack of sleep. Staying up all night having sexy time and getting up early every morning."

I nodded. "I'm going to have to change something up. I don't think I can sustain this pace."

"Have you talked to either Marnie or Phaedra about it?"

I'd been going back and forth about this very thing. I wanted to and could probably do it with Phaedra, who was easy to talk to about anything, but I was worried about Marnie's response.

"Not Marnie. But Phaedra's supportive of anything I suggest. She's laid back and open about everything. I'm not sure what to do about Marnie, though. Plus, my parents are coming home soon."

"Oh yeah. Have your parents given a date for their return yet?"

"Not yet. But sometime before classes start in September."

"What about Marnie? Will she move back in with them?"

Sadness hit me. I'd been trying not to think about it. I liked having Marnie as a roommate. The last three years had brought their share of challenges, but the good had far outweighed the bad. I wasn't sure I wanted her to move out, even if it was to move back in with our parents.

"I don't know. We haven't talked about it. As far as I can tell, things will remain the same when they get back, but I never know what's on Marnie's mind."

Taryn nibbled her chips. "And you don't want to ask her?"

I shook my head. "Not until it gets closer to the time. She can get overwhelmed if she's faced with too many options. I should probably talk to my parents first and get a better understanding of what the options are."

"You'll figure it out." She'd finished her sandwich and fixed me with an intense gaze. "Tell me more about the sex."

Heat rose up my neck. "I'm not giving you details."

"Come on! Why not?"

"I'm just not."

She sat back on the bench, glaring. "You're violating the friendship code."

I laughed. "What code?"

"The code requiring the sharing of deep and intimate secrets, thus binding our souls in friendship for all eternity."

"Oh. I was unaware."

She nodded vigorously. "Now you know. Tell me, is it mind-blowing?"

Her sweetly earnest question made me remember the last time

Phaedra and I were in bed, and I forgot I was trying to remain discreet. "Beyond mind-blowing."

"Shit. I knew it. Is she wild in the sack? I have that distinct impression."

What did she think *I* did in the sack, lie there? I fixed her with a raised eyebrow. "Maybe *I'm* the wild one."

She patted my leg. "Of course, you are, honey. Anyone who knows you knows that."

"Really?"

She favored me with an expression of forced innocence. "Without a doubt."

I scowled. "I hate when you placate me. I *can* be wild. I *have* been wild."

"Absolutely. So." She shimmied her shoulders. "Have you been teaching Phaedra a thing or two?"

"It's not like that with us." I paused to think about how to explain. "It's more of a fundamental connection. She totally gets me and knows what I need. If it's slow and intense, she does slow and intense. And if it's fast and explosive, she gives me fast and explosive. It goes both ways. We're so absolutely compatible in bed, it's kind of scary."

She gestured in a circle. "Tell me more about the slow and intense thing. Scott is all about fast and explosive…for him, anyway. For me, it's over way too fast." She sighed dramatically.

"You need to start dating women. Nothing is too fast for us."

A wistful look transformed her face. "I imagine it's always intense, and there are orgasms for days."

I was nodding and about to respond when I realized she'd tricked me into talking my sex life. "You're devious."

Again with the innocent face. "*Moi?*"

"*Oui! Vous!*" Which was the extent of what I remembered of high school French. "You're sneaky."

She winked. "But now I have a little more to get me through the next lonely week until Scott gets back."

I turned my head, but I was laughing. "I didn't need to hear that."

Chapter Thirty-eight

Phaedra

The door to my loft was barely open when Daria stepped in, grabbed me by the waist, and spun me around to press my back against the wall. My center clenched as she rolled the door closed, pressed her mouth against mine, and kissed me hard.

It'd been a couple of days since we'd seen each other, and it was always like this when we met up again. I thought about and wanted her touch all the time, but when we were apart for more than twenty-four hours, the want became a craving, plaguing me until we were together again. I'd been thinking about being with her all day. Apparently, she had, too. I moaned when she put her leg between mine, pressing into me.

No one had ever consumed me the way Daria did, not even Loredona. With the others, time apart was like foreplay, and I'd actually wanted a little time to myself to flame the desire. But with Daria, being apart was almost painful; the need I had for her wore at me. I didn't wish for time apart to increase my desire. It was always full throttle, never slaked. So time apart wasn't my favorite thing.

Now, with her body pressed against me and her lips claiming mine, my single focus was to get her into bed and under me as soon as possible. Making out with Daria was an erotic thrill. Her lips knew the exact right way to tease and excite me. Her tongue found spots on and in my mouth that shot currents of electricity directly to my erogenous zones. Within seconds of her mouth finding mine, I was wet and ready, a quivering mess. I was glad she only used her power over me in good ways. If she ever used it for evil, I'd be a goner.

I pushed my fingers into her hair, sweeping it back, enjoying the silky texture. She trailed kisses down my neck, causing all sorts of tingles and goose bumps to spread across my body.

"I thought about being with you all day," I whispered.

"Me, too. I was completely distracted." Her breath was warm against my neck as she spoke between kisses.

"Oh yeah? Distracted by what?"

"A few things, actually. These, for example…" she said, pushing her hand up my shirt and cupping one of my breasts over my bra. I shivered when she squeezed my nipple, and a moan rumbled in my throat. "Then there's the dip on your lower back that makes me want to do dirty things to you." She let go of my nipple, trailed around to my back, and grazed her fingertips along my spine until they dipped into the waistband of my skirt.

"What kind of dirty things?" My voice trembled, and the muscles of my lower back flexed as she continued to stroke the now extremely sensitive skin.

"Oh, the dirtiest, filthiest things, starting with this," she said as she dropped to her knees and lifted my skirt, pressing her face against the fabric of my panties, nuzzling me. Her hands were warm as she caressed my legs and pulled my panties down to my ankles. I stepped out of them and spread my legs.

She gripped my thighs, kneading them as she dipped her tongue into the cleft between them, swirling and tracing the swollen flesh. She guided my right leg over her shoulder, careful to shift my balance to my left foot. The position gave her better access to do what she wanted, and when her lips found my clit, I held on to the door handle to keep me standing. She sucked me in, and my entire body responded to the pulses in my center, expanding outward. I rocked against her face. When she slipped her fingers into me, a shattering orgasm exploded within me after just a few thrusts, creating a light show behind my closed eyelids. I almost forgot to breathe, the sensation was so strong, so powerful. When I sucked in air, shudders flowed through me, down my arms and legs, and out through my fingers and toes. If my leg hadn't been flung over her shoulder, I would have slid to the floor. I'd lost all strength in my limbs.

Daria continued to nuzzle and lick my center as the last of the orgasm faded, and I caught my breath. Finally, she gently shifted my leg back to the ground and held me up against the door as she stood, wiping her chin, flashing a victorious smile.

"I can't walk," I said.

"Then I did my job." She chuckled before she kissed me. I could smell and taste myself on her.

I pushed her backward without breaking the kiss. We took a few steps before I grew impatient, took her hand, and pulled her to the side of my bed.

Her laughter echoed in the open loft. "I thought you couldn't walk."

"I lied." I stood before her, unbuttoning her pants and then her shirt, pulling it off along with her suit jacket. It turned me on to see her in business clothes, but it turned me on even more to take them off. When her shirt was gone, I pushed her onto her back, and I removed her shoes before I pulled her pants and underwear down. She unclasped her bra as I threw her clothing to the floor.

When she was completely naked, I started to crawl up the bed to her, but she put a hand on my shoulder.

"Uh-uh-uh. This is strictly a no clothing zone." She waved at me. "You'll need to remove it all before you enter."

I stood next to the bed. "You mean like this?" I asked, lifting my tank top over my head.

"Perfect."

"And like this?" I unhooked my bra and pulled it slowly down my arms until it dropped to the floor. She swallowed visibly and nodded. I smiled.

I hooked my thumbs into the waistband of my skirt, and all my confidence fled. She'd seen me naked multiple times over the last month, but not when I was so on display, all of me, from head to toe. Everything.

"That's it. Go slow. You're killing me." She was watching me intently, her eyes on mine, a small smile curving her lips, her warm eyes telling me she liked what she saw. "Push it down." And I did. She licked her lips. "A little more." I lowered one side and then the other. Her eyes never left mine. "You're unbelievably beautiful. I can't wait to touch you." I inched the skirt even lower, until it was down to my knees. "You need to know how ready I am for you," she said as I stepped out of the skirt, one foot at a time. Her eyes bored into me, and heat was churning inside me. "Take your shoes off now and straddle me." I did as she asked, finally kicking out of my prosthetic as I crawled onto the bed until I was kneeling above her hips. I felt sexy and beautiful and unbelievably aroused.

"What's next?" I asked.

She took my hand and guided it between her legs. "Do you feel how much I want you?"

"Yes," I whispered. I traced her slick folds, circling her clit once, twice, and then again before trailing down and dipping shallowly into the liquid heat between her legs.

"So good," she sighed, lifting her hips.

I pulled some of the moisture up, slicking it over her clit, circling it a few more times before pushing my fingers into her again, more deeply this time. She lifted her hips again. I repeated this until she wrapped her hand around my wrist to keep my hand in place, fingers deep inside her.

"Fuck me, please." Her voice was ragged, barely a whisper. It took everything in me to start slowly, rubbing her clit with my thumb as she set the pace. It wasn't long before I was pistoning into her, her hips rocking, her muscles grabbing at my fingers as they moved out and back in, until she came with a shudder. She pulled me to her, holding me tightly as her chest heaved with each breath.

With a contented sigh, I snuggled into her, resting my head on her shoulder. The sweat we'd worked up made our skin slip against each other in a nice way, and I moved my hand in a circle across her abdomen.

"I didn't ask you how your Friday went," she said after she caught her breath.

I laughed. "There wasn't much opportunity. What with all the kissing and taking advantage of me as soon as I opened the door."

She grinned. "Yeah. About that. I'm not sorry."

I had to tickle her, which led to more kissing and touching, and once again, I was recovering from an intense orgasm. I snuggled into her, relishing the softness of her skin against mine. A rush of affection and something even stronger filled me. I squeezed her to me, trying to touch her with every possible part of me. I couldn't get close enough. She'd become undeniably important to me in such a short period of time. I rested my hand between her breasts, her heartbeat soothing me. I wanted her to be a part of the emotion coursing through me via the warmth of my hand. I imagined an electrical current running back and forth between us. It was like we'd been together for a millennium; our bodies just knew each other.

She placed her hand atop mine, pressing it to her chest. "Your hand is so warm. It's like it's radiating heat throughout my body."

I knew what it was then, the heat. It was my heart speaking to hers.

It seemed too soon to use the L-word, but I was sure that was what was flowing through me. So I kissed her instead, and I thought I felt her answer to my heart in the way she kissed me back.

When she pulled back, holding my face between her palms, her eyes were vibrant and dark, piercing me with the depth of her emotion. She hadn't spoken a word, but I knew. I didn't need to hear the words. I stroked her face, kissing her eyes, her cheeks, her mouth. She melted into me, and we held each other for a few minutes.

"Hey, do you remember the show we did at the Royal Standish?" I asked.

She rolled to her side and propped her head on her hand, smiling down on me. "It's kind of up there as one of the most amazing nights I've ever had."

I rolled to face her, intertwining our legs. "Mine, too."

"Why do you ask?"

"Well, the lead singer from the band we opened for asked me and Leigh to join their band."

"What? That's amazing. How did it come about?"

I explained what Nick had told me about his record label asking him to alter their sound a little. "Anyway, they're going to be in town this weekend, and the Royal Standish is letting us play there tomorrow. We're going to check out how we sound together. The Standish is almost always booked on Saturdays, and we got lucky that they don't have a show."

"If you sound good together, are you going to do it?" Daria asked.

That was the big question. The hugely enormous big question. The one that hadn't stopped rolling around in my head. "I don't know yet."

She ran a hand along my arm. "Regardless of what you decide, it's a huge compliment, don't you think?"

"For sure. You'll come watch, won't you? Tomorrow?"

Initially, I wasn't going to tell her about it until after I'd made up my mind. But it was good to share it with someone other than Leigh, who was ready to sign up as soon as she'd heard about it. Daria had a cool head. She'd help me work through this.

"I wouldn't miss it," she said.

I could always count on her.

CHAPTER THIRTY-NINE

Daria

I studied the heavy material of the red curtain next to me. Up close, it was worn and stained, the signs of wear that came with the traffic of hundreds of bands over the years.

I didn't want to be there. Not at all.

When Phaedra had told me she'd been asked to join Nick's Army, the crushing vise of loss took hold of my heart. I'd tried to hide it. On the outside, I was all happy smiles for her. And I really was. It wasn't a total act. Being approached by Nick's Army was a big deal. But on the inside, I was dying. Nick's Army worked out of Nashville. She'd have to move there to play with them, right? I couldn't sleep at all last night thinking about it. I'd just wrapped myself around her and held her as she slept. I didn't want to tarnish Phaedra's excitement by asking her the logistics of everything. She probably wasn't even thinking that far ahead yet. She was still elated about the possibilities. Plus, it wasn't as if she and I had ever discussed our future together, and this was definitely not the time to bring it up.

I knew what I wanted, though. I wanted a chance to see if we could make it work. I'd never grown this close to someone so quickly. She was smart, funny, talented, gorgeous, kind…among many other things. I should have been scared by how much I cared for her already, but I wasn't. It felt right. She was everything I wanted in a girlfriend, but now, I wasn't sure we'd ever even get there.

I'd spent the night holding her as she slept, knowing I loved her, hoping I could tell her someday.

Now, in the wings at the Royal Standish, I wasn't at all happy to be watching as our fate was being decided for us. Of course they were going to sound great together. I'd seen Phaedra sing all genres, and her talent with the violin meant she'd have no trouble incorporating it into the sound of Nick's Army. I wasn't even a musician, and I knew. Nick, who *was* a talented musician, wouldn't have asked her if he didn't think it.

From my vantage point next to the stage, they sounded even better than I expected, a funky mix of rock and bluegrass. There was an excited energy infecting everyone as they tried out different songs, infusing them with their own styles, which somehow blended into a completely different sound. There was noticeable stage chemistry between Phaedra and Nick, too, amplifying their individual charisma into an engaging and vibrant duo. They were unbelievable together. The record company was going to love them.

I hated it with every selfish inch of my body.

I wanted to be happy for Phaedra. And in a lot of ways, I was, but as every minute ticked by, she was slipping away from me, and my heart was breaking into a million pieces. It wasn't fair. I'd just found her.

In contrast, Nick's voice was brimming with excitement. "We'll take the tapes back to the studio and play with them, but I think what we have here is gold." He took Phaedra's hands and held them to his chest. "How soon can you be in Nashville to record with us?"

I couldn't take it. I didn't wait to hear what she would say. I took the winding hallway to the back door and stepped into the alley. Memories of the last time I'd been here with Phaedra invaded my mind, making me feel even worse.

I leaned against the brick wall, plunging my hands into the pockets of my jean jacket even though the night was warm. My hand wrapped around something in one of them, and I pulled it out, knowing exactly what it was. The tarot cards from the reading with Madamee Eugenie. I stared at the Two of Cups and the Two of Pentacles. The two paths she said I could go. She didn't tell me which one was better, only about the choice. But which could I choose, assuming I had a choice at all? I held a card in each hand. Which one would it be? I stared at them with such intensity, I started to get a headache.

"If you're so smart, which one will it be, huh?" I asked to no one in particular, but if I was honest, I was asking Madamee Eugenie. She was the one with the magical vision. Where was she when I needed the advice?

A breeze caught my hair, blowing it into my eyes. When I transferred the cards into one hand to move the hair back, the wind blew them out of my hands. I chased them and caught one, but the other rose on the draft before I was able to get to it. I watched it rise high above the alley, over the building, and out of sight.

A door slammed inside the theater, and I heard footsteps and voices coming closer. One of them was Phaedra's.

I couldn't remember the last time I'd cried, but I was fighting back tears, and I had to leave before she saw how much I didn't want the band to work out. I jammed the card I had left into my jacket pocket and took off at a run down the alley. When I reached the end, I imagined Phaedra's voice calling my name as I turned onto Broadway, but I kept running.

Chapter Forty

Phaedra

My phone calls kept going straight to Daria's voice mail, and I tried not to get angry. First she'd left the Royal Standish without saying good-bye or telling me why. And when I finally had gotten hold of her, hours later, she hadn't apologized for leaving or given a reason. She'd simply said something came up, and she was busy, so she'd have to call me back. That was two days ago, and she still hadn't called.

"Why are you glaring at your phone like you want to throw it against the wall?"

Barb was leaning against the conference room doorjamb. I dropped the phone onto the stack of papers before me and pushed my hair away before leaning back in my chair.

"Because I *want* to throw it at the wall."

She entered the room and sat in the chair next to me. "Is it the new Apple update? I hate the way they changed the photo storage. I can't find anything now."

"It's not the phone. Daria isn't taking my calls."

"Did you two get into an argument?"

"No. That's the most frustrating thing. I don't know why she's avoiding me. Everything was perfect until she shut down on me."

She crossed her legs and smoothed her skirt over her lap. "Is it possible she misunderstood something?"

"I've racked my brain trying to think of something I might have done or said. We'd had a great day, and she was with me at a rehearsal. Everything was going well until she up and left. She didn't even say good-bye."

"Maybe something happened there? Maybe she got sick?"

"She wasn't sick. I'd just talked to her. I can't imagine what could have happened." True, I'd been busy working with Nick and his band, but my eyes were never off her for long. It felt good to have her there, grounding me. She'd been quiet, but I assumed she was letting me do my thing. Maybe something was bothering her, and she hadn't said anything. I should have asked.

"Is it possible something happened with one of the others, and she's afraid to tell you?"

I scoured my memory of the evening. "I don't know. Unless something happened with someone from Nick's crew. I think I would have seen it, though."

"Who's Nick?"

"You know, the band I played with about a month ago, who told us he wanted us to open for them anytime they were in town?"

She nodded. "I remember something about them. They aren't the first band to tell you they wanted to play more with you."

I loved her support. "It's been a while. The thing is, I was sort of trying out for them."

She rested her chin on her hand. "You have to try out to be an opener?"

"I wasn't trying out as an opener. I was trying out as a co-lead singer."

She looked confused. "Interesting. But they're not from here?"

I shook my head. "Nashville."

She sat back and tapped her pen on the conference table. "How would that work?"

"I told them I wasn't going to move."

Relief flashed across her face, but just as fast, concern took hold of her features. "If you didn't have responsibilities here, would you make the same decision?"

"You mean responsibilities at Calamity? Or responsibilities in Denver in general?"

"I was primarily thinking about Calamity, but, yeah, in general."

"I'd make the same decision. I love Denver. I've lived in lots of places, and I love to travel, but my home is here." I didn't need to tell her that I loved Calamity Graphics, but my passion was music. Barb knew it. I just didn't want to have to say it out loud. There were other things keeping me in Denver.

Was I a fool to consider Daria in my decision to stay in Denver instead of moving to Nashville? After less than a month and a half of dating? But her face was what I saw when I closed my eyes, and she was what filled my heart with dread when I thought about leaving. She was who I thought of when I thought of home.

And she wasn't even talking to me.

CHAPTER FORTY-ONE

Daria

Marnie's routine was the only thing getting me out of bed in the morning these days, but today, even that wasn't doing it. My alarm had gone off three times already, but I kept hitting snooze. So what if I was late for work? I could sleep in a little if I wanted to, right? But I wasn't just sleeping in. I was avoiding being awake. Big difference. The thing was, being awake meant thinking about how much I missed Phaedra, and thinking about how much I missed her made me want to call her. And if I called her, there was a good chance I would beg her not to leave, and who was I to ask her to stay? To pass up on her dreams? With someone she'd only known for six weeks?

Sleep stopped all those thoughts. I pulled my pillow over my head and squeezed my eyes closed.

My bladder, however, wasn't down with avoidance and self-pity. Blearily, I used the restroom and was returning to my room, ready to get back into bed, when I noticed Rowdy sitting patiently by the front door. Uh-oh. I'd triggered our morning ritual by getting up, which set off the rest of the sequence, meaning someone had to take him out to the little dog park before we had an accident.

Morning walks were my job, but I went to Marnie's door, hoping the noises I'd heard earlier were her getting ready for work, and she was already dressed. I raised my hand to knock, but Marnie opened the door before my knuckles made contact. We were both startled.

"Hey, I'm running slow this morning. Would you be awesome and walk Rowdy for me?" I asked.

She was dressed, which was a relief. Movement in the room behind her caught my eye, and Courtney was next to the bed, pulling on a shirt.

Marnie looked over her shoulder. "Um. Courtney spent the night last night."

I waved to Courtney, who froze, probably because I saw her dressing. She wasn't one of the soccer players who stripped down to her sports bra to change shirts on the field. She was one of the shyer ones. I would have laughed if I wasn't feeling as down as I was, but I averted my eyes. "Hi, Courtney."

All I heard was a muffled response as Marnie stepped the rest of the way out of her room and shut the door.

"Yeah, I was about to take him for his walk," she said.

"Thanks. I didn't mean to get him excited to go outside and rush you. I thought I heard you up already. Otherwise, I would have tried to keep him in my room until you were ready."

It was weird, this whole thing. We had a routine, and this wasn't it.

"No problem," she said, clipping him into his harness and leash. "Come on, Rowdy. Let's go do your business."

They left the apartment, and I realized I was awake now. I figured I might as well get ready for work. I was making a cup of coffee when Courtney came from Marnie's room.

"Hey, Courtney," I said as I took the half-and-half from the refrigerator. "You want a cup of coffee?"

"Um, sure," she said, pink creeping up her face. "I'm gonna…" She pointed toward the bathroom and ducked down the hall.

I was grateful she'd been keeping Marnie company these days. I was pretty sure her presence was the primary thing keeping Marnie calm with all the disruption in her life. My stomach clenched. That made me think of Phaedra, my own favorite disruption.

Courtney came back and sat at the kitchen counter. The coffee was still brewing, and I leaned my elbows on the counter, waiting for it to finish. The tired that consumed me was deep. I hadn't been sleeping very well since I'd run like a coward from the Royal Standish, but that wasn't the cause of the absolute absence of motivation to stay awake. This was depression. And I knew the reason for it. I missed Phaedra.

"Thanks for staying with Marnie when I'm not here. I know it keeps her from worrying."

Courtney smiled, and her cheeks turned pink. "It's no problem."

"I'm probably not going to be away much anymore. You've been such a great friend, but you don't need to keep her company all the time."

Her cheeks grew red. "She's teaching me how to play some of the games she works on."

The front door opened, and Marnie and Rowdy came in. Marnie unclipped the leash, and Rowdy came sniffing around the floor, hopeful for any food I might have dropped. When he realized there wasn't any, he sauntered to his bed, flopping down as if he were exhausted.

Courtney swiveled her chair to face Marnie. She chewed on her thumbnail. "Daria says she won't be sleeping over at Phaedra's house anymore, so I don't need to stay the night here with you."

Marnie stared for a moment, furrowing her brow, and then she turned her gaze to me. "Okay."

Something felt off, but I couldn't tell what it was. If I hadn't known Marnie better, I would have thought she and Courtney were passing glances with one another, talking without speaking. But that wasn't how Marnie operated. At least with anyone but me. They *had* been spending a lot of time together. Maybe they'd figured out Phaedra and I weren't seeing each other anymore. Either way, I wasn't in a frame of mind to discuss it with anyone yet. My heart was too bruised.

Chapter Forty-two

Phaedra

I stared at my phone, willing it to ring, but like every day over the last two weeks, it just sat there. Silent. I hated it.

I left my last message for Daria a week and a half ago, after having left at least a dozen other voice mails and twice as many texts, asking her to call me. After a few days with no response, I'd given up. It didn't mean I didn't think about calling or texting her at least a hundred times a day, though.

My desk phone buzzed, interrupting my staring contest with the phone.

"Hello."

"There's someone here to see you, Ms. Jean-Julien."

"I don't have any appointments."

"She says she's a friend of yours." My heart rate spiked. Daria?

"I'll be right out." I rose from my desk but took a moment to take a couple of breaths. If it was her, I didn't want to act like a scattered fool when I finally saw her.

The front desk was down the hall from my office, and I tried not to race-walk to get there. When I came through the frosted glass doors, my heart stopped. She was right there with her back to me, staring at the art on the wall behind the couch. I took a few steps toward her, and she turned. Disappointment flooded my chest. It was Marnie. Not wanting to be rude, I tried to keep my expression neutral to hide my reaction, but the letdown was almost more than I could bear.

"Hi, Marnie. It's nice to see you."

It hit me then. Why was she here? Had something happened to Daria? God, my emotions were leaping all over the place.

She gestured toward the portrait she'd been studying. "You have Ansel Adams prints."

"My boss is a huge fan," I said.

"Me, too. Black and white is easier to enjoy. Too many colors make my head spin." Her smile was so like her sister's, it made my heart ache.

"How are you?" I wanted to ask if Daria was okay, but I wanted to play it cool until I found out why she'd come. Besides, Marnie seemed too serious to smile through a crisis.

She ignored my question, though she met my gaze for a fraction of a second before her eyes darted away. "Do you have a few minutes to speak in private?" Her fingers were flicking out in a repetitive motion next to her thigh. Daria called it stimming, something Marnie did when she was overwhelmed. Aside from the lack of eye contact, it was the only outward sign I'd ever noticed of her autism that couldn't be explained away with social awkwardness. I wondered what was on her mind.

"Sure. Let's go to my office."

She followed me down the hall and sat when I closed the door and walked around the desk.

"I came to ask you to speak to Daria for me."

She didn't beat around the bush, but I was sort of used to it by now after the handful of times we'd interacted over the last month and a half. I wondered if she knew Daria was avoiding me.

"You need *me* to speak to Daria? For *you*? Why?"

She met my eyes for a second and then focused on a spot near my shoulder. "She thinks Courtney and I are just friends. But Courtney's my girlfriend."

"I see. Why do you need me to tell her?"

"Because Courtney and I don't want to hide our relationship from her. I'm afraid she'll freak out if *I* tell her."

"Why have you been hiding it in the first place? Why do you think she'll freak out?"

"She doesn't like change. She likes things to be a certain way. When things change, she gets weird."

Interesting. That was exactly how Daria described Marnie.

"What do you think she'll do if you tell her?"

"I don't know. I'm bad at reading people, and I haven't been able to talk to her about it."

"What do you *want* her to do?"

"She worries, and her worries make her sad. I want her to stop worrying about me and to stop worrying about our mom and dad. I want her to stop worrying about you, too. I want her to be happy. I want her to branch out, do her own thing and live her life. She used to be fun before Mom and Dad left, but now she's so…responsible."

"Have you ever told her this?"

She shook her head. "I think it would hurt her feelings."

It made sense. Marnie was concerned about Daria not living her life because of her responsibilities. She was also irritated about Daria impeding her relationship with Courtney. Above everything, she didn't want to tell her any of this because it could hurt Daria's feelings. I understood, but I still wasn't convinced I was the best person to relay it to her.

"Don't you think it might come better from you since you're the one closest to her?"

"She's in love with you. She'll listen to you. I'm only her little sister, a responsibility to her."

Oh, wow. What a loaded response. At first, I only registered the first part. Love? Had Daria actually said she was in love with me to Marnie? I wanted to interrogate Marnie to find out, but this conversation wasn't about me. And then I realized the rest of what she'd said. It made me sad that she didn't know how much her sister adored her.

"You're her sister. She loves you. You're not just a responsibility."

Marnie sat forward. "I'm not sure if you know this, but I'm autistic, right in the middle of the spectrum. I used to be further down the scale, but I think I'm moving in the other direction, dealing with it better. Things don't overwhelm me as much anymore, and I know how to compensate. I don't read people very well, but I'm a good communicator, and I try to figure people out through talking about it. My boss is helping me. He's autistic, too. He passes, though, and doesn't tell many people he is, but I knew right away."

This was the most I'd ever seen her speak. It was a little disorienting how little emotion she conveyed about the heavy subject. I struggled to figure out how all of this was affecting her. It must have been bothering her. Otherwise, she wouldn't have come to my office to talk about it. More importantly, I wanted to know, why me? Why now, when Daria was actively avoiding me? Marnie's visit was laden with emotional baggage I wasn't ready to deal with.

"You do know your sister loves you, right? You're her number one priority."

"That's the problem. I need her to know I'm capable of taking care of myself. But I think it will make her feel…" She appeared to search for the right word, and in the process, displayed more emotion than she had during the entire conversation. "Useless? Or maybe like she's been wasting her time trying to take care of me?"

I wasn't very knowledgeable about autism, but I remembered Daria telling me about Marnie having alexithymia in addition to autism, so her expressing such empathy for Daria was interesting…and touching. I wished Daria was there to see it. A sting of tears made me blink several times before answering.

I cleared my throat. "You're very sweet to worry about her response, but I'm sure she'd rather hear all of this from you."

"She tries hard to keep the world consistent. But the world isn't consistent. It's chaos. You can apply logic to explain it, but you can't control it. She's going to burn out trying to control it." She looked at her hands, and the finger flicking stopped. "I think I'll screw it up if I try to explain."

Having heard Daria's perspective made Marnie's account that much more poignant. They were both trying to be good sisters, but in doing so, they were holding each other back from the lives they'd hoped for each other and for themselves.

I studied a paperclip I'd picked up and unbent it while I mulled over Marnie's request. I hadn't tried to call Daria in almost two weeks. I still felt like a fool for having left her the slew of unanswered messages and texts in the days after she took off without telling me why. Part of me wanted to agree to Marnie's request just for a chance to be in the same room with her again. But another part of me was reluctant to use this as an excuse when it was obvious she didn't want anything to do with me.

"She misses you," Marnie said.

My head shot up. "So you *do* know we haven't been seeing each other?"

She nodded. "She's been sleeping too much."

"Did she tell you why?"

"I think because she's tired."

I would have laughed if I wasn't so depressed about it. "Not about the sleeping. About why we aren't seeing each other."

"She hasn't told me anything, but she's home all the time when she's not at work these days. She's not happy, either, so I know she misses you."

"I'm not sure about that."

"You won't know until you ask her."

"Assuming she answers my call."

"Come home with me, then. She'll be there."

The thought of showing up at Daria's unexpectedly filled me with dread. "I'm not sure she'll be happy to see me."

She held up both of her hands. "You won't know until you try, right?"

I couldn't argue with her.

CHAPTER FORTY-THREE

Daria

I could always count on Rowdy to boost my mood. Not one hundred percent, but definitely better than I'd felt most of the day. When I got home from work, he showered me with kisses and doggie hugs, and when we went down to the dog park, he was so sweet with a nine-week-old corgi, I couldn't stand it. It was the first time at the park for the little corgi, Mr. Bean, and he'd been timid to explore, but when Rowdy saw him, he took it upon himself to be Mr. Bean's guide, and soon they were playing. It was nice to smile for the first time in a week.

Rowdy was wiped out when we got back to the apartment. I unclipped his leash, and he took a long drink of water and went straight to bed. The quiet of the apartment pressed in on me as I went to the refrigerator to get dinner started. Despite the menu having been decided on Saturday, I spaced out between the time my hand wrapped around the handle and I opened the refrigerator door, and I was leaning against the door without seeing anything before me. The only thing I was aware of was the same thing that had been running through my mind over the last couple weeks: how much I missed Phaedra.

I finally roused myself, forgetting entirely what I'd been meaning to do, and when I turned and Marnie was right there, I was startled. I hadn't heard her come home. I put my hand on her shoulder and dropped my head to rest on it. "Shit! You scared me."

She laughed. "I said hello when I entered. I thought you heard me."

"I was totally out of it. I can't even remember what I was supposed to be doing."

I shut the refrigerator door, and my eyes landed on Phaedra.

She was standing so still right next to the door that at first, I thought she was a hallucination. The way her eyes bored into me was the only indication she was real. If I had imagined her, I was sure she would have been glaring or, worse, not even acknowledging me. I deserved either of those. This questioning stare, a look that held such emotion, was almost worse. I didn't know how to answer it.

An uncomfortable quiet descended over the room.

Finally, Marnie broke the silence. "I begged her to come home with me."

I cleared my throat. "Hi."

She raised her hand. "Hi."

I wanted to run to her. But I'd screwed things up. I wasn't sure what to do, how to act.

"Do you want something to drink?" Marnie asked.

"Water would be great." She answered without taking her eyes off me, and I realized I was staring, too. I averted my eyes.

"I'll get it," I said, needing something to do to keep me from doing or saying something stupid.

By the time I got us all glasses of water, Phaedra was perched on the edge of the couch as if she were ready to leave at any minute.

I took a seat on one of the barstools at the kitchen island, and Marnie took her usual place at the other end of the couch.

"How are you?" I asked.

"I've been better," Phaedra said. She was always beautiful to me, but I knew what she meant. I felt about an inch tall. "And you?"

"I'm good." I was such a liar. I wasn't even remotely good, but I said it, and when she lowered her eyes, I wished I could take it back.

Nothing had changed. She was still moving to Nashville. And I wasn't about to ask her to stay and give up her dream. But damn. All I wanted to do was to go to her, wrap her in my arms, and beg her to stay. It was lonelier with her in the room and not being able to touch her than it had felt even when I'd never expected to see her again.

"Um. I asked Phaedra to come over to help me with something."

I'd forgotten Marnie was even in the room. "What's that?" I asked. I was ashamed of my selfishness. All I could think of was my own pain.

"I asked Phaedra to come over here to help me talk to you about something." Marnie was flicking her fingers against her thigh, indicating her agitation was pretty high.

"What do you need help with, Marn?"

Marnie cast her eyes at Phaedra, who nodded and turned to me. She appeared to be trying to figure out what she wanted to say.

"Marnie loves you very much." She glanced at Marnie, who nodded solemnly. "It seems she's as protective of you as you are of her."

I turned toward Marnie. "I know. You're an awesome sister." I had a million questions about what Marnie wanted to talk about and why she thought it was necessary to enlist Phaedra's help. There was a little irritation, too, since I'd always been there for her, and it made me sad that she hadn't come directly to me. I might have been a little jealous. Okay, I wasn't going to lie…I *was* jealous, and not just a little bit. She'd gone to someone else, but the thing that eclipsed all of it was that Marnie was comfortable enough with Phaedra to trust her like this. It was kind of huge. She didn't naturally lean on people. Too bad Phaedra wouldn't be around much longer. My heart clenched as soon as I had the thought.

"Marnie's worried about you. She thinks you focus on her, and you don't live your life the way you should. She'd like you to do more on your own, have more fun. She doesn't think you need to take care of her all the time. She wants you to live your life for you."

What? I felt defensive. I turned to Marnie. "I do things, Marnie. Being your sister doesn't keep me from doing the things I want." Even as I said it, I knew I wasn't being truthful, and I knew she knew it. Her expression grew even more serious.

Phaedra took a deep breath and continued. "One of the reasons Marnie asked me to come over was because she was afraid of hurting your feelings." She checked in with Marnie, who nodded. Then she turned back to me. "She's grateful for everything you've done for her. She made sure I knew that, but she's afraid your protection over her is a little much at times, not only for her, but for you, too."

"Too much?" So many emotions flooded me, I had a hard time identifying them. Indignation. Irritation. Embarrassment. Failure. Among others. But mostly, I thought that I'd actually been slacking off lately, first with my obsession over being with Phaedra and then in my obsession of losing Phaedra. I didn't know how to respond.

Phaedra shifted in her seat. "Maybe I'm reading into this, but I think what she means is both of you are being a little too gentle with one another. Neither of you wants to rock the boat." She gestured toward me. "You with keeping routines so strictly and her not telling you when she needs a little space to do her own thing. Did I say it right, Marnie?"

She nodded again.

I looked at Marnie. My feelings were hurt, and I felt like crying. "I'm not sure what you mean. Have I not given you enough space?"

Marnie got up and started pacing. The finger flicking turned into wrist flapping with one hand. I hadn't seen her this worked up in a long time.

"You...you...you..." Her eyes darted all over the room, and her head was bent forward. It reminded me of when she was a little girl, and she'd become so overwhelmed she couldn't control her movements. Then she stopped pacing and clasped her hands together, which stopped the stimming. She straightened her shoulders, lifted her head, and closed her eyes, breathing deeply. I'd never seen her do any of this, but then again, it had been a long time since she'd been agitated to this extent.

Then she spoke. "I'm thinking about the time we went to Capital Reef National Park. Remember when you gave me the ring you bought at the museum?"

I remembered it well. I'd given her the ring out of guilt for having made her fall over the cliff. It was one of the worst days of my life. "I remember. It had a Kokopelli on it with an amethyst for the head."

"Yes. I still have it in a box next to my bed." She opened her eyes and smiled. "Thinking about it makes me feel good. Calm."

"Is that what you just did to calm down?" I was in awe. She'd done a great job just now of distracting herself from a meltdown. "How did you learn that?"

"Sam taught me how to use a good memory to help ground me. He calls it redirection. It helps me at work all the time. It's been a tremendous help and keeps me from walking out of the room when something needs to be addressed."

"Did you want to walk out of here?"

She nodded. "I wanted to walk out as soon as I got here. I knew what we were going to talk about."

"And you're afraid of hurting my feelings?"

She tilted her head as she thought my question over. "I'm afraid of that but more afraid that you'll think everything you've been doing for me has been worthless. Because it hasn't been worthless."

"Why would I think it's been worthless?"

Her fingers were flicking at her thighs again. "Because you've worked so hard to build a bubble around us, and I don't want to be in a bubble."

I got up and put my hand on her shoulder and left it there for a second before I rubbed it up and down. She stopped the flicking.

"I get it. You don't want the bubble," I said. "We can definitely work on that."

"There's something else."

"Okay."

"Um, it's about Courtney." She looked past me to Phaedra. I turned to Phaedra, too.

"What about Courtney?" I asked.

"Marnie and Courtney are girlfriends, but Marnie has been afraid to tell you."

I turned back to Marnie, who was staring intently at me. It made sense. Courtney had been spending a lot of time at our place lately. I tried to think if there had been other signs. But did there need to be other signs? Marnie didn't do casual. The fact that Courtney had been hanging out was telling all by itself.

A shadow of guilt fell over me for being so caught up in my issues that I didn't catch it. "Really, Marnie? That's great. I know she's been hanging around a lot, but I thought it was because I was gone a lot of the time." My stomach dropped as soon as I said it, thinking about why I'd been away so much. And how it was over. A knife turned in my heart. I struggled not to cry, and I couldn't look at Phaedra. "When did you two become more than friends?"

"April third. Four months and eighteen days ago."

"On your birthday." How had I not known this was going on?

She nodded. "She sleeps over a lot. We wait for you to go to bed, and she comes over."

I leaned forward, clasping my hands together. "Why couldn't you tell me?"

"Because you said no more girlfriends sleeping over after you and Lisa broke up."

"I meant for me, not you."

Her brow furrowed in confusion. "Why would it be one way?"

"You had a bad reaction to Lisa coming over to the house. I assumed it was because your routine was disrupted."

Marnie appeared even more confused. "I wasn't getting agitated when Lisa came over because you disrupted my routine. I was agitated because she tried to kiss me."

What? Did I hear her correctly? "She tried to kiss you?"

"I told her I was sad because I'd never kissed anyone. I thought she was my friend. She said she wanted to kiss me to show me what it was like. Like romantic kissing, not a peck. I didn't let her, and it made her angry. But *I* was angry at *her* because she was supposed to be your girlfriend. You don't kiss other people when you already have a girlfriend, especially if it's my sister."

Rage flared within me. Lisa was so far in my past that none of this affected me personally, other than what she'd done to my sister, but that was unbelievably cruel. Marnie's fingers were flicking against her thigh faster and faster. I put a hand on her shoulder, and it slowed down and then stopped.

"Why didn't you tell me?"

"Because she said you would get angry if you knew and throw me out of the apartment."

"*That's* why you got so worked up when she came over." I had to concentrate not to display my anger. I didn't want Marnie to get even more stressed out because of me. But then something inside me shifted. Marnie needed to see me angry at this. It was unforgivable what Lisa had done. "I would never throw you out. It was not okay what Lisa did, and it's even worse that she made you think I would get angry at you for something she did."

Marnie looked relieved. My anger didn't seem to increase her agitation.

"I was glad when you broke up with her. But I was sad when you decided not to date anyone again. I liked seeing you happy. And when you met Phaedra, you were happy again. But when you broke up, I was sad for you. I was sad for me, too, because I wouldn't have the excuse to have Courtney over anymore."

"And here we are," I said. I wondered what Phaedra was thinking about all this family drama. What was she feeling about being dragged into it? I didn't have the courage to look at her, but I could feel her watching me. I sat on the barstool again and studied my hands.

"Why did you two break up, by the way?" Marnie asked.

I'd been expecting the question, except I wished it hadn't come when Phaedra was sitting right there.

"We didn't break up," I said.

"Could have fooled me," Phaedra said, which made me glance at her. Her face wore the surprise I felt. I didn't know why I said we weren't broken up. Sure, there was no fight, and it wasn't like we'd agreed *not* to see each other, but that was only because I'd been a coward, and I'd walked away and then avoided all of her calls and texts. I'd never given her the chance to talk it through. I never even gave her a reason. I'd just disappeared on her. I was a jerk.

I shifted in my chair to face her. "I'm sorry."

"For what, exactly?" She sounded angry. I didn't blame her.

I shrugged. "For everything. For disappearing. For not returning your calls and texts. For being too scared to talk to you. For being a jerk. For all of it but mostly for hurting you."

She leaned forward with her elbows on her knees. "All I want to know is why?"

God, I didn't even know how to explain it. Why was a good question.

"I guess for preemptive reasons."

"Preempting what? I don't understand."

"I keep telling myself it's for you. You need freedom to pursue your dream. You don't need me hanging around to complicate everything for you. But in reality, I'm selfish. I wanted to control the inevitable pain of you leaving me."

I hadn't even known this until I said it. All this time I'd been telling myself I was helping her realize her dreams when I was really just protecting myself. What kind of person was I? I'd been trapping my sister in a bubble, and now I was a coward, too? I didn't even recognize myself.

Phaedra stood and turned to Marnie. "Are we good now? Have we brought up everything you wanted to talk about?"

Marnie stood, too. "Yes. Thank you."

"Okay, good. I'll see you later."

She walked to the door and left without looking back. I watched, unable to move, unable to say anything. My heart felt as if it had left my body.

"Why are you sitting there?" Marnie asked. "Why are you letting her leave?"

"I don't know."

"Follow her, then."

How had my sister become wise about matters of the heart? I got up, flew from the apartment, and descended the stairs. I had no idea what I was going to say, but I wasn't about to let her leave without talking to her.

When I got to the bottom of the stairs, she was nowhere in sight. I searched the sidewalk both ways and across the street, and I waited for her to come out of the parking garage where the elevator let out. After several minutes of waiting and not seeing her, I decided to go back up to the apartment. A sense of numbness overtook me, making the stairs an insurmountable challenge, and I went to the elevators. I pushed the button and waited, leaning against the wall, facing the doors. They were so slow, all I wanted to do was slide down the wall and fold up into a ball. When one of them finally opened, I stepped in and almost stepped on Phaedra, who was sitting on the floor, pressed into the corner under the button panel. Her face was hidden against her knees, which were pulled to her chest. I dropped to my knees before her.

"Are you okay?" I asked.

Without lifting her head, she rocked it from side to side. "No." Her voice cracked, and I knew she was crying.

My heart broke wide open. I had done this to her. It was my fault. I sat as close to her as possible and pulled her toward me, grateful she let me do it. I held her tight, resting my face against the top of her head as huge sobs ripped through her, and tears ran down my face. We sat that way until my butt fell asleep, and I lost track of time, but I didn't care. I didn't want to let go of her.

After a while, she said something, but I missed it because it was muffled against my chest.

I loosened my hold on her and raised my head off hers so she could lift it. "I'm sorry. I couldn't hear what you said."

"I asked if I'm that easy to walk away from."

The words cut through me. I squeezed her to me. "No. No. No."

"Then how come you wouldn't talk to me? Why didn't you tell me what was on your mind? You just walked away like I didn't mean anything to you."

It was a minute before I could trust my voice to speak. "It was the opposite. I couldn't trust myself to be strong enough to stay away if I saw you."

"Why didn't you tell me what was on your mind? I thought everything was going well right up until you left. What happened?"

"I heard how good you sounded together. What you have is gold, like Nick said, when he offered you a spot in his band and asked you to go to Nashville. I could tell how excited you were. There was no way I was going to stand between you and your dream. No way." I wiped the snot from my nose. "And like I said, part of me wanted to protect myself from the pain of you telling me you were leaving. I'm not proud of myself for it, but I can't bear to hear you tell me you need to leave."

She moved until I could see her face. Her eyes were swollen and red. It broke my heart. "Well, I'm not leaving, and you're a big reason why."

"What? No!" Although I loved having her in my arms again, I extradited myself and stood. "See? This is what I mean. I can't be the person to stand in the way of your dreams. You have to go."

"But I'm not."

A tiny part of me was ecstatic. She'd given up her dream for me. But the bigger, more rational part of me was absolutely against it. "You can't stay here because of me. We've only been dating for a month and a half. What if you decide you made a mistake?"

She stood, too. "I know we're not a mistake. I already told Nick I was staying in Denver, and he understood. In fact, he—"

"Phaedra, listen to me. You can't stay here because of me. I'm…I'm…" I struggled to find words to explain. I'd always have responsibilities here. I couldn't leave Marnie or my family. Regardless of how independent Marnie was, my family would always be important to me, and I'd want to live near them. I couldn't find a way to say it without hurting her or giving her a reason to stay.

"You need to listen to me, Daria. None of this matters because Nick's Army is moving here to Denver. Two of them have family here, and they've been talking for a while about moving somewhere more centrally located to make it more convenient for tours and closer to their label, which is located in L.A."

"They're moving here?"

"Yes. It was part of the reason they were looking for a singer in Denver."

"Does that mean you get to pursue your dream *and* stay here?"

"That's what I'm trying to tell you."

I hung my head. "I'm the biggest jerk on the planet."

"They have a studio here in Denver, too. It works out for the band to be here, and with Leigh and me being here, it works out even better. Besides, it's not only about you, even though you're a huge part of my decision. I'm going to continue to play with Washtub Whiskey as much as I can. I can't just ditch them. I've grown up with them, so I'm going to play for both bands."

"I can't believe what an idiot I've been. I made an assumption that you needed to move to Nashville if you wanted to be part of the band, and since I couldn't move, I made the decision to end it. I should have talked it over with you."

She nodded, and I couldn't be mad at her for the "I told you so" expression. "That would have been the easiest way, yes."

I ran my hand down my face. "I'm a pig-headed fool."

"Hey. I'm not going to say I don't have emotions about how you just disappeared on me, and we need to talk it out a little bit more but maybe later. However, this is definitely something we can work on. If you want to. You've spent your life trying to learn how to communicate with a person who isn't wired to communicate in traditional ways. You've learned to make assumptions because it's all you've had to work with. It's bound to affect the way you do things. But I witnessed how you two figured it out today. You're capable of adapting and learning new ways. It's a wonderful thing. Together, we can learn how to do it, too."

"You know Marnie is always going to be a huge part of my life, right? Sure she wants to be more independent, and I think it's super cool, but we're close. I'll always want to be engaged in her life, and I want her to be in mine. That comes with certain challenges sometimes."

Phaedra stepped closer to me and took my hands. "Hey. One of the things I love most about you is how close you are to your sister. I wanted a sibling so bad when I was a kid. Family's important to you, and I like being around it."

I stepped closer, and we were almost touching. I wanted to wrap my arms around her again, but something held me back. "Can you forgive me for the terrible way I behaved?"

She pushed my hair behind my ear and cupped my jaw. "As long as you promise not to disappear on me again. We need to talk things through and work on not making assumptions with one another."

I leaned my head into her hand. "I promise to talk everything out with you, and I promise to never walk away again. In fact, you might have to ask me to leave you alone sometimes. I hated not seeing you. I was miserable. I don't know how it happened so quickly, but you've become enormously important to me."

"You aren't the only one feeling it. It killed me not being able to see you. I've been a mess these last two weeks."

"I guess I have a lot of making up to you to do."

"You certainly do. Starting here." She took the final step closer, bringing our bodies and lips together. A wave of relief crashed over me while at the same time, my body responded with a flash of hot desire. The kiss was soft and sweet at first but quickly became something more. God, I'd missed her. I couldn't get close enough to her. She must have felt the same way because she pushed me against the wall of the elevator, which drove the heat of the kiss way up.

I'm not sure how long we kissed, definitely long enough to get me almost painfully aroused. I had to keep myself from removing her clothes. As it was, I had my hand up the back of her tank top and was moving it around toward her breast when a ding sounded through the elevator, and the doors whisked open.

Little Mr. Bean stood in the doorway, along with his dad, who wore an embarrassed expression.

"Um, sorry." His eyes were everywhere but on us. And I suppose we appeared a little indisposed with our bodies pressed together and our hands in places. We were so shocked we didn't even think to move apart, which probably added to his discomfort. "Didn't realize you were…yeah…um…we'll take the stairs."

He disappeared from view, but we heard him talking to Mr. Bean as they walked away. "At least someone is getting a little action, huh, buddy?"

Phaedra dropped her head to my shoulder, and her body shook with quiet laughter. I covered my mouth to mute my laughing.

Phaedra stepped back just enough to take my hands again. "Maybe we should take this somewhere else."

As much as I wanted to drag Phaedra back to her place and ravish her, I thought about Marnie up in the apartment. She'd seemed okay when I left, but I wanted to make sure she was okay before I lost myself in Phaedra's arms.

"Are you hungry? Do you want to have dinner with me and Marnie? And then, maybe you can stay the night, and I can try to make up for some of our missed time?"

Her eyes were dark and soft, and she stared at me for a long moment. I wasn't sure she was going to answer. "My answer is yes, but before we go anywhere, there's something I need to tell you."

An anxious seed started to grow in my stomach. "Sure. Go ahead."

"Daria Fleming, it is imperative I tell you now that I love you. I wanted to tell you before, but I felt like it was a little too soon, but then I was afraid I was never going to tell you. So I'm telling you now, inside this dank little elevator." She looked around, taking in our interesting environment. "I love you. I think I fell a little in love with you the first day when we were at the street fair, and it's been growing ever since. Please don't let it scare you away. I just needed to say it."

My heart was in my throat. *She loves me!* I was so happy, I wanted to scream, but my throat was tight, and I wasn't sure I could speak. I needed to say something, though. Her face wore a rapidly changing collage of love, expectation, fear, hope, and a myriad of other expressions, and here I was standing silently making her wait to see how her words were received.

She squeezed my hands. "You don't have to say it back. You don't have to respond at all. In fact, I—"

I flung my arms around her neck and held her close. "I love you, too," I said, and I buried my face in her neck. "So much."

Her arms wrapped around my waist, and we clung to one another. "You do?"

I leaned back to gaze into her eyes. "Something stirred in me the first day I saw you playing on the mall, but like you, I knew there was something happening between us at the street fair. I want to show you how much I love you, and it's killing me. I need to check on Marnie first. But as soon as I know she's okay, I'm going to drag you into the nearest bedroom and show you how much."

She kissed me softly and slowly before answering. "We have all weekend."

"Do you have a problem with that?"

"My only regret is the weekend is only two days long."

"We have all the time in the world after that, though."

EPILOGUE

Phaedra

4 months later

Eerie quiet surrounded us as we stepped onto the snow-covered sidewalk in front of the building Daria worked in. Two inches had fallen since our arrival, and we carefully picked our way down the sidewalk. The holiday party was still going strong, her company having taken over the entire top floor of the fifty-five-story building with open bars, rowdy raffles, and secret Santa exchanges, but we were headed home.

There were few cars on the road, and most people were indoors on this cold night. It was as if we had the city to ourselves as we walked the block to the 16th Street Mall to catch the shuttle to Blake Street, where we'd get off and walk the last three blocks to home, taking in the brightly decorated sights of Union Station and all of the historical buildings along the way. We walked slowly to enjoy the bright lights and hear the snatches of holiday songs pour from establishments along our way. Denver was magical this time of year, and the magic was intensified by the presence of the woman I was walking with. I squeezed her hand. I couldn't imagine a more perfect moment.

I'd been on tour for the last three months, with infrequent trips back home, and I was ready to spend the next two weeks relaxing and making our first holiday-together-memories. I had a pretty good idea what most of those memories would be about because all evening, I hadn't been able to take my eyes off the sexy backless pantsuit she'd worn to the party. The temptation to touch her was undeniable, and I couldn't keep my hands off her soft, warm skin. We'd spent a lot of time on the dance floor as a cover for my almost mindless near-constant caresses. Now I couldn't wait to get her back to our loft so I could explore the rest of her body in private.

Daria blew out a stream of breath, and a cloud billowed before her. "I'll bet you're wondering if you should have stayed in San Diego for Christmas."

We'd played two nights at the Belly Up in Solana Beach and then a night at the House of Blues in San Diego. The warm weather had been awesome, but it didn't feel like the holidays with the sun shining every day and people walking around in shorts. Even the bedazzled palm trees lacked the festive spirit of seeing all the lights shining in the snow.

"Christmas in Denver is my favorite thing next to you, and since you're here, this is the only place I want to be right now."

"You and your smooth tongue." She stopped and gave me a quick kiss before we started walking again.

"Oh yeah," she said a second later. "Marnie wants us to come over to the apartment for a little while before we head over to my mom and dad's place for Christmas Eve dinner. She wants to show off the tree she and Courtney put up."

"Sounds like fun. Those two are funny. As soon as you moved out, they moved all the gaming stuff into your old room and put in a huge puzzle table. I giggle imagining them putting together puzzles like a couple of old ladies."

She swung our hands between us. "Dude, the puzzles they do are super complex, like, 3D. They're not puzzles for geriatric patients. Besides, you and I do puzzles sometimes."

I stopped and looked at her. "Did you just call me dude?"

She laughed. "I have no idea where that came from. You are most definitely not a dude." She gave me another kiss, and this one was steamier. As much as I wanted to get back to our place and ravish her, I liked walking with her in the snow, enjoying the solitude and muted quiet so much that when the shuttle came by, we chose to continue walking rather than join the louder crowd on the bus. It appeared from the ugly sweaters and tipsy passengers that several companies were having their holiday parties tonight.

When we neared the end of the mall, red light reflecting off white snow caught my eye. The neon hand in the window of Madamee Eugenie's. Daria must have seen it at the same time because she stopped. As we stood there, a stooped, dark figure stepped out from under the window overhang to brush off the snow settling on the little table out front. She waved us over. I wondered if she was cold because she didn't wear a coat. I doubted the long-sleeved black dress and thin black shawl provided much warmth.

"I see you found each other," she said when we approached. Her eyes were bright, as if lit from an internal light.

"We did," I said, glancing at Daria, who nodded and smiled.

She waved her gnarled finger. "The cards, while they allow for an infinite number of paths and outcomes, are never wrong." She finished brushing off the table. "You should go in and get warm. My daughter just made a fresh pot of tea. She'll enjoy the company."

We hadn't planned on stopping, but a cup of tea sounded good. Daria and I went into the shop where the younger Madamee Eugenie sat on one of the couches in the front room, pouring hot water into a cup on a saucer sitting before her on the coffee table. Interestingly, there were two other cups sitting in saucers across from her, where two chairs sat next to the table. I turned to see if the old woman was following us, but the door shut without her coming in.

"It's a cold night out there. I was about to have some tea. Will you join me?" she asked as if she'd been expecting us. She gestured for us to sit, and Daria and I did.

"We were walking by, and your mother said we should come in," I said, settling my dress over my prosthesis.

The younger Madamee Eugenie selected a tea bag from an open box next to the teapot and dipped it into the hot water. "My mother has been gone for a while."

"Should one of us go ask her in to join us?" I asked, and Daria started to get up.

The younger Madamee Eugenie glanced up. "I mean, my mother passed on several years ago." She pointed to a framed picture on the front counter I'd never noticed. It was a picture of the old woman. A cold shudder worked its way down my spine while the younger Madamee Eugenie offered us the box to select our tea bags, seemingly unfazed by the topic of conversation. As if she expected people to see her mother all the time.

If someone had asked me what I would have done in a situation like this, I'd have told them that I would run out the door and keep on running without looking back. However, the next half hour was both relaxing and unusual. Madamee Eugenie was a good conversationalist and kept us talking about our plans for the holidays, my recent tour with

Nick's Army, and a variety of other things. It was unusual because, at the same time, we were sitting in a psychic's shop, two days before Christmas, visiting as if we were old friends after a woman who'd been dead for several years had invited us in for tea. The superstitious part of me, which sounded unsurprisingly like my mother, wondered if we were treading on mystical ground best left untrod. The rest of me was surprisingly at ease with the visit.

"Well," said the younger Madamee Eugenie, "I appreciate you stopping in. But I should probably close up now. No one else is coming out in this weather."

I wondered if she knew this because of some sort of vision or if it was a guess based on the weather. I leaned toward the second one until she walked us to the door and said good night.

"You two are good together." She smiled at both of us and then turned to Daria. "The Two of Cups was the right path."

We said good night and headed toward home again. Neither of us spoke for about a block.

Finally, I spoke. "Was that weird, or was it just me?"

Daria grabbed my arm as if she'd just been waiting for someone to acknowledge what had just transpired. "I'm freaking out a little, to be honest."

"Right? We talked to the old lady, didn't we? She told us to go in. I didn't imagine it, did I?"

She shook her head. "Not unless two people can imagine the same thing at the same time. I had a card reading by her the same week I met you. I didn't imagine that. She seemed as real to me as you do."

There was a time not too long ago when I would have tried to brush it all away, knowing there was a plausible explanation that just hadn't been revealed yet. I didn't feel the need to explain it now, though. "What did she mean about the Two of Cups?"

"At the end of the reading, two cards came up at the same time when she flipped them over to read my future. The Two of Cups was one of them. The other one was the Two of Pentacles. She said my path could go either way, but ultimately, it was my choice."

"What do they mean?"

"She said the Two of Pentacles was about balancing priorities." She squeezed my hand. "The story of my life. The Two of Cups was about romance and connection. She handed me both of the cards to keep before I left, but I lost one of them."

"Which card did you keep?"

"The Two of Cups."

Another cold shiver ran down my spine. The strange thing is, it wasn't completely uncomfortable.

"It's a good thing neither of us believes in this stuff."

We both laughed, and I snuck a glace behind us and saw the neon sign blink off in the shop window. From this far away, it appeared to be like any of the other shops around it. I could see how easy it would be to look right past it.

About the Author

Kimberly Cooper Griffin is a software engineer by day and a romance novelist by night. Born in San Diego, California, Kimberly joined the Air Force, traveled the world, and eventually settled down in Denver, Colorado, where she lives with her wife, the youngest of her three daughters, and a menagerie of dogs and cats. When Kimberly isn't working or writing, she enjoys a variety of interests, but at the core of it all she has an insatiable desire to connect with people and experience life to its fullest. Every moment is collected and archived into memory, a candidate for being woven into the fabric of the tales she tells. Her novels explore the complexities of building relationships and finding balance when life has a tendency of getting in the way.

Books Available From Bold Strokes Books

A Love that Leads to Home by Ronica Black. For Carla Sims and Janice Carpenter, home isn't about location, it's where your heart is. (978-1-63555-675-9)

Blades of Bluegrass by D. Jackson Leigh. A US Army occupational therapist must rehab a bitter veteran who is a ticking political time bomb the military is desperate to disarm. (978-1-63555-637-7)

Hopeless Romantic by Georgia Beers. Can a jaded wedding planner and an optimistic divorce attorney possibly find a future together? (978-1-63555-650-6)

Hopes and Dreams by PJ Trebelhorn. Movie theater manager Riley Warren is forced to face her high school crush and tormentor, wealthy socialite Victoria Thayer, at their twentieth reunion. (978-1-63555-670-4)

In the Cards by Kimberly Cooper Griffin. Daria and Phaedra are about to discover that love finds a way, especially when powers outside their control are at play. (978-1-63555-717-6)

Moon Fever by Ileandra Young. SPEAR agent Danika Karson must clear her werewolf friend of multiple false charges while teaching her vampire girlfriend to resist the blood mania brought on by a full moon. (978-1-63555-603-2)

Serenity by Jesse J. Thoma. For Kit Marsden, there are many things in life she cannot change. Serenity is in the acceptance. (978-1-63555-713-8)

Sylver and Gold by Michelle Larkin. Working feverishly to find a killer before he strikes again, Boston homicide detective Reid Sylver and rookie cop London Gold are blindsided by their chemistry and developing attraction. (978-1-63555-611-7)

Trade Secrets by Kathleen Knowles. In Silicon Valley, love and business are a volatile mix for clinical lab scientist Tony Leung and venture capitalist Sheila Graham. (978-1-63555-642-1)

Entangled by Melissa Brayden. Becca Crawford is the perfect person to head up the Jade Hotel, if only the captivating owner of the local vineyard would get on board with her plan and stop badmouthing the hotel to everyone in town. (978-1-63555-709-1)

First Do No Harm by Emily Smith. Pierce and Cassidy are about to discover that when it comes to love, sometimes you have to risk it all to have it all. (978-1-63555-699-5)

Kiss Me Every Day by Dena Blake. For Wynn Jamison, wishing for a do-over with Carly Evans was a long shot; actually getting one was a game changer. (978-1-63555-551-6)

Olivia by Genevieve McCluer. In this lesbian Shakespeare adaption with vampires, Olivia is a centuries-old vampire who must fight a strange figure from her past if she wants a chance at happiness. (978-1-63555-701-5)

One Woman's Treasure by Jean Copeland. Daphne's search for discarded antiques and treasures leads to an embarrassing misunderstanding and, ultimately, the opportunity for the romance of a lifetime with Nina. (978-1-63555-652-0)

Silver Ravens by Jane Fletcher. Lori has lost her girlfriend, her home, and her job. Things don't improve when she's kidnapped and taken to fairyland. (978-1-63555-631-5)

Still Not Over You by Jenny Frame, Carsen Taite, and Ali Vali. Old flames die hard in these tales of a second chance at love with the ex you're still not over. (978-1-63555-516-5)

Storm Lines by Jessica L. Webb. Devon is a psychologist who likes rules. Marley is a cop who doesn't. They don't always agree, but both fight to protect a girl immersed in a street drug ring. (978-1-63555-626-1)

The Politics of Love by Jen Jensen. Is it possible to love across the political divide in a hostile world? Conservative Shelley Whitmore and liberal Rand Thomas are about to find out. (978-1-63555-693-3)

All the Paths to You by Morgan Lee Miller. High school sweethearts Quinn Hughes and Kennedy Reed reconnect five years after they break up and realize that their chemistry is all but over. (978-1-63555-662-9)

Arrested Pleasures by Nanisi Barrett D'Arnuck. When charged with a crime she didn't commit, Katherine Lowe faces the question: Which is harder, going to prison or falling in love? (978-1-63555-684-1)

Bonded Love by Renee Roman. Carpenter Blaze Carter suffers an injury that shatters her dreams, and ER nurse Trinity Greene hopes to show her that sometimes love is worth fighting for. (978-1-63555-530-1)

Convergence by Jane C. Esther. With life as they know it on the line, can Aerin McLeary and Olivia Ando's love survive an otherworldly threat to humankind? (978-1-63555-488-5)

Coyote Blues by Karen F. Williams. Riley Dawson, psychotherapist and shape-shifter, has her world turned upside down when Fiona Bell, her one true love, returns. (978-1-63555-558-5)

Drawn by Carsen Taite. Will the clues lead Detective Claire Hanlon to the killer terrorizing Dallas, or will she merely lose her heart to person of interest urban artist Riley Flynn? (978-1-63555-644-5)

Lucky by Kris Bryant. Was Serena Evans's luck really about winning the lottery, or is she about to get even luckier in love? (978-1-63555-510-3)

The Last Days of Autumn by Donna K. Ford. Autumn and Caroline question the fairness of life, the cruelty of loss, and what it means to love as they navigate the complicated minefield of relationships, grief, and life-altering illness. (978-1-63555-672-8)

Three Alarm Response by Erin Dutton. In the midst of tragedy, can these first responders find love and healing? Three stories of courage, bravery, and passion. (978-1-63555-592-9)

Veterinary Partner by Nancy Wheelton. Callie and Lauren are determined to keep their hearts safe but find that taking a chance on love is the safest option of all. (978-1-63555-666-7)

Forging a Desire Line by Mary P. Burns. When Charley's ex-wife, Tricia, is diagnosed with inoperable cancer, the private duty nurse Tricia hires turns out to be the handsome and aloof Joanna, who ignites something inside Charley she isn't ready to face. (978-1-63555-665-0)

Journey to Cash by Ashley Bartlett. Cash Braddock thought everything was great, but it looks like her history is about to become her right now. Which is a real bummer. (978-1-63555-464-9)

Love on the Night Shift by Radclyffe. Between ruling the night shift in the ER at the Rivers and raising her teenage daughter, Blaise Richilieu has all the drama she needs in her life, until a dashing young attending appears on the scene and relentlessly pursues her. (978-1-63555-668-1)

Olivia's Awakening by Ronica Black. When the daring and dangerously gorgeous Eve Monroe is hired to get Olivia Savage into shape, a fierce passion ignites, causing both to question everything they've ever known about love. (978-1-63555-613-1)

The Duchess and the Dreamer by Jenny Frame. Clementine Fitzroy has lost her faith and love of life. Can dreamer Evan Fox make her believe in life and dream again? (978-1-63555-601-8)

The Road Home by Erin Zak. Hollywood actress Gwendolyn Carter is about to discover that losing someone you love sometimes means gaining someone to fall for. (978-1-63555-633-9)

Waiting for You by Elle Spencer. When passionate past-life lovers meet again in the present day, one remembers it vividly and the other isn't so sure. (978-1-63555-635-3)

While My Heart Beats by Erin McKenzie. Can a love born amidst the horrors of the Great War survive? (978-1-63555-589-9)

Face the Music by Ali Vali. Sweet music is the last thing that happens when Nashville music producer Mason Liner and daughter of country royalty Victoria Roddy are thrown together in an effort to save country star Sophie Roddy's career. (978-1-63555-532-5)